THE
DEAD
LIFE

THE
DEAD
LIFE

MATTHEW SPROSTY

atmosphere press

To my first editor.
Thanks, Mom.

1

"Ugghhhh...."

Sounds. I can hear them. The voice vibrates through my skull, my own throat, my teeth, my lips. Something flutters in front of my mouth, and I open my eyes to see green, fuzzy ...green ...

Grass? Grass. I'm on a ... "lawn".

Words are the first thing to come back to me. But not all of them. My mind, it seems, as my body begins to operate on auto-pilot, *flutters*. As I lay here, whoever I am, I feel like I was collecting breath inside of myself before releasing it out to dance with the infinite blades of *grass* spread out in the *lawn* before me. Now, I breathe effortlessly. In, out, in, out. I remember at one point I was able to do some breathing through my ... *nose*, but that seems out of the question now. Oh well, this mouth breathing seems to work just fine.

I try to focus on where I am—a small lawn that I barely fit on lengthwise. My right arm is outstretched above my head and my hand is palming a border of a garden made out of rocks. One individual rock in particular seems light, perfectly rounded, and perfectly sized so that my fingers can be wrapped around it. The way I grip it, I wonder if I was being attacked before I fell asleep and this was to be my weapon. Not feeling attacked anymore, I let my death grip loosen and fall from the stone, every knuckle in my hand cracking as I do so.

My toes are almost touching the cement of the ... *sidewalk*. The sidewalk where people *walk* be*side* the road. Where nobody is walking currently. Where somebody might be wandering about at some time and come across me and perhaps help me out. Should I be embarrassed I'm splayed out in the yard or should I be concerned?

Blades of grass that touch my skin are beginning to make me feel *itchy*, or *ticklish*; I can't remember which of those feelings I like less, but the current feeling is the lesser of the two. Rolling my limbs side to side, I find it obvious I've been here awhile as my body has made an indent in the ground. Either being in this lawn has created a grass-angel or I fell hard. I fell fast.

I don't remember falling...

I absolutely cannot remember anything.

I'm wet, soaked from the ... *dew*.

"Uuuugggggghhhh ... "

I groan again, unable to help myself. Waking up from a sleep you don't remember taking is quite the disorienting experience. Letting moans escape my chest is like pulling the cord of a lawnmower, trying to jumpstart my brain.

"Uuuugggghhhhh!"

The questions come flooding in: Where am I? How did I get here? What happened? Why am I in so much pain? Who lies down in the middle of a yard anyway? Was this for a laugh? If so, why is nobody laughing? Why is nobody around? Was I drugged? Oh dear God, was I drugged?! What diseases or babies am I carrying now?

Who am I?

I continue to lay there for a couple more moments, seconds, minutes, hours ... hoping that maybe everything just needs to catch up with me, and like a kid lost in a grocery store, if I just wait where I am, somebody will be the wiser and come looking for me. They'll find me, and rescue me, and tell me all about me, and remind me of everything leading up to this moment, and we'll have a laugh about it over a chain restaurant's sampler platter.

Although, in my mind, the sampler platter is filled with red, uncooked meat, and for a moment, I can smell it, and my belly rumbles its approval of my brain's newfound ability to project images of *food*.

I try to discover more of my surroundings.

It is dark, which is *night*. There's a light lighting the street: a *street light*. The brightest streetlight I feel I have ever seen in my life, although I can't recall a streetlight before this one. Beyond the streetlight above me, random sporadic clouds are blocking out any chance of seeing any stars or the *moon*. Matching streetlights that are tall, and black, and giving off orange artificial light line the street in the direction my head is currently facing.

The curiosity of whether or not the streetlights are lining the street the opposite way gets the better of me, and all I want to do is turn my head to look that way. My first movement of lifting my head probably appeared like a small twitch to anybody watching, and my mind exploded into an immediate panic. My head is stuck! Stuck to my body, facing left forever! What a cruel world I have awoken to! I'd have to go for runs sideways!

Another twitch of the neck and something grinds inside. A ... *tendon* rubs against something else underneath the skin of my neck, and there's popping, and more grinding, and suddenly I'm moving my head up off the grass with all the strength I can muster. I can feel wet blades of grass drop from my cheek as I hold my breath with concentration, and it escapes from my throat with short bursts and whimpers. I force my head to the right, and have such an extreme pain from something tearing that I immediately collapse my heavy dome back onto the lawn and rest there—eyes clenched shut, grass tickling the inside of my ear as I wait for the pain to cease.

Finally, I open my eyes to see the street is long and straight, and from my vantage point through the blades of grass, I can't see where it ends.

I feel I'm quite visible from all directions because of this streetlight. Why didn't the streetlight protect me? Dang nabbit, I stayed in an obviously well-lit area and I still found my body dumped and abandoned and undiscovered in this lawn. Shouldn't I have awoken in an ambulance asking somebody "what happened?" Is this a normal occurrence in life? How many other people have completely blacked out and woken up dazed and confused and had to put their lives together? Is there amnesia of amnesia?

It seems I'm in a neighborhood where all the houses look the same, as if all built by the same person or construction company. All of them are two stories with the same white, plastic railings around first and second floor balconies. Most of the homeowners have replaced their lawns with pebbles, except for a few. Except for the one I have woken up on.

All right you, take notes. You don't know:
-Who you are
-Where you are
-Why you're here
-Why you were laying in the lawn

A male, British voice enters my head: *"Why, Dr. Watson, it seems we have a mystery to solve!"* Is that me? Is that my Dad? Who is Dr. Watson? I'm getting nowhere fast laying here.

Feeling every muscle in my shoulder contract and ache from being stiff, I pull my limp hand from the rock and bring my arm down next to my body; slowly, like a snake slithering through the grass back to my side. The feeling of moving and working my muscles, my skin, and my bones feels similar to breaking down a cardboard box— finding the weak points where you can bend them and crease. The pain dissipates as I rest my arm and so there I stay—*immobile*. I'm afraid to move any more. Afraid to discover any more pain.

Call me weak, I don't care. Here I lay, in an eight-foot-long lawn waiting for dawn. Waiting for someone to discover me, lift me up, and say:

"Hey! Your name is ____! And, you were _____ on _____ because _____!"

I'd breathe a sigh of relief. Not because I felt any safer or there was no more pain, but for the fact that I finally knew. I knew the questions I was pondering laying in the grass, staring at the street light, watching the street with no traffic, the sidewalk with no walkers, feeling the dew soaking up into the cloth of my clothes, tickling my sides and armpits.

You would think the owners of this lawn would discover me sooner or later. Maybe they are older, more elderly. Maybe they go to bed when the sun sets because they have no use for the night. Maybe it's still the early hours of the morning and I still have hours before anybody is going to find me. Maybe the cold of night mixed with the wet of the dew will slowly give me pneumonia and as I lay here waiting to be saved, I'm slowly allowing nature to kill me, turn me into *mushrooms.*

Mushrooms. Fungi. Fun guy. I knew a joke once about this stuff, but I've forgotten it.

If I die, what will people think?

Maybe I shouldn't just resolve myself to death because I just want to lay here and not feel any more pain. Maybe I should just get up.

Or, at least, try to.

"Uuunnnnnngggggghhhh ... "

My body no likey as I slowly push myself up off the grass. Just putting my palms down on the ground bends and creases muscles in my side that I swear split and tear open upon any movement, almost as if my ribs are breaking out of my body. Pain screams through every nerve ending in my abdomen and lower back as I push myself up off the lawn and curl my spine. Once I get a little elevation, I rock back to my knees and bend my legs underneath me. A yoga pose. *Child's pose?* Random knowledge coming back to me just in time for me to take a break and reflect on it. I rest my forehead in the cool grass and mouth-breathe in between my knees that I am too scared to move.

In, out, in, out.

Bbbbuuuuurrrrrrrgrrrrrrrrrrr ...

A new sound comes from me but not out my mouth. No, this one came from my guts. My stomach. With my body bent like a "G" that fell forward, I can hear my stomach clearly as it tells me that I have been neglecting it for too long. That's a good sign, right? Mortally wounded people are not hungry, are they?

In my mind, I see a black-and-white plaid coat detective with leather patches on the arm of his jacket, and a long, bent smoking pipe turn to a shorter man and say, "Well, Dr. Watson, it seems we have a mystery of the stomach to solve." And I remember—this man is *Sherlock Holmes*. The voice I heard earlier was a TV show. TV is Television.

Television is vision—visual—images that tele— tell ... a ... tell you something....

That's not right.

But, television is ... *shows*. My favorite television show is ...

Note #5

-Find out your favorite television show

My list is frustratingly getting longer and longer....

Suddenly, the thought that maybe I'm on my own lawn invades my head, and if that's the case—I'm very close to my own food. The thought invigorates me to continue my ascent to my feet, and as I peel my arms back to ninety-degree angles at my side, I hardly feel the excruciating pain of muscle contractions.

I quickly ignore the one moment of hesitation I could have, the one thought of how badly this might hurt, before I push up and off the ground. It's been so long since I've stood up, (forever, actually, with my memory) that I feel like a rocket ship bursting five feet into space before my knees creak, crack, fail, and I go crashing back to the grass. My butt acquaints itself with the dewy grass, soaking a new body part. I hold my knees close to my chest, and find no noise in my body to convey how much pain I'm currently in.

Whimper, I think, but I don't. I have no idea how or why I should cry.

My knees practically throb in pain as the rest of my body remains sore. Using my fingers, I probe around the knee bone. The *placenta?* No. That's something else. It doesn't matter now as I try to make sure the cap of my knee won't move if I attempt to walk again. I massage down the calf, shake the snap, crackle, and pops out of that foot joint. It seems the only issues I have in my legs are my knees. Maybe I just have bad knees.

Maybe I'm old. Much older than my skin suggests.

Maybe I'm just being a baby.

I try again, rolling forward so one leg is beneath me, and one leg is set to push myself up. *Genuflecting.* And, with the gentle reminder that everything will be fine in the end, I push up on that one knee. It appears the worst was yet to come as something *snaps* in my leg joint, but as soon as it does—like a rapidly peeled bandage—the pain immediately relents and I find my strength. I stand like that for a while, a flamingo in the grass, one leg cocked behind me while I balance on the leg I had just broken in.

Can't be scared forever, I tell myself, and I swing the other leg down underneath me.

CRACK!

Cheese us Christ!

But then—nothing. No pain. I am a new being. I evolved from being a wriggling creature in the grass to a *homosapien,* a walker of two feet, in just a couple of hours. Proud of myself, I look down at my outfit that is probably five shades darker than what it's supposed to be due to the wet of the night and my willingness to lie in it for so long.

No shoes.

Well-manicured toes.

Grass-stained, dirty blue jeans.

Tight-fitting, wrinkled, dirty, drenched purple tank top with a stain at the bottom of it....

I grab the bottom of my shirt and fold it up for a better look in the streetlight. Saliva escapes my lower lip, and I try to slurp it up, but I'm too tired, so it waters the grass.

Reminding my body of mobility, I find it difficult to balance at first, but soon figure out how to stand without wobbling. I prod the stain and the dark spot smudges more into the fabric. It's fresh and it grows bigger the farther up my shirt it goes. The stain leaves the tips of my fingers red, and I'm finding it more and more difficult to figure out just what is all over my clothing. I crane my neck to see more of it as it looks to grow toward my shoulder.

I place my hand on my shoulder, pressing down into the fabric so whatever the stain is seeps out around my fingers. I bring my hand back out from my body so I can see it in the light of the streetlamp.

Blood.

No doubting it.

That light red that turns dark red in every line in my hand, which are exceptionally line-y and crack-y and prune-y from being in the wet grass all night.

A handful of blood.

There's blood all over my shirt. Why is there blood all over my shirt?!

As I wonder who I killed, or if this is Halloween. My hands fumble at the strap of my tank top, moving it aside to check and make sure my skin has been unmarred by violence. I run my fingers down the smooth skin of my shoulder, and I touch something gooey. Something hard and something gooey. There's a weird texture that I reach past and...

I reach *into* my shoulder....

I see stars and streetlights.

I feel like I swallow my tongue.

I see black.

2

Apparently, this time when I fell, my head hit the rocky border of the garden. Although, instead of finding the soft rock I was palming all night, my temple smacked against a pretty hard one. I touch my temple with my finger. No blood there. No pain really. Fascinating.

Cautiously, I venture to touch the wound in my shoulder again.

That's a good word for it. *Wound.* A hole in my shoulder where blood is leaking out with jagged edges where skin has been ripped and some of it is frayed up off my body and some of it is just missing. I wonder if I'm in shock because my fingers are clearly inside my shoulder now and I feel no pain. My wound feels like a mini-cherry pie left out in the rain. I probe at the gooey fibers of muscle covered in tissues covered in pieces of skin covered in—

Ants?!

Dear God, are these ants?!

I begin scraping away and off what I can at my shoulder wound—

That's right. It's MY shoulder wound. I claim it and ants can't have it!

Something insect-y is crawling around my flesh and I rub fast and furiously over the uneven hole and hopefully clear it out. I don't know much. I mean, I know I'm probably not a doctor, but I know having insects in gaping wounds is counterproductive to the healing process.

What did you expect, a female voice says in my brain, *laying in nature all night. Nature finds you.*

If that's my voice, I sadly find it a little raspy and annoying.

Well, "G" must be my favorite letter to resemble sitting, because I'm in an upright one on my bum. I look up at the house before me and, like all the houses on the street it is light colored, two story, and pitch black inside. In fact, it doesn't look like anyone lives in it. Upon closer inspection, the whole long street doesn't have one porch light on.

Get up and go silly.

I will! Pushy, raspy voice from Hell.

With a fraction of the pain from earlier in the night, I stand up. I get over the customary wobble of my new feet in the grass and give a compulsory brush over my wound. When I feel no new pieces and parts moving underneath my fingertips, I reach out and grab the railing for the porch stairs, celebrating as I take my first step.

Once the first foot was planted, I grab onto the railing hard and lift up my second foot to start ascending the stairs.

I feel like I'm a natural at this walking thing. Even if my sore, bruised, and stiff knees don't necessarily bend like they're designed to do. I adjust to the straightness by swinging my leg around the side instead of bending the knees. I pretend that I look like the one dancer guy in that black-and-white rainy movie, although I probably look much more foolish.

After a couple of steps, I realize the more I move, the better I am getting at it. There's less pain from creased muscles and joints, and I climb the last couple of steps without even holding onto the railing. My thighs are already laboring from the effort, but the rest of my body seems good to go. The stairs creak, my footfalls echo off the silent night, and I find myself on a dark porch looking at a run-of-the-mill wooden front door flanked by two windows that are closed with white curtains drawn over them.

I step up and ring the doorbell.

Ding. Dong.

Nothing. No lights come on. No noises scurry on the other side. No hushed voices arguing over who should get the door or whether they should get the door at all. Nothing.

I ring it again.

Ding. Dong.

At this point hope begins to run out of me and I wonder if I made all of this effort of moving about to find myself at the wrong house. I look down the street in both directions. The clouds have lost interest in my story and moved on, giving the moon an unadulterated view on my current porch swan song. There is no way any sight on this street will trigger my memory, for it's really "if you see one, you've seen them all." Have I obsessed about getting to this front door only to arrive at the wrong house?

Is there a right house? Is there a MY house?

Ding. Ding. Ding. Ding. Ding. Dong.

Call me rude but if anyone is sleeping in this house they better wake up now and take me in, ask me what happened, ask me if I am all right, ask me if I need a shower, ask me if I would like to borrow some clothes, ask me if they should call my parents, and ask me if I'm hungry. Because I am. Oh God, am I ever hungry! I could eat through this door if I thought that it would not ruin my teeth, not taste like wood, and not take forever.

I run my tongue over my teeth. It seems like I have a good set.

Eat through the door....Beat through the door....

Answer!

How rude is it that I would put all this effort in climbing the porch stairs, and they won't even meet me halfway?

I try the knob but it's locked. I try to knock, but with my balance and dexterity, I actually just lean against the door, and slam my forearms against it, all the while moaning. This house is impenetrable. No surprise there. I stumble about the porch as I look up and down and around at what might be possible hiding areas for a front door key. Everybody hides one, don't they?There's no welcome mat and it doesn't look like there's enough space above the door frame to hide a key without showing it off to the neighborhood. Other than that, the porch is comprised of wooden floorboards and a white plastic railing that goes around it, protecting the ungraceful from falling into the front hedges. So, no metal, which means a "hide-a-key" magnetic box would not work. How else do people hide keys to their houses?

Brrrruuuuurrrrggggrup!

My stomach tells me to hurry it up and figure it out like my own Dr. Watson urging me on.

"Jawr whonent, Dior Wa nnn."

I try to name my stomach Dr. Watson and tell it "just a moment" but my words come out like I'm speaking to a dentist. I realize I'm going to have to work at the talking thing. Why must I *work* at everything? Perhaps something to drink would lubricate my tongue and help in conversation....

Well, I would love to if I could just get past this pesky front door.

I have faith in myself, which is probably silly, because I am a stranger to myself, and who knows if I've ever been a critical thinker? Even as I stand there soaking wet with a bloody hole in my shoulder and my head hurting from where I fell on the rock....

...

That's it!

I try to descend the stairs faster than my skill set will allow and end up sliding down them on my back. Several vertebrae meet wooden edges and a pain eases in which I'll feel later but adrenaline is kicking in now. I stare at the rock border of the garden. There has to be a hundred rocks, but only one of them has a wet palm print from where someone was grasping it all night long.

And, it just so happens that the palm-printed rock is a false one with a compartment inside holding a dead bolt key.

Elementary, my dear Watson....

3

Ah, "home."

Whether this is my home or not, it is hard to tell. I can't rightly identify myself let alone anything that might just be mine. It doesn't smell completely weird, like when you entered into a childhood friend's home that had a different nationality than you and you couldn't quite get used to the smell until the moment you were picked up. And, then you'd smell your Mom as she hugged you hello, and she'd smell like laundry, and you'd immediately grow tired, because, unbeknownst to you, you were entirely too stressed out being surrounded by unfamiliar smells so when you're back in your habitat, you'd instantly relax and fall asleep on the way home in the car.

For the record, I have no mental image of my mother. She wears jeans and a sweater and smells like fresh linen and cinnamon gum. I'll have to put the word out that I'm looking for a lady that matches that description.

As I stand there in the doorway, I have a conversation with myself about what in the heck is actually happening inside of my mind. I have the stupidest recollections of things and I don't even know if they're mine or movies or television, and yet I can't seem to sift through all the brain cells in my head to find a name or anything useful. I'm sure Sherlock Holmes is family fun entertainment that teaches as well as entertains but knowing his tagline is not currently helping in this situation.

Is this my home?! I scream in my head, only to be met with utter nothing.

What's my name?! Again, ignored, but this time I feel almost a suggestion to just make one up. Name myself something. Who cares if it's not right? If I don't meet anyone that has met me ever again, supposedly I can be whoever I want.

I have a moment of not knowing whether or not to slide off my shoes, but it's brief because I'm so hungry I start to stumble forward and grab the stair railing in front of me. I'm stiff all over and it feels like every time I move one foot forward that I need to unstick it from the floor first, as if constantly moving through muck. It gives a whole new meaning to "stick and move," a phrase I can recall which adds to the frustration of not knowing anything really useful. I jerk my foot forward and plant it, then jerk the other one forward and plant it. Eventually, I'll work on getting the smoothness of my gait down, because, like stated before: this walking thing is my bag.

"Aauughhh brraaaah."

Mental note—figure out how to talk like a sensible human being and not like a breathy horse with its snout in an oats bag.

I make my way down the tiled foyer hallway with a soft runner rug that makes me appreciate these homeowners even more. The squishiness of the rug feels great under my rigid, calloused feet. I make my way into what I feel is the kitchen, slamming my hand across and over the wall to my side, looking for a light. Nothing seems to be there until my wrist hits that tiny peg and the room awakens with the brightest, yellowiest, five-million-gad-jillion-watt bulbs I have ever seen. Perhaps I'm exaggerating from feeling my way down the dark foyer, but I feel as if my retinas were burned from my skull for a second, that I awoke to see just to be blinded, and I scream—

"Ayyyoooaarraaaagghhhgooooo."

I sound like Tarzan's menopausal widow asking the gorilla gods why large, yellow, metal spiders are tearing down all of the trees. I cover my eyes with my hands and buckle at the waist. I almost fall and that reminds me of my new fear of falling and having to get back up again, and I brace myself.

No falling for me. I've been fall-free for fifty-or-so steps.

I should get a token, like they do in Alcoholics Anonymous. Walkers Anonymous.

I blink.

My pupils adjust to the room. This is the emptiest kitchen I have ever seen. My memory is one of the most random things as I suddenly recall at least a dozen of other nameless, label-less kitchens I have been in before—but not remembering why or when I was in them. A sudden fear hits me that I might have just broken into a model home; a home to show off what other homes could look like before they are built. I stumble to the fridge and open it, and it's just as I feared.

Empty.

And not just empty, mind you, like these people don't have any money, and so they must just open the fridge to stare at the Arm & Hammer Baking Soda, but we're talking *empty* empty. Nothing. Nada. No cold air even. Not even on. The fridge isn't even plugged in. Nobody lives here. There's no saviors upstairs tucked into their beds waiting to come down and make everything okay.

I realize the biggest lie of my life currently is the home-like, cozy runner rug in the foyer hallway. Everything else is just empty. Like my stomach, Dr. Watson, who still is grumbling like a troll underneath a bridge.

I think about crying for a moment but forget how and I move onto the pantry. Refrigerators are nice because they keep perishable things not perished, and pantries are how we stored things "back in the old days". Pantries are old fashioned. Pantries are for the foods preserved by either chemicals or salt, and I wouldn't mind shoving either down my throat and filling my stomach with them.

Something happens and I don't unstick a foot and plant a foot properly and end up stumbling forward, putting my shoulder into the swinging closet doors of the pantry, knocking them off their rail. The frail, fake wood things don't support me, so I stumble down into the food closet, bringing shelves down with me. Products fall on top of my wounded shoulder, hitting my rock-assaulted head. I hardly feel it as I lay there underneath the rainfall of hard-edged canned products. All I have thought about is food, and I have found it.

Glorious aluminum cans of it raining from Heaven.

Un-openable cans of it.

Somewhere in the beginning of the turn of the century,

food packing companies decided to help the common man out and instead of making cans where you needed the tool of the "can opener" to get the lid off, they invented the "pull tab." As far as I could tell, none of these cans that made their impressions on my skin had the pull tab. I'd have to have a chat with the grocery shopper of this house when I could.

(Don't you love that I know all of the above stuff, but I couldn't tell you what my favorite color is? *I know I do!* I say to myself, in that annoying raspy voice I guess I have, blatantly dripping with seething sarcasm.)

But, a house that has non-pull tab cans of foods must have a can opener, right?

I growl as I wipe the pieces of splintered door and cans of food off of me, and reach up to grab the sides of the pantry to lift myself up, and stumble over to the kitchen island.

Most of the drawers are empty until I open one filled with dish towels. Another drawer contains the silverware, but it is all plastic-wrapped. I begin to suspect the pantry as just scenery. The cans are props to show potential buyers—*this is what could be in your house.* Perhaps they are sealed with rocks inside to give them weight.

No. Now I'm just being ridiculous.

Ridiculously hungry.

Finally, I find a can opener in a drawer with a wine bottle opener and I take them both, because—why not? If anything, I have learned that I am going to need all the tools I can get as I proceed with this bumbling life. The key to the house is jammed into my back jeans pocket. It's my key now. That makes this my house now. And these cans are all mine as well. My can opener. My wine opener. At this rate, I'm going to be very rich in very little time.

Strength is one thing.

Balance is another.

Now, finger dexterity is a trait I have to master. One day, I'm going to look up when babies start to get their motor skills, but for now I feel like an overgrown one as I try to manipulate the can opener in my hands. I know how one works—I remember that. You clamp down the mini compact disc-looking thing around the border, and the sharp blade slices into the lid as you crank the wheel with all of your finger-y might. But, even as I know this, I can't seem to make my hands work.

As I have done since my rebirth in the yard, I go with whatever Plan B is.

I return to the silverware drawer, and tear into the plastic wrap, using my nails to dig into the multiple layers of thin, plastic-y sheets and get at the separate but equal piles of butter knives, forks and spoons. I grab two butter knives working hard, with my tongue between my lips, to force my fingertips into wrapping around just one of them. I grip it as hard as I can. I can't quite grasp (*ha, pun intended*) the mobility of my hands at the moment, but I feel like they're asleep and someone pounded on them with a sledgehammer. I'm currently trying to grab things as if I'm on the bottom of a current-y, undertow-y ocean.

That's exactly how it feels.

Got it?

Good.

So, I grab the knife in my hand. I have it in my *grasp*. I'm so focused on just wielding this new weapon of mine, I can feel another drop of drool free fall from my bottom lip and down to the floor. I waver back and forth as I try to lay a can of Farmer's Baked Beans in front of me.

I find out quickly, as you probably knew already, that thrusting a knife into the side of a cylindrical container is not the proper route to go as the can won't hold steady, and/or the knife will roll off the side of it and either stab the counter top or the hand you have negligently elected to hold the can in place.

So, I stand the can up and hoist the knife over my head like the shower killer in that old black-and-white film I saw once. Sadly, I know that I will probably remember the name of that before my own name.

I stab the knife down onto the top of the can and before I can see that it only makes a dent, my grip slips, and my hand slides down the blade to be slightly sliced and certainly crushed on the side of the can.

"Aaaaywwwooooo."

I howl like an orphaned wolf.

Perhaps I was bit. Perhaps I'm a werewolf.

For a second I think of how cool that might be and hope for it.

But, no, chances are I've been diseased with a new virus that turns you into a mushy-brained elderly person overnight. Perhaps a zombie? But zombies are dumb, brainless dead things, and I'm clearly pretty smart, just mobile-y challenged. I'm about to spend the rest of my days blundering through life, crying over unopened cans of beans. Eventually, I'll lose the desire to keep trying. I'll slowly crumble with the realization that it won't get easier. I'll starve to death. One day—I'll give up.

But, not today, folks. Mama needs her beans.

I right that can up on the counter and I raise the knife over my head again, lining up my eyes to the half-inch dent

I left moments before, and I stab down with all the aggression of a silver-backed gorilla pounding down on the back of its enemy. And, baby—that knife sinks right in.

Like a child getting its first taste of sugar, it only takes a moment for me to realize how sweet life is about to become before I'm grabbing the can, holding it as I slide the metal knife out from the aluminum wound at the top. The knife is covered in a brown, sticky substance, and I stab down again, making another hole, needing to at least get my finger in. I stab again. And, I stab again. And, I stab again. Metal through aluminum, the can slamming down on the counter, the mushy insides sounding like tiny feet getting stuck in the muck.

"Aaaaaarrrrrgggggggghhhhhhh!"

Crazy.

I fall to the ground with my opened can of beans and I sit there, staring at the insides. Room temperature pork and beans. I don't even know if I like this, but it looks like a delicacy to Dr. Watson who is telling me to just shove it all in my mouth, including the can. *Be the Goat*, my stomach tells me.

I dip two shaky, dirty, bloody fingers into the beans, and using them as a scoop, slide about half a dozen toward my waiting outstretched tongue. I get about three into my mouth and crush them with my teeth, mouth breathing the whole scenario and swallow. Okay, I guess. Not spectacular. But, I do it again, and again, angling the can to get more beans into my gullet. I chew sometimes. I have to remind myself to chew.

...

"Bllllurrrrgggglllleeee," Dr. Watson says, hoping that he has my attention.

I'm in trouble, I think to myself as my stomach violently rocks inside me. And before I know it, without even heaving forward, I regurgitate the can of beans down the front of my shirt. I feel the sauce made from brown sugar and ketchup drip slowly off my chin. I feel my vomit weigh down my shirt to my chest, and then ooze down to my stomach. I wretch again, sending more fluids down the front of me as I sit back against the center island of this person's kitchen. This house which has brought me nothing but misery, and heartache, and ...

Hunger. Still. I'm hungry.

I don't think I have ever been immediately hungry after I vomited. I have beans still stuck in my molars, under my tongue, between my lips and teeth. My sought-after meal now mixed with warm stomach acids soaking through my shirt, surprisingly warm. And, here I was, still hungry.

I looked over at the can, tipped on its side on the floor, and I reached forth. Between my index finger and thumb, I picked up a small, cube-ish piece of unrecognizable bacon. I ransacked my mouth with my tongue, cleaning the corners of it for any chunks of wayward throw up, and spit them out. I cleared out the real estate of my mouth hole and moved in the piece of bacon.

Slowly, as not to risk another upchuck, I bit into the pig meat, moving it from side to side, letting all of my teeth meet their new, edible friend, and when it was turning into more liquid than solid—I swallowed.

And waited.

I then found myself reaching out for more of the bacon in the can, sifting around the beans to find it, cursing the makers for promising Pork before Beans when there was obviously more Beans than Pork. Jerks. I empty the can of its contents onto the kitchen floor, sifting around it with my fingers, spreading out all the beans in their gelatinous sauce to get a better view of the bacon.

Once the can was empty of meat, and my belly was still rumbling, I disgusted even myself by sifting through the barf on my chest for the darker brown matters of already chewed bacon and I returned them to my tongue. To be honest—the taste buds weren't there. I was enjoying the sustenance of the bacon but tasted it like I had a hundred and two degree fever and the flu and a stuffed nose and a dry throat. Everything was dulled down, so it wasn't as if I was tasting the stomach acid.

After that can was done, I went searching for another can that might have meat. A can of chili perhaps. Already, I was feeling stronger. My hands were working a little better, shaking less. I wasn't as dizzy. Wasn't as hungry. Wasn't feeling as under the weather. I was feeling better all around, and the next can of meat I found, I would try the can opener once again.

Who'd a thunk, huh?

I'm a meat eater.

4

Excuse me while I take this moment for some product placement.

SPAM is actually really good. Perhaps it's just because for some odd reason, recently I'm obsessed with meat and SPAM is canned meat of an unknown origin that tastes like salty gold. I must say that my savior is the pig flesh inside the rectangular blue cans with the sparkly top and the genius pull tabs. I mean, I now totally side with the wolf in the fairy tales as, I think, we all should because who doesn't love a tasty bite of pig? How many hypocritical times was I read that story with some kind of pork product in my stomach and hoping the wolf didn't win? I'm sorry, Wolf. I understand now. I hope you get those pigs in their stupid brick houses. If not, I highly suggest the liquefied and re-solidified ground pigs in each can of SPAM. Just ignore the fact the meat comes out like oversized, peg-less Lego brick.

So, SPAM aside, I truly have found a new appreciation for canned chili without beans—stuff is amazing. Chewy morsels of meat with the occasional molar hit of pulverized bone and the definite feeling that it's not just cow you're eating but perhaps pieces of horse and roadkill. Either way, my compliments to the chef. And speaking of chefs, Chef Boyardee, relax on the sauce and noodles and I will give you my heart because those tiny meatballs are delicious to slurp back. Kind of odd that they have the texture of grapes, but who am I to judge? The ravioli was tough to open with my hands and lick out the meat without everything crumbling down into my lap, so ... I have to reluctantly take a star away.

As far as canned seafood goes, tuna was difficult to open and wasn't as satisfying as, say, the brown canned meat, but it still went down and stayed down, so who am I to complain? Why does tuna own the market for their weird-shaped cans? Why did everyone else follow soup's can, and tuna go with the hockey puck can? Either way, hockey pucks are horrible for shaky hands to try and open.

Still hungry, but not as much.

Still shaky, but manageable.

Still have no idea what happened earlier tonight and who I am, just as much.

Feeling satiated but without proper nutrition, I put my palm down on the sauce, noodle, and bean-soaked floor and stand myself up. Even covered in food and puke, it seems to be much easier to move around than before I ate. I bend and close and wave my fingers, and look about the kitchen, seeing that my vision has cleared. It is still empty, but at least now with the broken pantry door and the canned products and food everywhere, it looks slightly lived in, albeit by drunken homeless people.

A piece of bean-y throw-up plops off the bottom of my

shirt and to the floor, and I realize it's about high time that I clean myself up.

I trudge out of the kitchen, turning the light off as I go, because I don't know who's responsible for the electricity bill in this house, but I'm certainly not being stuck with it, and I head off into the foyer. Mental note—I should be a good houseguest and clean up all the food from the kitchen floor after I have straightened myself out. Mental hope— that this house doesn't have any cleaning tools and I don't *actually* have to clean up the kitchen.

I look around the first floor of the house, primarily trying to spot a bathroom that I can wash up in, but really just taking in the lay of the land. The front door opens into a foyer where to the right is a living room with plastic-wrapped furniture and to the left is an eight person dining room table with oddly generic paintings on the wall in the form of seascapes. Counting the kitchen I've destroyed tonight, what appears to be a utility room with a washer/dryer, and a bathroom that only has a toilet and sink, that is the tour of the first floor. *What I need is a bathtub*, I think to myself as I hold the bottom of my shirt out to catch any food falling from the front of my body. At least, I need a shower to undress in and wash everything off of me.

I begin to ascend the steps, feeling the weight of my shirt as each stair shakes a little more of my night of binge-eating from my clothing. If I have to clean the whole house because of my eating habits, it's going to be a long day tomorrow.

The second floor of the house is just one long bracket-shaped hallway connecting two master bedrooms at each end with a full bathroom in the middle.

Excellent.

I move into the bathroom and shut the door behind me, allowing myself some extra privacy in the empty house of unknown origin. Once inside, I realize that I am probably standing in the dark in front of a large mirror that will tell me more about me than I ever have come to remember in this evening. I take a deep, ragged breath. Even before flicking on the light, I feel like crying. I almost don't want to see.

What if I'm ugly? I mean ... isn't there a good chance by the way I'm acting?

Not ugly, like, how people call you ugly because you are either prettier than them or because you are just not their type, but I mean ugly as in hairy warts on a face of greenish skin, knotty black hair, yellow teeth accentuated by the fact my gums are black and bleeding. What if I'm the Wicked Witch of the West and this is Dorothy's house I jumped out of the way of just in time?

Why do all my visual references deal with television or movies? Did I have a life before I had *this* life?

I flick the light switch on.

A glance around the room shows a seashell border around the top of the room, and a toilet with plastic wrap over it. My pupils take a quick moment to adjust as I look upon myself in the mirror over the sink and am pleasantly surprised and horribly disgusted at the same time.

I do believe I am kinda pretty. I wouldn't say I'd stop buses or launch ships, but what I see is shruggably not bad. Unfortunately, it's hard to tell because I am soaked in my own sick of barely digested, and haphazardly chewed baked beans. That's not the worst of it. I also have a pretty large gash in my shoulder that has bled all the way down the front of my shirt. If that's not the worst of it, the mere fact my eyes seem sunken in, my skin seems gray, there's a bruise on my temple from the rock, several marks on my body from the cans, and the fact I look like a zombie could be the most frightening part.

Focus on the good....

I have pretty thick, healthy-looking brown hair that goes halfway down my back. I'm okay-ish-ly fit with green eyes, medium-full lips, splendid cheek bones, straight white teeth, and good posture. Overall, I'd say I'm about sixteen, maybe seventeen years old, but I could pass for younger. My age is quite the relief as that means I have only forgotten about my childhood, and I haven't lived a full life only to awaken on a strange lawn to live another.

What also is great about it is ...no teenager goes through life completely unnoticed, right? Somebody has to know who I am. Either parents are looking for me or social services. I have to have classmates that either love me or ignore me, but will still realize I'm absent when the homeroom teacher calls my name, and nobody says "Here!" The guy who sits behind me in class will tap his pencil on the back of my empty chair and look around to everyone else and say, "Hey, where's what's-her-face? Anybody seen her?" And the other students in the class will take a cursory glance at my empty desk and wonder where I am.

I'm a kid. Somebody loves me. I mean, I'm a kid covered in vomit and blood, but nonetheless, I'm somebody's angel, right? Somebody is crying tears of worry right now because it's the middle of the night and I'm not home, yet. I hope I didn't run away.

First thing's first, nobody likes anybody covered in

vomit, no matter how passably attractive they are, so I have to correct this situation.

I begin to fill up the sink with water as I don't know if there are any clothes for me in this house and I have to make do with what I have. I slowly peel my shirt off, feeling the cold of dampness on my dry skin that hasn't gotten used to it. I feel the shirt unstick itself from my shoulder wound—still no pain. I put the shirt into the sink and begin to do my best at getting the upchuck-y bits off and suds it up using the hand soap.

I look in the mirror at my body. Nice. Curvy but not mature. Soft but not jiggly. My bra is pretty basic; clearly picked out by a girl with an eye for fashion but not for the purpose of seduction. As if.

Should I assume I don't have a boyfriend? Which I'm totally cool with as I have more problems now than I know what to do with.

With the shirt off, I notice that blood has run down my skin to also soak into the waistband of my jeans, and I unbutton, unzip, and peel the denim away from my legs and throw them onto the white fake marble of the bathroom counter.

Weird.

I glance in the mirror at my underwear clad self, and— *Ooof,* granny panties that don't match the bra or outfit. So much for being fashionable, but they are comfortable.

Thinking about a missing purse makes me wonder if there's anything in my pockets, but after checking them, I only come up with a Wrigley's gum wrapper, a receipt to a pizza shop which I apparently paid for whatever with ten dollars in cash (but the pizza shop, named In The Sauce, printed their address on the receipt).

Which is a clue, Dr. Watson.

Dr. Watson gurgles his approval at going to a place that serves Pepperoni and Sausage anything.

And the last thing found in my pocket helped to better define the first thing found in my pocket—a pack of Wrigley's Double Mint gum. So, it's *my* gum. Apparently, I like to be really trendy and buy the five stick packs of gum for a quarter.

With just gum, a gum wrapper, the house key, the wine opener, the can opener, and a receipt in my pockets, I can now confirm that my purse was stolen because what kind of self-respecting teenage girl like myself doesn't carry a cell phone on her? It obviously was in my purse that somebody stole. The same somebody, probably, that left me for dead on the front lawn of this house. The same somebody that I have every intention of finding and slapping around, perhaps even slowly hunting down with my car.

What car?

I don't know.

Exactly.

So, okay, add the question to the list:

What happened to my purse, and/or cell phone, and/or wallet, and/or any identification I probably had and therefore need to get replaced?

I sit up on the counter and lean over the sink, making sure to turn off the water before it overflows, and get a look at my shoulder wound. Upon closer inspection, there is absolutely no denying that a chunk of my body was bitten off by something very rude. I have to be in shock because all I feel is curious as I stare into my own shoulder and watch as blood grossly pools up in between the chewed out crater of my skin before the crater gets too full and slowly begins to trickle blood down my collar bone and chest again.

I see the dark red muscle fibers underneath, and the veins and arteries, I think, crisscrossing amongst each other. I feel the edges of my skin that have hardened because who knows why, and the gray discoloration around the wound as the skin slowly dies becoming frayed flesh. I look closer, trying to make sure no more ants are crawling around on it, and don't see any, but am very worried about the fact that it is still bleeding. That, and the fact that it seems black veins are spiraling out from it, going closer to my neck and down my shoulder to my arm as if evil is webbing around me.

Wouldn't be long until I wasn't even slightly pleasant to look upon.

Think, dummy, think.

No wound is a good wound, that's for sure, so I have to get this properly attended. Judging by the graying skin around it, something is spreading, like an infection, and I'm sure the tough skin around the hole is not a good sign either. It's deep, oval, and about three inches long. I try to think in my head of every animal I know and the shape of their mouth. Dogs, wolves, and coyotes—anything that seems like it might bite poor little me and have snout-y bite marks. Cats don't have this big of mouths. I begin to think about birds when I realize that I am just being ridiculous.

It's a human, I think to myself. *You were bitten by a cannibal.*

"Ayyooouugggghhhh."

How awful of a feeling it is to know that someone ate

a piece of you. I immediately groaned with the realization I was somebody's protein bar for the evening. Somewhere out there in the world are my parents, my friends, and there is an arrogant person who is digesting my shoulder. I have the odd thought that hopefully the person is homeless and that I can rightly understand the extreme case of hunger that might have risen where they felt like they needed to bite me. But, really, I bet it was just some wretch who thought he was entitled to feast on me.

Thank God they only took a bite and not a meal.

... said—only me, ever.

Add to the list—*Find out who bit me.*

I have a walk ahead of me as I don't have a cell phone and I didn't see any phones in the house. I have no idea where any human life might be in this neighborhood, but I have to get to a hospital. I need a professional to look at this bite and make sure I'm okay and not infected with rabies or AIDS or some flesh-eating virus from Paraguay. *Oh, good, I'm glad I know that country's name....* Maybe the hospital can also run my fingerprints and tell me who I am. Maybe they can call my parents. Maybe my parents can take me home and feed me SPAM and bologna roll-ups.

Don't judge me.

With a sense of hope for a more promising future, I unclasp the bra and kick off the granny panties, start the shower, and hop on in it, letting the cold water wash away blood, dirt, grime, and puke from my skin and down the drain. As the water heats up, I instantly grab for the handle to keep it cold, as I enjoy the ice-cold water against my skin. Warm water, for some reason, makes me feel like I'm on fire, and I have no intention of finding out what hot water might feel like. The cold water feels like it surrounds me and protects me, and I languish in it.

At this point, I assume that I probably have a fever. Infections do that, right?

5

Puke and bloody clothes will have no luck coming clean in an upstairs bathroom sink. So, as I wait, wrapped in a bed sheet because there are no towels in this house I am aware of, my clothes are rumbling around in the dryer.

The stains did not come completely out of my clothes after the wash, but at least I won't look like a ravenous villain walking down the street as I try to find my way to a hospital. My wound is not bleeding much anymore, at least outwardly. The muscle fibers underneath are still soaked in my genetic liquid of life, and a curious slimy film has begun to grow on the outside of the wound. I am hoping it is some kind of biological shield to prevent further infection, but I honestly feel that it is some kind of sci-fi flesh-feeding algae that is feasting on me. Either way, every once and awhile I turn my head to my right, and blow cool air into the gaping hole, feeling my breath wisp around the crater like wind in a valley, and listen to the dryer tumble. I try not to think about the black rash spreading outwardly from the bite. And, every time I feel I have too much saliva in my mouth, I have visions of rabid raccoons.

I could clean up the kitchen as I wait, but that would make me appear to be more dutiful than I actually feel like being, and so I placidly sit at one of the chairs in the dining room and listen to the sounds of the house in the dark. Subtle creaks as wind tries to find its way through it. Water drips out from the shower head upstairs, smacking against the shower curtain that hangs inside the tub.

I have scavenged this house. *My house, as the door key in my pocket protests.* And, I have come up with the following discovery of this domicile:

This is not a model home. While it has the appearance of not being loved nor lived in for a very long time, there still seems to be a lot of items one wouldn't expect to be in a place where people are just "browsing." Like, honestly, is there a reason for working plumbing and toilet paper? Who enters this house and goes: "Umm, I don't know. Maybe, I'll buy it? Let me use the john." No reason for bed sheets either if nobody is going to sleep in here. The wine opener is also confusing because if I was the real estate agent, I wouldn't be opening wine for people unless they had bought the house. And one couldn't buy the model home, so the wine opener is simply an addition to somebody's summer home.

My current assumption is that this is a timeshare house, and since it has neither the necessary supplies of living in it, nor a living member of the human race sleeping upstairs that this is not the time that people are sharing it. Could this house be mine, or maybe owned by my family? Maybe. There has to be a reason I knew that rock was where the Hide-a-Key was. Unless, by shear dumb luck, I was attacked in the yard, and my hand fell upon the rock of my destiny. What was I doing in this front yard anyway? If I'm in a place where nobody else is, what reasonable explanation did I have to be somewhere I shouldn't be? I'm playing scolded child and concerned parent all-in-one, lambasting myself for my poor decision-making while thanking Heavens that I was still alright.

Still wanted to ground myself, though.

Teach myself a lesson.

What were you doing here, you rambunctious child?! I ask myself, ready to cry at my own inner meanness. I want to run to a room and slam the door in my own face. God, I'm such an overbearing parent/negligent child.

I want to cry, but I have no idea why. Every time I think about how lost I am, I realize that I might not be that lost at all. When I realize how alone I am, I think about the last time I knew I wasn't—and that was when I was getting robbed and eaten alive, and really, wasn't it better to be alone than that? I want to cry thinking about how scared I am, but as I sit and think about how I am about to head out and find a hospital, I realize I'm not scared. I'm determined. I have a plan. I know where I'm going. I know how I'm going to get there. To be sad or scared at the obstacles in the way is just inexcusable or an excuse to fail.

I might have been a damsel in distress before, but now I am Bite Woman; determined, quiet, and bleeding.

When *my* dryer beeps and signifies that my clothes are done, I go to grab them excitedly and the mere touch of the freshly laundered clothes feels like my hands are melting off. I immediately let go, moan at the excruciating pain that my scalded palms feel, especially the palm that already has a small cut in it due to the butter knife and beans incident, and I recoil quickly. I let the door stay open and hope that my clothes breathe and cool down fast.

Man, am I super sensitive to heat or what? I remember laundry. I remember my mom smelling like laundry. I remember the feeling of jumping into a pile of laundry my mom had just taken out of the dryer and thrown on her bed to fold, and how mad she'd get when I dove belly first into the pile, relishing in the feeling of manufactured warmth. Perhaps I was always a brat, looking for that one good feeling, that one warm cuddle, and to Hell with the consequences of my actions.

Those days were past, though, as my shower was cold, and now I wait for my clothes to get down to a comfortable room temperature.

After what I assume is enough time passes, I remove myself from the couch and head back to the dryer of my infernal outfit and test the denim of my jeans like one would test an iron. A quick pat at first, followed by a series of pats, followed by laying my hand on it and realizing— yes, it's safe to touch. My clothes are not the same temperature of Hell fire anymore.

At least my underwear's clean, I think to myself as I slide into my antonym-of-appealing granny panties and clasp the bra behind my back. The jeans are still blood-stained around the waistband, but nobody will see it when I put on my shirt, which is worse for wear. A bloodstain, which now appears black in some spots and yellow around the edges, rains down from the right shoulder to my hip and there are still blotchy spots from the belched baked beans. Regardless, it smells like fresh linen, is dry, and no longer carries the worry of creating a mess wherever I walk.

I slide the shirt over my head and check myself out in the full-length mirror in the laundry room.

Not bad if I do say so myself.

Maybe I am an alien, and I have commandeered this body for myself. Maybe it was me who attacked her as she walked to check on her family's timeshare home. That is when I knocked her out in the front yard, and what I think is a bite wound is actually an entry wound from myself and my consciousness invading her body. Maybe, the reason I know so much about television and movies is because I studied those two mediums when I knew I was going to be visiting Earth, and Sherlock Holmes was a part of my research. Maybe I'm a parasite and this teenage girl is my host.

I have a mental image of chewing on a human being. Of ripping flesh from muscle and chewing everything, blood pouring down my chin.

Creepy, I think as Dr. Watson grumbles at me.

Still, being an alien doesn't explain my missing purse or cell phone. I doubt body snatching would leave me without memories of who or what I am, or what my home planet or mission was.

In all actuality, I have a sinking feeling that maybe, before all of this, I was just a weird girl with a weird imagination. Maybe who I am thinks outside the box, and maybe I didn't have any friends because of this. Maybe nobody would care if I wasn't at school the next day. In my head, my mental image of the boy tapping his pencil on the back of my chair is replaced with my empty desk, all the way to the back left corner of the room. If I did get a second chance at life, I should add making as many friends as possible to the list.

6

Armed with the corkscrew wine opener, I step back out into the night, locking the front door behind me, and put the key into my pocket for safekeeping. Easily, I walk back down the steps, remarking to myself about how hard it was to do earlier. The meat I had consumed has obviously helped my mobility. I'm not a graceful dancer by any means, but my feet no longer feel like they're sticking to hot tar. I do notice that I'm having problems bending my knees and am walking like a pirate on two peg legs. Aside from making my upper body rock back and forth like a lightly struck bowling pin, it's not that bad. Not nearly as bad as before when I felt like a toddler.

I turn around and look at the house, memorizing the address of 2256, and thinking to myself that I will have to find a street sign to have any hope in returning here. Every house on this street looks the same, and knowing my luck tonight, every street in this town will look the same as well. Perhaps I'm dead and this is Hell, and my Hell is a never-ending suburb with no Arby's.

I pass my grass angel and notice something new within the blades of greenery—a curious track of a left foot, and one long line next to it. Almost as if whoever else walked through the grass was dragging its right foot behind them. Did the person walk through when I was in the house feeding and showering? Or before I had arrived? Or as I was laying in the yard? I catalogue it like I've had to catalogue everything else tonight. Man, there's a lot to think about and remember and figure out.

I look up toward the sky and see things are brighter to the left, almost white even, and no stars are visible. I can remember this is called *light pollution;* artificial light that bounces off the atmosphere, blocking out the chance of seeing stars on clear nights. The number one reason why it would be *no bueno* for an astronomer to live in a metropolis.

Great job, genius. Now tell me your name.

Even talking to myself, I hope my brain responds—

"What's wrong with you? My name is ____!"

But nothing comes. Nada.

So, with a new lease on life, *literally,* and with utter disregard for the fact that I was attacked and my attacker is, probably, very much so, still out and about somewhere by me in this neighborhood, I begin to waddle down the sidewalk toward the effervescent light of the horizon with the corkscrew wine opener lodged between my fingers, just ready to punch anything that threatens me. The night air has a certain mustiness to it that I can't place, and an unyielding breeze constantly tickles my neck with the wayward hairs of my head.

There's another sound out here, almost as if the Earth is breathing. It's rhythmic, peaceful, and seems to be all around me.

I find myself at an intersection, and take note of the street signs. *My* house is 2256 Atlantic, about ten houses away from 21st Street. I say this to myself mentally as I continue to walk.

At 15th Street, I stop and look both ways down the street. I can only see a couple blocks before there's nothing but blackness beyond. To my right, it seems the road ends at a wall of wood. To my left, it seems the road ends at a field of high, dry grass. It's very unsettling that it feels like the world ends two blocks away left or right, and my only options were forward or back.

When I arrived at 12th Street, I smelled something in the night sky. At first, it was subtle. Just something I would catch every once and awhile in my nostrils, but the more I walked, the more the smell grew. Like warm, baked bread with hints of cinnamon and sugar. My stomach gurgled again at the delicious wafts and I began to just follow my nose and not my eyes. My bare, scraped feet waddling faster the closer I got to 10th Street, the more I could smell something like fried chicken with a side of roasted turkey smothered in butter.

When I passed the intersection of Atlantic and 10th Street, I could sense I was leaving the smell behind. And even knowing that I should be trying to find a hospital and get my festering wound looked at, I turn around. I have never smelled food like this before in my life. It was succulent meatballs and prime rib with woody spices. Like Mom's chili meets your favorite Chinese place meets a spit of roasting lamb meat, I honestly was about to swallow not just my tongue, but my entire lower jaw.

"Oooh aye Gawg, eh heh oooh Goy!" I exclaimed, still

very much surprised at how horribly I spoke, but also agreeing that yes, *Oh my God, it does smell so good.* And then I drooled a little.

The next street was, as I assumed, exactly the same as Atlantic, but called Center. As far as I can see, it runs parallel to Atlantic both ways, and rivals it house-for-house with the same collection of timeshare homes with nobody living in them. Streetlights burn an orange-ish color and no other descriptive features to write home about. From what I could see at the intersection of Center and 10th, the perpendicular street only had another fifty feet to go before it met one more street, and then ended in an abyss of no light. But, the smell of BBQ and cornbread was up ahead and so I trotted off after it.

The third and final parallel street was called West and instead of being a two-way street, they had added two more lanes to it, making it four-lanes wide. On the opposite side of West there was nothing but tall grass and darkness beyond it. The street had traffic lines painted on it and for some reason, double yellow lines in the middle of the road (which, I knew, meant drivers couldn't drive their car over them without fear of getting a ticket or in an accident) meant that there were rules to this village. And where there are rules, there is civilization.

Of course, where there is the smell of mince meat pie happening, there must also be civilization. I had to find whoever was cooking all these lovely dishes and shake their skillful, culinary hands. I bet the person was stocky and jovial, because who couldn't cook this deliciously and not be eating and happy all the time? Not that I was a great judge of cuisine—I had just eaten SPAM with my hands.

I knew I was close to the smell as there was no more

losing it for a second. Every breeze carried it. But I could not see its origin. All there was was me, the streetlights, the empty houses, and the empty void across the street.

There was something, though, wasn't there?

A flash of movement in the dark.

Something white.

Something big.

Whatever it was, the smells of meat lovers' pizza, sage, and seasoned salt were coming from it, and so I just had to follow. I just had to see what it was. It couldn't be the thing itself. How could I smell the thing? But, it must be carrying something like a bag of food it stole from somewhere. I'm so hungry; I might even try and bargain for it. If it was just a large animal, I'd try to wrestle the food free from its snarling jaws, and run with it as fast as can be on my solid peg legs.

I advanced on my prey slowly. Dr. Watson leading the way, grunting and growling and moaning with a tenacious veracity that made me worried my stomach was going to rip out of me and leave me behind. While my memory was only a couple hours old, I knew I had never been this controlled by my taste buds, by my nose, by the overwhelming want to feed on the delicious aromas permeating off of this object which, as I got closer, I could make out slightly in the dark....

It wasn't facing me. It was facing the black nothingness. It was looking out, peering out, maybe wondering the same thing I was wondering moments ago, when it came to wondering what else is out there in the void. There was nothing in its grasp. I was smelling...

... it.

The thought almost repulses me as I realize that I am

in love with the way this being smells. That I could actually look upon a living thing as if it was a casserole dish of baked chicken breasts smothered in gravy and cheese. That I was mouth-breathing over being so close to this feast that was within my grasp.

This ... man....

He hasn't noticed me, yet, this handsome chap. I continue to waddle over to him, and I want to call out—to announce my presence, but at the same time, I don't. No. I want to get closer to him. I think, maybe. Maybe, I can run my tongue over his skin before he notices. Maybe I can bite down on his flesh and taste him before he fights me off and runs away, but then, I'll have tasted it. I'll have sampled this sweet smell of deliciousness.

Almost within reach, my arms now looking to grasp him, I stumble forward.

"Aoooohh goaaawwrrrr," I say, immediately cursing myself for letting the Lord's name escape my lips, but I'm just so hungry, so determined for a bite, that I can't help it.

He hears me and turns around. His eyes open wide at the sight of me in my bloody tank top and bare feet. I must look a mess. I can't close my mouth. I can't look away from him. I can barely blink. With sheer determination, I advance. He's shocked to see me as he throws up his hands in defense; all I want to do is rip into his flesh, and slurp down his life's liquid.

I mean ... I can barely process any of this.

"Alex?" he says, almost like a question.

Before I can wonder if he knows me, I fall on top of him, my teeth at his soft throat.

7

Of course, he's surprisingly strong. Or maybe he's not strong, and I'm just weak. Still shaky from all my previous experiences of the night, and still absolutely starved, he easily kicks me off him, and I have trouble trying to figure out whether I should go through the whole ordeal of rising to my feet again, or unpretentiously crawling after him, my beautiful dinner. As if on auto-pilot, my body begins to inch forward. I reach out and grip dry, dead grass and pull myself onward, the grass breaking off in my hands as I do it again and again, trying to get at this chap who is kicking away.

Grip grass, pull, kick out with my legs, and move a fraction of the distance that he is gaining on me. This crawling thing is hard, and I feel pathetic. Can't imagine how I look when I'm laboring so, and I can't quit breathing out my mouth as drool falls down my chin.

He's afraid of me. Good. He should be. If our situations were reversed, I'd be downright petrified of myself. I can't remember if I have always desired the taste of human flesh, or if this is something new, but I regret feeling disgusted at the thing who took the chunk out of my shoulder. I understand now how delicious I must have smelled. I don't understand why they took one bite and left me in that lawn. Did I taste bad? Was the smell of homo sapien cuisine false advertising and as soon as I ripped this man's throat out, was I going to regret my decision and choke the piece down? I didn't have the answers, but I sure couldn't wait to find out.

"Alex, what are you doing? It's me. It's Max!" the man says.

I ignore him. Or, I don't so much as ignore him as I absent-mindedly file what he is saying to the back of my mind as I imagine chewing the skin off of his shin, the closest body part to me as I kick forward on my belly, and he kicks backwards on his bum. I know it sounds gross, the act of eating another person, but imagine not eating for days, and suddenly somebody puts a fried turkey leg in front of you. Are you going to be all like, "Eww, the skin is crunchy, and peppery, and the meat is too juicy"? Or are you going to be like, "Yum, yum, gimme some" like how I currently am with this man who calls himself Max? (If you're a vegetarian, I have no idea how to describe my current predicament. In fact, we obviously will have nothing in common with our tastes.)

I admire his utter skill of standing up without having to crack his knees into place, without having to give conscience bodily thought to each and every movement, to standing up, straightening out his body. An impressive feat that I just can't duplicate so I continue to grab grass, and pull, knee thrust, kick!

Grab grass, pull, knee thrust, and kick!

This is how you crawl, children, through the grass. Demeaning, demoralizing, sure— especially when you're drooling, moaning, and have about as much strength as an earthworm on a hot sidewalk, but the struggle is real. The hunger pains have become entirely overpowering, and all I want to do is bury my incisors into his *epidermis* and peel back a piece of him, only stopping to chew the crunchy bits and slurping down the rest.

"Alex, what's wrong with you?"

I'm hungry, I say in my mind. My mouth says, "Awerrr owwgurra". This sounds like I'm making a request for arugula with a mouth full of cotton balls to a person who doesn't speak the same language as I. Honestly, if I had any intention of talking, I probably would put it higher on the list than:

1. Make this man's calf an appetizer. Whatever belly fat he has on his stomach, make the main course.

"Alex, do you remember me?"

Nope.

"What's wrong with you?"

Nothing. I'm hungry.

"Is that blood? Are you bleeding?"

Will you just stop moving so I can chew on you?

Crawling was not working as every time I scooted a little closer, Max would move swiftly out of the way like a teenage ninja. I have come to realize that I am so slow that he is able to get within inches of me, like a wildlife photographer snapping photos of a gorilla, and then dart away when I go to grasp for him. He'll bend down, eyes wide and staring, and I'll look up, a low, guttural groan escaping from my lips, and I'll swipe to grab a piece of clothing, and lose my balance to fall face-first back to the grass. Max jumps back to wherever-land and repeats his dance all over again. If I wasn't prone to gnawing off his face, he might laugh at my pathetic-ness.

That's it. *Mano-y-mano*, I thought to myself as I retrained my brain to stand like I did in the front yard of "my house" earlier tonight. Bent elbows, palms on the ground, and push ... up ... steady legs ... find your balance ... and ... there? There.

Max's eyes go from wide and unblinking to wider with hidden eyelids. I felt like either the most beautiful person he has ever seen, the most famous person he has ever seen, or his dead great-grandmother come back to life looking for her missing teeth. Max just stares at me, and I stare back for a second, relishing in actually being seen, regardless of how dang creepy he was making me feel. And then I thought, *wait, I want to eat this man. I am creepy.* And then I thought about food, and my hunger, and how close I was to salvation.

That's when I lashed out to eat Max again.

And he hit me.

After that was the darkness I was born into.

8

Coming to, I realize that I can't move. Not like when I first came to and couldn't move because I had no remembrance of motor skills, but this time I was actually tied up. "Max" (if that was his real name) had taken my wrists and bound them behind me, and then, for added effect, had bound my elbows to my sides using his hoodie. My ankles were tied together with some kind of string that I assume came from his shoes which were now flopping and loose. As I wake, I groan a little bit and open-and-close my mouth to hear a clicking sound in my jaw. I dart my tongue out in all directions, because my mouth is incredibly dry, and continue to mouth breathe. The sounds I make are of a dog eating a delicious bone.

Great. I finally meet someone, who seems to be nice and a friend, and I go and try to eat him. Therefore, he broke my jaw. And honestly, I can't blame him.

I test the durability of his workmanship in the "bounding-girls department" and realize Max is quite the Boy Scout knot maker. If completely free, I wasn't going anywhere fast; now bound, I absolutely wasn't going anywhere at all. This brought the old mission up in my mind—if I couldn't move at all, I wasn't going to be going to a hospital any time soon. After that thought is the delicious aroma emanating from Max and how hungry I am. That's my life in a nutshell: either bandage me or feed me.

Max noticed I was awake, probably at my propensity to moan every time I smell him. And also at the fact I breathe through my mouth like a heavy sleeper with a stuffy nose. Or perhaps the wiggling got his attention. Either way, he stopped poking a two-foot stick in the mud (as boys do when in nature and bored, I guess) and walked over to me, still holding his new woody play toy.

"Alex? I'm sorry I hit you."

Could it be? Could my name be Alex? Is Max my savior I was hoping for when I first broke into the house tonight?

Regardless, he filled in a blank:

"Hey! Your name is <u>ALEX</u>! And, you were _____ on _____ because _____!"

Alex. My name is Alex. And I'm a teenage girl who dresses all right who woke up on a lawn tonight with a bite taken out of my shoulder in the middle of a ghost town.

Max is dressed like a typical teenage boy. Jeans, t-shirt, shoes of the tennis variety, but his laces are missing. (Remember? Around my ankles?) He's got a good build, average height, messy brown hair, and the kind of eyes that always seem like he's scrutinizing you. Which is probably for the best, because I am one to be scrutinized at the moment.

I struggle more against my binding, and Max kneels down to put his fingers between all of his knots and my skin to make sure nothing is cutting off circulation. To reward him for his kindness, I try to take a bite out of his arm. He quickly recoils, grabbing his stick, and pointing it at me as if it was some kind of projectile weapon. I snap my teeth at him and lay back down, letting him know that I might be this person he knows, this "Alex", but I still was going to eat him if given the chance.

"Your shoulder ... it looks infected," Max said, using his stick to probe around my wound. I wiggle away from him. Not because it hurt, necessarily, but because it was my wound of which I was able to claim from the village of ants and dirt and I didn't want his mud-poking, sticky wooden stick anywhere near it. "Do you remember what happened? What did this to you?"

He asks, and the want to cry again but not necessarily knowing how squelches up in my throat. I had strangely been hoping that the first person I met would have all the answers, and I now realized that life was going to be a long, hard road of questions.

"I should get you to a hospital."

My eyes open wide, and I agree. "Gaaaww-rrreeehhhh," I respond and he's momentarily lost in his thoughts as he looks closer at my mouth.

"Did you eat your tongue? Why can't you talk?"

I'm just about to answer him when I decide to hold back. It was a good question, a fair question. What did happen to my ability to talk, and why did I feel like it was getting worse than what it was back in the house? Every time I opened my mouth, it was like it didn't want to shut again. My lips didn't want to cover my teeth. My tongue felt like it does when I ... *yawned*—just a stiff, un-controllable piece of muscle. Max wanted to have a conversation, and all I could do was cough the spit from my windpipe and then string together the noises the vowels made in the English language one right after another.

When I'm alone, I'll remind myself to practice this communicating thing. Of course, if I wanted to get to the hospital, my best chance was for Max to take me, or untie me, or both. I stopped wiggling, stopped breathing all together, and simply looked up at the stars, waiting for Max to make the next move. Which he did by sticking his stick into my stomach. I winced.

"If you're playing with me ... I'm asking you to stop. I mean it. I don't want to be out here any longer, and you're beginning to freak me out. It's late."

I still lay there, staring up at the stars which are a little harder to see now, because, that's right, *light pollution* from the city that was only ten blocks away. Only ten blocks away but no, I had to go hunting for this man with the wicked right punch and the sailor's knot tying skills so now I'm laying out on another field of grass, except this one is dead grass, and less comfortable, and more itchy than ticklish which I think I hated more as a sensation. I look out toward the abyss and see nothing.

But, wait? Maybe it was Max who took a bite out of me and left me for dead earlier? It honestly isn't all that far-fetched considering he just decked me and this is all a little bit déjà-vu-y.

"I think I should take you to the hospital. Your shoulder is bleeding, and I noticed, when tying you up, that you're freezing. Your skin is really cold, and you seem a little bit—I mean, I'm no doctor, but you seem to be discoloring a little bit. Is that okay with you? You don't have, like, a fear of hospitals or anything, do you?"

I couldn't help but picture in my mind Max trying to lift me from this position like how heroes rescue girls in the movies—the carry where one arm goes under their legs, and the other goes across their backs, and the girl's head rests on the guy's shoulder—their lips next to the guy's neck. I couldn't help but picture grasping his skin between my front teeth and snipping through it like biting the casing off a sausage link and beginning to collect his blood on my tongue.

Maybe I'm a vampire.

...

I doubt it.

I feel if I'd woken up a vampire, I'd be a whole lot more verbal. Vampires seemed to have a cool Old English vibe to them. Like, as soon as you become a blood drinking member of the undead, you also got your Masters in English and talk like a lost member of the Eastern European royal family. I smile because mentally using multi-syllabic words amuses me where verbally, my speech is akin to gargling Listerine.

"I'm going to go get my truck," Max said as he began to run away, leaving me bound by the side of the road called West in the ghost town of unknown name by the tall dead grass that bordered the black area of nothingness.

Hospital, here I come.

9

Something about hospitals does unnerve me.

Perhaps it's the way that the doctor, a young Indian man, smelling of a certain blend of delicious spices that were succulent and sweet, and one stocky nurse woman just seemed to stare at me like I was an enigma that they couldn't quite figure out. Granted, this was before anybody began to treat me, or inspect me, or whatever it was health professionals did, but it must have been a slow night for these hospital workers for they had nothing better to do than stare at me bound and gagged in a chair in the lobby.

The receptionist nurse (*intake nurse person?*) had made a show about calling the police when Max brought me in, my stiffening body (from lack of use) dangling over his shoulder. My fantasy of opening up his jugular and drinking his pulse-y milkshake as it flowed from him like the outdoor faucet on a hot summer day was spoiled when he dragged me feet first into the uncomfortable bed of his pick-up truck, and left me there, sky-gazing, as we drove through the city, and the street lights, and the artificial light to the hospital. Heckuva friend, if you ask me, and if I ever did get the power of speech back, we were going to have words about this abusive treatment. In the parking lot, he apparently found a new piece of cloth in his cab and stuffed the sock, or the wash rag, or whatever grimy, itchy fabric it was into my mouth before I could snap off one of his fingers with a quick bite, and then proceeded to carry me into the hospital where a nurse admitted me with her lower jaw almost on her desk.

"I found her like this," Max was able to stammer.

"Tied up?" The nurse asked. It was an honest question.

"No! Wounded. I found her wounded. Well, her shoulder—I didn't do her shoulder. But, her face—I hit her. And then I tied her up. Threw her into the back of my truck and brought her here. All these other marks? I don't think they were me."

"You found this girl ... by the side of the road, hit her, tied her up, and brought her to the hospital?"

"She was trying to bite me," Max pleaded, as if further explaining the lunacy of it all would make him seem less crazy. But, I felt bad for him. I understood. It was that kind of night. "I don't know ..." he continued. "Bath salts?"

The name of the hospital was Ocean City Hospital which I'm thinking is the name of the town that we are in, but it still doesn't recall any memories of how I initially got here. The hospital was a couple of rooms, and there were no other patients: just moi. Ocean City must have been a really small city with not a lot of people for its hospital to be so ... dead. Which is probably for the best as I have not been let out of the waiting room, and surrounded by people, I might have exploded at the want to feed off all of them.

They did replace the wash rag gag in my mouth with a surgical mask which was nice of them. Right before they got the mask on me, I gave one of my best *recitations* of the vowel sounds and snapped my teeth close to the doctor's arm. He swore in an unfamiliar language, and looked back at the nurse to see if he had reacted in a way that was unbecoming, but she just looked at me like I was a piece of art. If I had awoken in a land where people eat people, as my appetite clearly suggested I did, she might be trying to figure out the best way to cook me.

As far as my hunger pains, I still felt them. Max smelled the best, and I wonder if it has something to do with his youth. The nurse smelled of flowers and tea, as if a pleasant snack. The intake-receptionist-person, the poor thing, smelled of rot, and it was all I could do to squirm in Max's grasp when he was checking me in so he'd set me far away from her. I hope the poor dear is okay, but I don't understand how nobody has told her to mask her scent of inner decay.

"Seems she has a bite on her shoulder. Rabies?" the nurse theorized.

"Usually doesn't work this fast. Bite seems new. Can we take off the mask?" Indian Doctor replied. "Get the usual rundown?"

"She'll bite," Max professed, with all the confidence in the world. Not even giving me a chance on this one.

"I can't see this being rabies, which is a good thing. If the symptoms present themselves, the victim is surely to die. Besides, it's just an old wives' tale that the person would become like a rabid dog. Usually just delirium. Dehydration. This girl might need a psychological evaluation."

"What did the police say?" the nurse asked the receptionist who was walking in with a wheelchair.

"Something about a man running through yards on the South side. Will get here when they can."

"Well, let's get her into the chair, and wheel her to an exam room."

Examination Room 1 was a sterile square room with a counter top of jars that held cotton balls and swabs, a poster of the muscles and bones and tendons in our body which looked, to me, like a menu, and an examining room table. The doctor almost didn't let Max in the room with us, preferring to keep him in the hall, but he demanded his way in as I was lifted and placed on the table. Perhaps they were bypassing the cooking, and just going to dig into me here. I envied them this. I could really go for some soft flesh as well. At the sight of how I was thrashing, they used leather and *fleece* straps to secure me to the table, giving Max back his pieces of cloth and shoelaces, to which he readily laced back up his tennies.

"Rabies usually takes multiple days for symptoms to show up, sometimes weeks. If she was bit tonight ..." the doctor continued to say, staring at me, but talking out the side of his mouth. "I mean, there's no fever.... Wound is almost experiencing necrosis."

All right, all right, we get it. It's not rabies. Move on.

"Couldn't we also be dealing with a drug overdose?" the nurse asked.

"How about that? She take any drugs we should be aware of? LCD? Bath salts?" the doctor scrutinized Max. "Heroin?"

"No," Max responded immediately.

"That you know of?" Nurse asked.

"Sure. What's with the black around her wound?" Max asked.

"Infection. We'll get her an IV. Antibiotics. See if that does the trick. You her boyfriend?"

"Uh," Max struggled with the question, and I struggled to hear the answer. "Technically?" He asked.

"Forget it," the doctor said, not wanting to get into our high school drama.

Even I had to be relieved I wasn't some druggie. I could have totally fried my brain tonight with some mood-altering drugs, and passed out, and woke up without memories. Then, while passed out, an animal came by to take a bite of me, but was scared away when I woke up. Still didn't explain my bloodlust and/or those creepy footprints in *my* front yard.

"I mean, I don't know. We only just met this week. At school."

Well, shoot, apparently Max really wasn't my savior. What kind of guy goes out with a girl he barely knows, loses her so that she's attacked, punches her, and gags her to take her to the hospital? Well, Alex, you certainly got yourself into a pickle, and if you don't start calming down, it's only going to get worse. It's never a good thing when doctors pore over you. They write journals of unusual cases and you become less of a human and more of a study. Quality of life doesn't matter at that point, just individual doctors fighting for accolades.

The other bad thing that can come out of this is the police officers using me as a way to solve some of their more unsolvable crimes. Picture this, a girl that nobody knows who can't communicate, and seemingly, likes to bite people. If the person who bit me is still out there somewhere, biting people, but the cops can't find them, who's to say "nay" when they point the finger at me? Then my life becomes doctors poking and prodding me, and at the end of the day, a jail cell, a cot, and a thin blanket to warm me up at nights. If I didn't start acting normal any time soon, I was going to lose any hope of normalcy.

And I wanted normalcy.

And blood, and flesh, and organs down the gullet, Dr. Watson, my stomach, reminded me.

I know the two aren't connected. Shut up. Life is complicated.

Of course, another concern is if Max and I go to the same school together, he's going to tell everyone I'm some psycho chick who tried to eat him. I'm sure that won't go over well and I'll lose serious brownie popularity points from being homecoming queen or prom queen or student class president or whatever makes whoever cool at our school. Probably just call me Hannibal Lector and throw different pieces of meat at me during lunch time. The latter of which, as of now, I'd totally be fine with.

"I assume you don't have her parents' numbers, then?" the receptionist questioned.

"No. She had a purse and a cell phone, but she didn't have it on her when we reconnected," Max explained, looking this-way-and-that. I'm thinking the incoming police were going to have more questions for him, and he was starting to get more nervous about that.

"Well, we'll have to wait for the police to hopefully track down this young's girls parents before we give her anything she might be allergic to. In the meantime, I want to address the wound, clean it out and dress it. Her hand doesn't look like it will require stitches. We'll wrap it up. Let's get an IV in her arm to address the loss of fluids issue. Might just be this girl got bit by a dog and is just going through a state of shock at the moment. What's her name again?"

"Alex," Max said, and I loved hearing him say it.

"Well, Alex, my name is Doctor Patel, and you are going to be all right. You are at the hospital now, and we're going to take care of you."

The doctor seemed like a nice enough man, but Dr. Watson was the only thing I was privy to listen to, and Dr. Watson was hungry. The nurse found a vein in my arm, and after disinfecting the area with alcohol, she stuck in the needle, and suddenly—I was feeling pretty good. I couldn't tell what exactly they were putting in me, but it was clear, going in cold, and spreading throughout my entire body. She was an angel, and quickly becoming one of my favorite people. I laid back and enjoyed the ride. She then disinfected the butter knife wound on my hand, and began to wrap it in gauze, all the while peering at Max.

"How did she get this wound on her hand? Looks as if a sharp object cut her."

"I don't know."

"Looks like a defensive wound."

Max knew enough to know when he was being accused of something that he had no answer for, so he stopped talking and stared at the floor. The nurse finished her bandaging, and cleaned up her area.

"I will be waiting for the police and doing some research on our friend here," the receptionist said, excusing herself.

As my eyes grew heavy, the doctor left the room, and

the nurse pulled up a chair closer to my head to begin to do her magic on my shoulder wound. Max checked his phone for messages, and finding none, replaced the phone back in his pocket. He sighed, running a hand through his hair, pretending like he wasn't tired, but his body slumping against the countertop told a different story. It wasn't helping that I was about to pass out myself on the table.

"She looks like she's feeling pretty good," the nurse said.

"What did you give her? Morphine?" Max asked, a twinge of jealousy in his voice.

"No, it's something to help her get her fluids back up. We don't know how much blood she has lost, and when a patient loses a lot of blood, them going into shock is a bigger risk. So, we're giving her—what's almost like a saline solution. It's called a blood replacement."

"Like blood but not."

"Basically."

I heard every word they were saying, but I did not care. Dr. Watson gargled, and grumbled, and purred, and grumbled, but he wasn't the crazed Mr. Hyde I have come to know and loathe tonight. He actually was restful. My mouth was no longer dry, and I was able to, behind the surgical mask, lick my tongue over my teeth and lips, and swallow, swallow, swallow until nothing felt dry and sticky anymore. Actually, laying on my back, I almost choked on my spit going down the wrong pipe which, for somebody dealing with extreme cotton mouth all night, save for the momentary lapses of drool, was almost a pleasant experience for me.

The nurse, who I might begin calling Angel, and maybe

even claiming as *my* angel as to lay claim to her like I have so many things today, begins to clean out my shoulder wound with a saline solution, and put gauze over it. She has the same smell of flowers, and tea, and soft cheese, and parsley as she did before. I don't feel like eating her anymore. In fact, I don't feel like eating anyone. I'm now just enjoying their scent.

That includes Max, the hunk of prime rib over there. He can keep his body.

"I'm not hungry anymore," I say, dreamily. I'm slow blinking and taking everything in, not even really realizing what's transpiring. The light above me seems fuzzy and I'm almost in a state of euphoria.

"Alex?"

I forget that's my name, or at least that's what Max calls me and I continue to look about the room and up at my angel who is smiling down at me with her eyes as she secures the last bit of gauze to my skin. My wound itches, and I go to scratch it, but am instantly reminded that I have been tied down, and a new panic of claustrophobia or *cleithrophobia*, the fears of small spaces or being trapped, (*why in all the Sherlock do I know this?*) hits me hard. I instantly feel like I'm going to freak out. My ankles and wrists have been tied down so closely to the table that I only have an inch or so of wiggle room, and that inch or so of freedom is just enough to drive me absolutely crazy in a new and different way tonight.

"Let me go!" I scream, sending Max with sheer panic as far away from me as possible. He palms the wall, and stares at me, not unlike the first time I stood up in front of him. The nurse also flinches back, hands in the air, like there's even a possibility of biting her through the surgical mask. "Let me go! Please. Let me go!"

"Calm down, sweetie; the straps are for your own good."

My brain screams in my head about how much I hate being tied down while at the same time trying to tell me that they'll never undo the straps if I appear uncontrollable, but it doesn't matter. I want free as badly as I want to go insane, so I repeatedly kick, and pull, and tug at my straps. If you ask me, nothing is for your own good if it is driving you completely bonkers.

"I can't breathe! Please. Please do something for me. Please, take the mask off!"

The magic word loses its nicety when screamed viciously.

"If I take the mask off, will you try and bite me?"

"No! I promise! Please!"

"Calm down."

Her hands hover over my face, and I watch them, and I fight all the muscle reflexes in my body to lash out against the bindings. I feel like I'm loosening them, but that just might be my brain telling me to try harder to get free. Her hands inch closer, and I'm shaking, and sweating, and the straps are digging into my wrists and ankles, but I don't relax. I don't give in. I just feel more comfortable (but not comfortable at all) stretching the leather to its giving point rather than laying placidly on the table. In the movies, when the walls are coming in, the hero will continue to pointlessly push back on the walls until the hero is flattened, because nobody allows themselves to be crushed. They'll fight back until it kills them.

Was I insane?

Anybody would appear insane if you tied them to an

examination room table, I feel.

My angel of straps and stress quickly pulls the surgical mask from my face and I breathe deep, trying to control my emotions. I lay meekly down, but my whole body is itching with pins and needles just knowing that the straps are still there, and that I can't readily move how I want to. My brain tries to tell me that I have made headway with the straps, and if I just fight a little more, I can break them. But, Dr. Watson argues that brains cannot be trusted.

Brains get you into the messes the gut gets you out of, Dr. Watson grumbles. *Lie there and wait.*

I do as my stomach commands.

A couple more controlled breaths, a couple more thoughts about how if I just act natural, they'll free me. A couple more moments and I won't be living the life of a test subject / wrongfully convicted serial biter.

"What is your name?" the nurse inquires, and I already know this is going to go south.

"Alex."

"Your full name."

Crap, you got me there. But, if I admit to the amnesia, they'll want to do further tests, and if I can't explain where I've been and where I'm going, the police can pin whatever on me.

Don't let them know you don't know, Dr. Watson coaches me, and I'd hate to say it, but my stomach is right. Although I know that its intentions are purely to go back out in the world and hunt.

"Please, if you'll just let the straps go. I hate it. I hate this. Please."

I feel tears welling up in my eyes, and I smile. Holy smokes, I have to look crazy, but I finally remembered what it was like to cry and I felt embarrassed and lighter at the same time. I look over to Max, and lock eyes with him—I know I have him. I beg him silently to let me go.

"We can't loosen the straps until we get more information out of you, Alex. What happened to you tonight?"

"I was attacked. Please."

"What attacked you?"

Hey! Your name is Alex! And you were attacked on _____ because _____!

"I don't know. I didn't see it. I woke up in my front yard and I was bleeding, and my purse was gone."

"Do you know your parents' phone number?"

"It was in my phone."

"You don't know your parents' phone number?"

"No."

"Did they get a new number recently, or...?"

"No. I just... don't know it."

"What is your last name, dear?"

That's when I screamed. It wasn't, probably, a minute or so after she told me that if I just answered all of their questions that they would let me go, but it felt like their questions would be forever coming. I had rights. As an American citizen and as a minor who had really not done anything wrong criminally—

You might have broken into someone's home and trashed the place.

Okay, but that's hearsay or whatever—

There was no reason I should be tied down the way I was.

"Why am I being restrained?" I ask with a cool voice.

"So you don't hurt yourself or anyone else."

"Who have I hurt?"

"Max here says you tried to bite him." This woman was beginning to lose her status as *my angel* and just becoming the woman with the good saline drip.

"But, did I? I'm fine now, but these are driving me crazy. They are making this worse! I would like them removed."

"Now that you are coherent, let me go get Dr. Patel and he can make that call, okay? I'll be back in a jiffy."

The nurse cleans up the mess she made while bandaging my wound and throws her rubber gloves and wrappers out in a biohazard waste unit. All the while, she keeps her eyes on me as I stare back at her, neither of us trusting the other. She also doesn't trust Max, which is apparent as he is the last thing she glares at as she ventures down the hall. I turn to the only person who might be my ally in this whole mess—the guy I tried to eat.

"Max! Max, please undo these straps."

"We'll just wait for the doctor," Max dismisses me, arms crossed, as far across the room as he can be.

"Max, I'm sorry I tried to bite you. I wasn't myself. I was dehydrated or mental or feverish or something. But you punched me and gagged me, and threw me in the back of your truck. I think we're even."

"Hmmph," Max responded, maturely. "What even happened to you? You ran off."

"I don't know."

"You don't know?"

"I don't remember."

"A couple hours ago?"

"I have amnesia," I say, blurting it out in a blatant form of trust that could seriously ruin me, but I was racing against the clock, against the doctors coming back and being all clinical, against the police getting here and being all... *procedural*. I wonder if I'm always the kind of girl that doesn't test the waters with her toe, but rather jumps in headfirst.

But, this did get Max's attention, "What?"

"Close the door."

Max does as he is told, *good boy*, mouth open, completely enthralled by my latest confession, and I'm seeing why I might have begun to like him. There is a possibility he's my only friend and confidante in the world, and I must utilize him if I am going to get out of here and figure out what happened tonight. Max and I could sit down, and he could tell me everything he knows, and from there, we'll start formulating something. But, as of now, doctors and police are not going to help.

"I don't remember anything of tonight. Or yesterday. Or who I am. I only know my name is Alex because you said it was."

Max thought about it, clearly over his head in the situation.

"Well, then, we need to get you help," Max responded, and I could tell he just wasn't confident in handling my case. But, if one thing is easily inflated, it's paper bags and male egos.

"No, please, Max, you're the only one who can help me. They'll want to keep me here. The police, they just like to solve crimes—"

"It's their job."

"What do you think they'll see when they walk in here? A girl who was beat up, and a guy who admits to, at least, punching her. They'll arrest you, Max, and I don't want that. And then they'll arrest me."

"Why, what did you do?"

"Nothing—"

"That you remember."

"Well, I did break into a house tonight, eat some food, and take a shower. I did do that. That's on the spectrum side of illegal. Look. We're both in hot water here, and I think—"

"I had to punch you. You were going to bite me," Max says more so to remind himself he is a good person. His voice is shaking, betraying a whimper, and I feel bad that I have practically broken the kid. "I didn't want you to get hurt."

"I know. I know. And, I understand. But, they won't. Please, help me. I don't want to be some medical experiment, in some cage the rest of my life. I need everything to appear normal, until I get my memory back."

"What if you never do?" he asks.

"Help me. Just help me."

Max sits there, in that lonely chair that faces my bed, chewing his lower lip like I want to do. It's not necessarily that I want to eat him anymore, but if he's going to sample himself, I wouldn't mind a taste, either.

"What do you need me to do?"

"Untie me."

"But—"

"If you untie me, and I stay calm on this table when they return, they'll have no reason to tie me back up."

Max thinks about it quickly and shuffles his feet closer to me. He takes deep breaths, trying not to appear scared of the girl that he is definitely scared of as he reaches for the strap by my ankle. He works the buckle like a kid that has never put on dress pants before. Once the first strap is off, I fight the urge to kick up and out like a Rockette. I let my foot enjoy its freedom and bend my knee up, resting my foot flat on the table. This saline solution IV drip is wonderful for my dexterity.

And my speech.

"Thank you, Max. Thank you."

"I still don't trust you," Max responds, getting control of his fear.

Once all of my restraints came off, Max backed quickly away from the table and toward the wall. Crossing his arms, he stood there, scrutinizing and staring at me as I rubbed my raw skin from where the fleece didn't protect quite enough with me fighting against it. With my limbs now free and the coolness of my IV, I actually felt "normal" for the first time.

And, for the first time, I *remembered* what it would feel like to be normal.

I liked the feeling.

Normally lying in a bed, staring up at the ceiling, breathing through my nose, relaxed.

And that's when the police entered my examination room.

10

Hello.

Perhaps I should start there. I don't know what a blood replacement necessarily is, but it is working wonders for who I am and who I want to be. My thoughts are clearer, my tongue works phenomenally better. Instead of letting the spit fall from my bottom lip to the ground, I am now able to suck it back to my molars, to my throat, and then swallow it down to the grumbling stomach, which, for now, is a slumbering Dr. Watson.

This, I remember; this feeling of feeling.

And it feels amazing.

So, hello, whatever is out there, watching me; whatever wants to see whether I succeed at this new-life thing. If thoughts carry no weight, much like the human spirit, and my thoughts and memories have escaped me, does this mean that my former self is out there somewhere, walking about? When whatever happened to me, good ol' Alex, and I fainted, or whatever, on that front lawn, and I forgot who I was, and where I was going in life; did my spirit go off, taken from my body? Are people who fall under amnesia just separated souls? And if all of this is the case, which, let's be completely honest here, it probably absolutely is not, does this mean to get my memories back all I have to do is find my spirit and reunite it with my body?

Let's hope so, kids, eh?

It does no good to hope about such trivial matters, Dr. Watson flutters in my abdomen as if grabbing the comforter, rolling over in bed, and wrapping it tighter around him. *What we need to do is rest and then find food, the basic need for survival for any living human being. And ours. Rest and find food, then find food and rest. On and on, we'll go.*

Look, I understand my stomach isn't actually talking, but I feel like it is, and really, I feel like it is the only voice I can trust. "Go with your gut," they say, right?

Who's they? And why do I remember such stupid little sayings and nothing else?

I'm a red-blooded female, staring at this clear blood replacement bag, while laying here in the hospital bed as two police officers enter the room, sending Max into a full-blown panic attack. He stands up out of his chair, probably in a way of greeting, but the cop who entered first is a female, African-American, strong core leading to great posture and a jawline that could cut glass, and eyes that don't miss the flap of a wing of a hummingbird. She's instantly pointing a non-manicured hand at Max who goes to shake her hand before realizing it's not a hand of greeting.

"You, sir, you can remain seated," she says, everything lining up perfectly; lips, teeth, tongue. The enunciation intoxicating.

"Yes, yes, okay," Max says and sits back down.

The female specimen of a civil servant is followed up by the biggest mountain of a man I have ever seen. His shoulders barely fit through the doorway. His head is sheared into a buzz cut, and I swear I see the longest hair on his head, which is the length of a dandelion petal, hit the doorframe. If a velociraptor is pound-for-pound the deadliest dinosaur ever to live, this man is pound-for-pound the solidest policeman to ever police.

Did I mention this scared and attracted me at the same time?

Did I seriously compare this man to a dinosaur? Do I have dinosaur facts stored in me somewhere? Am I that much of a nerd?

Dr. Watson snores in response, apparently satiated.

I look over at Max, who looks like he could be somewhat of a bad ass. The boy with the dark bangs that could fall into his eyes, sitting there, his knee moving a mile a minute, his bitten fingernails bleeding from his picking at them, and his eyes darting from me to the police officers to the buckles he'd undone from my wrists and ankles to the policewoman's hand as she gets out a pad of paper to write notes on. This boy who saved me, who tied me up and threw me in his truck as I was... not myself, he double-takes the female officer. He licks his lips and swallows, as if at any moment she will ask him to make-out. So, this is what two hormonal teenagers are like, eh?

But, Max looks... cool to me. He appears to be someone who would have a trove of friends in school, and so if he's popular, and he took me on a date, that must mean...

I'm a cool, dinosaur-fact knowing chick!

Who needs to stop shouting in her head and go to sleep,
Dr. Watson says.

*Who's feeling desperately better and should order
some blood replacement for the road!* I tell my stomach.

I don't disagree, my stomach responds.

"Are you Alex?" The female police officer, double-
checking Max to remain seated, starts with.

"Y-Yes," I stammer, still getting used to common
conversation. When I first knew I could talk, I used it to
shout at strange nurses who had tied me to the bed. It had
come so easily that I almost missed that I could now talk
and not howl like a diseased wolf. To be honest, I had a
smile dancing in my mouth with the fact I was speaking
clearly now, and my chest grew warm knowing that I was
not as weird as I had been earlier. What I was earlier was
a tough pill to swallow and would have been a tough way
to travel. This more normal version of me is something I
don't want to let go of.

"Do you have a last name, Alex?" The officer asked
politely.

I paused, looking at her. I don't know how my face
appeared, but Max jumped on the boat instantly to help
me out.

"Jordan," he said, getting the officer's attention. She
turned to him, regarded him with mild annoyance, and
turned back around to me, jotting my "new" last name in
her book.

"Is that correct? Alex Jordan?"

I smiled weakly and nodded, meek.

"How old are you, Ms. Jordan?"

I thought about my reflection in the mirror earlier. The
way my body looked, mainly my boobs and the amount of

hair I had in places, I figured that I was pushing driving age.

"Sixteen?"

It had come out more a question than I actually wanted it to, and I wished that I could get that verbalization back. These officers weren't as dumb as, maybe, I would have liked them to be, because the female's officer's eyebrows went up instantly. The mountain of a man behind her just folded his arms, and leaned back on the counter that held pamphlets, glass jars of swabs, and a stainless steel sink that was only used by doctors to quickly wash their hands.

"Are you not sure of your age?" came the female inquisition.

"I didn't catch your names," I replied, veering off the subject.

"My name is Officer Grillings, and this is Officer Ispy," she said, holding out her arm like a white, blonde lady used to do in front of a large board full of light up letters while game show contestants spun a wheel. I couldn't recall what the show's name was, instantly feeling off track in the conversation and trying to find my way back to it.

"Officer Grillings. Officer Ispy. Do you know what kind of bite I have on my shoulder?"

"Do you know what happened to you tonight?"

"I was on a date?" I said, still lambasting myself at how the end of my sentences were going way up in octaves to purvey questions. *Statements, Alex!* I demanded of myself. *Compose your questions like statements!* But, once again, I was raising my eyebrows to go along with my voice and looking over at Max for clarification on what was transpiring between us two youths late into tonight. I wondered if the inflection of my voice at the end of every statement would be taken as a Valley-Girl-Southern-California accent instead of, you know, recent temporary amnesia.

Unfortunately for Max, who was picking his fingers to the bone, his knee bobbing in rhythm to a woodpecker, and sweat forming on his upper lip, the two officers turned to face him. That was when the mountain spoke, and the room vibrated with the gargantuan detective's voice.

"Should we ask him to leave, Ms. Jordan? Is he making you uncomfortable?"

To say his voice inspired something in me would probably be putting too much weight on it, but the way that man talked made me want to crawl into his arms and say goodnight. The physical stature, the ultimate conceit of this man, had me feeling like he was a father to the world, and we would all be safer under his protection. I could not remember who my own father was, but this officer, Officer Ispy, would do.

"No, please, he's my friend? He's my friend." I had heard the question on the first statement, and quickly corrected it. "We were on a date, a friend-date thing, we went to get pizza? Pizza! At—" *(what was on the receipt?)* "In The Sauce and then we did something, and got separated—No! I was going to my family's timeshare. Yes, I was going to my family's timeshare to, uh—use the bathroom! Because... I don't like public toilets, and—date, and all... Didn't want to actually use the bathroom near him, so I separated to use the bathroom somewhere else, and as I was going to the house—something jumped out and attacked me. Someone, obviously. Not some *thing*. Unless you believe there are such things as Bigfoot and werewolves and mothmen, and then I would totes be blaming one of those entities, because I'm usually not a careless person. I mean, I usually have my wits about me, and for some reason, not even with that bright-as-hell streetlight, you know, the one of many that I was—that I woke up in—well, not in—but in its light—as it—above me— you know—I was in its light, was when I woke up—and Max found me and brought me here."

And, without missing a beat, as if I didn't go on some crazy little rant right there, Officer Ispy turns to Max, stares down at the boy that he could probably bear hug until Max's whole body turned into a lump of slime, and Officer Ispy accusatorially said: "He brought you in hogtied."

"She was trying to bite me," Max said, repeating himself.

"Were you trying to bite him?" Grillings grilled me.

"Yes, but I was not myself. I was very dehydrated, it was dark, I didn't see him, I didn't recognize him. I was disoriented. This—" I said, tapping the IV bag, which was almost empty, that was delivering heaven to the vein in my arm, "this is bringing me back to perspective."

Officer Grillings looked at Max and then back to me, very clearly trying to see if one of us was lying, if both of us were, or if we were telling her straight. I felt bad for this police officer as she was just trying to do her job, and while I would love for her to be on my side, and help me find the person who bit me, I could not just let her completely into my world. I didn't really know what my world was, to be honest, and that is what scared me the most. I assumed people who suffered from amnesia were taken to some hospital or other, perhaps even a psychiatric ward, until some sense could be made of their situation. I didn't want that at all.

Let me be clear, I am not disparaging psychiatry, psychiatrists, psychologists, psychology, psychiatric wards and the people employed by them or currently (or have) been helped by them; I simply don't want to be involved, surrounded by, partake in and/or told what to do by them. Not only do I not think that I am crazy, and believe me (I understand the offensive nature of the term, but let's not let the offended take away the fact the term is an easy, broad brush stroke on the canvas of psyche wards) I don't even want to be perceived as someone who might need the help of one of these places. I feel that the best therapy for me, and for a girl in my present situation, is to live life like it was normal, and then, hopefully, get back to where life is normal. Right? Isn't a common piece of advice when you're sad to smile, thus tricking your brain into thinking you are happy?

I have this fear, somewhere in my chest, that if I am taken to a psychiatric hospital, that I will suddenly *need* a psychiatric hospital. While trying to bite people might be crazy, I wasn't full on crazy until they tied me down with the same straps they tie down actual crazy people, right? Treating someone like they are crazy will sometimes actually make them crazy, right?

Anyway, enough crazy talk, because I'm not. And you're not. And we're not. I'm just a girl who has lost her memory and wanted to eat her friend, Max. Totally normal, no?

Let's face it. God gave the leaf-eaters incisors and molars, right? He gave the sharks, shark-teeth. And he gave us bi-pedaled pink fleshy people incisors and canines.

He gave us molars and pre-molars. Why? Because we'll dig into the meat, baby. We're with the lions, tigers, and bears, oh my.

"But, those are all animals!" someone would say if I voiced this out loud.

Let's take out that broad brush, and say, "We're all mammals here." And then lump me into that, and if I was a tiger, and Max was on the side of an Ocean City road, or wherever we were, Max would have been torn into and eaten, and we would have said, "Well, that's what happens when you run across a tiger in the middle of the road." Right?

Maybe the situation I am suffering from is not some form of rabies but a were-carnivore situation. Like a werewolf, or were-tiger, or were-lion, or were-alligator, or were-hippopotamus, and if you're thinking to yourself *I think I just got a great idea for a run of young adult novels,* beautiful, go with it, and start them with a word that doesn't make any sense. For a fact, I know that my name is Alex Jordan, and I am not crazy. I'm a new thing, a new breed of human. I'm a were-human. I was hungry for a boy who took me out on a date, and I was attacked, and so therefore, ergo, vis a vis, I do not belong in no psychiatric ward.

Got it?

Good.

And that is the long version of why I continued to lie to the police officer.

Officer Grillings looked at her giant partner and gave him a sign by cricking her neck, and Officer Ispy held out his paw toward Max.

"Let's go, sir," he said.

Max's eyes went wide.

"Am I being arrested?" He asked, his voice cracking on the 'I' and we all heard it, and all reacted differently. I felt embarrassed for him, Grillings looked surprised at the sudden reveal of continual puberty, and the corner of Ispy's mouth curled into a smile. Obviously, the police officer's puberty went swimmingly.

"No, I'm just taking you into the hall for some questions."

"Okay..."

Max followed Ispy into the hallway. When they were gone, Grillings shut the door and turned to me. She sat down on the chair, her shoulders slouching, getting more comfortable than she had looked since arriving.

"Ms. Jordan," she began in a way that looked rehearsed, that looked like she had done this several times before. She closed her eyes, sighed, and then opened her beautiful brown irises and looked into my eyes and down into my heart, and she connected with me on an emotional level. This officer was beautiful, and I wondered; *Am I gay? Or just very observant on attractiveness?* Because I was on a date with a boy, I wanted Ispy to wrap me in his arms, and now I wanted to bend forward and smell this woman's neck.

And bite... Dr. Watson grumbled, and then I realized, that no, I didn't want to make-out with this woman—I wanted to eat her face.

"Alex," she said, and I paid attention. "Do you remember the attack?"

"No. Like I said, it came from nowhere."

She stared at me, but not in a threatening way. Her eyes were a quarter-closed, as if pleading with me.

"I was attacked once," she started. "I was about your age, yeah, and this boy, his name was David, he was the running back of the football team, and he asked me out. Which was weird for me, because I was into books, studying. I liked to stay in on Friday nights, help my mom cook, and watch shows with my parents. When David asked me out, it was exciting, yeah? I felt like the coolest person in the school. He took me to a movie, asked if I wanted to drink out of his flask. He had taken some alcohol from his parents.

"I had never drank before. It smelled and tasted awful, yeah? I mean, alcohol is literally poison we put in our systems that gives us a euphoric feeling, you know? Why would I want to put poison in my system? But, this wasn't my world. David was graciously inviting me into the cool kid's world, and this was their... elixir. This was the potion that made you cool! So, I drank a little, yeah. And if you didn't know, if you have never drank..."

She looked at me, looking for a sign, and I shook my head that I had not... remembered ever having a drink before.

"It doesn't take a lot the first time. Suddenly I start feeling... numb. And after the movie, after the popcorn, and the soda, and the flask, yeah, and David's hand sometimes touching my hand, sometimes touching my leg, he parks the car on a road I don't think I had ever seen before, and he unbuckles his seatbelt, throws my seat back, yeah, where I'm laying down, and then he's on top of me, pinning me with all of his weight to the point I can't breathe."

"Whoa," I say, listening, wondering why, all of a sudden, a police officer is telling me this huge secret of hers. I feel Dr. Watson in the pit of my stomach, sitting up in gut-bed, clenched. "Why?"

"David realized the cool girls, the girls he was surrounded with, the ones who had rich parents, or protective brothers, yeah, or were pretty enough to call their own shots, or were with a clique who destroyed lives with rumors against reputations, the girls with higher alcohol tolerances; those were the girls who were hard to prey upon. But, little ol' me, yeah? Someone who was excited just to be invited to the party, someone who would drink from a flask because he smiled as he asked, someone who wanted her dad to look at her like she was always his little girl, who would be embarrassed to say a boy took advantage of her.... A girl, who if she tried to say the star running back raped her, would be terrorized at school, smeared in the local papers, and called a whore by the town's alumni with no lives. This is why David invited me out. Because he was a predator, yeah?"

I looked at her. She didn't look hurt. She didn't look sad. She just looked like a woman with a story.

A story which didn't make much sense to say in the situation.

"Did Max attack you tonight, Alex?"

Oh... I get it...

"Max? No."

"That's a human bite mark on your shoulder, love," Officer Grillings asked, using a soft voice, but pointing a very authoritarian finger at my wound. "And from the position of it, it wasn't made from someone behind you, but in front of you."

I absentmindedly reached up and felt my shoulder, felt the stitches in it, felt the rough skin around it which was now very tender to the touch.

"You saw whoever it was that bit you. You and Max, go out on this date—"

"It wasn't Max," I said. "I don't know who it was, but I know it wasn't him."

"Why did you try and attack him, then?"

Because I was hungry...

"I felt crazy," I said, telling the truth, really. "I was attacked, I woke up alone, in the grass, I didn't know where he was, I took a shower, and then when I found him... I guess I blamed him, maybe. For leaving me alone to get attacked? I don't know. But, he brought me here. Stayed for the police. It wasn't him."

"Honestly, Alex. I never trust people a hundred percent. It's not in my nature anymore. Not since David. But, if you tell me it wasn't Max, I'll say it wasn't Max, and we'll let that kid go home...."

"Thank you," I said, not really knowing if she was doing anything for me personally.

"Can I ask why you showered?"

The thought of the throw-up, the chili beans, the blood, and the dew mixed with grass, the ants, and the overall discomfort flashed before my eyes. "I felt gross."

"The only pain you felt was on your shoulder? Nowhere else?"

"Just my shoulder. My head felt groggy."

"Mind if I look?"

I sat there as she used her fingers to feel around my skull, looking for a lump or a bump or more blood, but not finding anything. In the meantime, I was able to smell her skin; the oil that she used was a kind of butter, something she covered herself in. I wondered if she had a problem with mosquitos biting her. I wondered what it would be like to be one of those mosquitos, to sink a sharp object into her, and let the blood fill my mouth, the warm, metallic liquid oozing down the corners of my mouth, and congealing on my chin....

"I don't see anything," she finally said. "Any of this hurt?"

I shook my head no.

"Alex..." she began, sitting down in front of me, her eyes finding mine, a reassuring smile finding her lips. "I'm just going to ask. When you woke up in the grass, did you feel like you might have been... sexually assaulted?"

I thought about it. I honestly didn't know what "sexually assaulted" felt like and I absolutely did not want to know. I knew I didn't feel myself, but I hardly felt the wound on my shoulder. I thought that I would have some sense of being raped. I was pretty sure I had been attacked when I woke up in the lawn, but not sexually. While not a hundred percent sure, it was close enough for me.

"No. No, I don't think so."

"I had to ask."

"I don't think I was raped," I stated again. "I think they just bit me, knocked me out, and took off. Whoever it was. I'm sure it wasn't Max, though. I'm sure of that more so than anything specific that happened to me."

Grillings smiles, all teeth.

"My partner is probably scaring him enough in the hallway right now."

"Your partner is pretty scary," I reply.

"Nah, he's a teddy bear if he likes ya," she says, smiling and getting up. "He's as vicious as a real bear if he doesn't."

"Like a were-bear?" I ask.

She laughs. "Yeah, I guess so. A were-bear... I like it."

She opens up the door, and there he stands with his Popeye-forearms crossed. Max stands in front of him, sweat soaking his bangs, his clothes hanging off him like the stress and pure terror of his interrogation had him starve for a week and *atrophied* all of his muscles.

"What are we talking about?" Ispy says, realizing his partner's smile means he doesn't have to arrest the scared teenage boy in front of him.

"She says you might be a were-bear," Grillings says, and he looks at me, and I smile, and he looks back at Grillings, now confused. "Like a werewolf? A werebear?"

"Oh, I get it!" He says and smiles.

Grillings turns to me, smiling as if we suddenly became good friends in this short amount of private time.

"I swear," she says, clapping an arm on his shoulder. "Sometimes, I think half his brains are in his feet, and it just takes awhile for the two to connect."

I smile at their joviality.

"Alex?" Max says from the hall, his arms crossed, his phone open and he's reading a text. "Your parents are here. They're parking."

"Will I be able to go home?" I say, looking at Grillings.

"Absolutely, I'll tell the nurse we are done."

Ispy ducks out of the room, and his big frame forces Max to step nervously to the side. It was apparent that the two boys did not bond as well as us two girls did. Grillings began to follow her big lug of a partner into the hall, until I spoke out to get her attention.

"Miss?" I said, thinking I was asking her a question as a woman and not law enforcement. She turned back, her eyebrows up, anticipating some big reveal, instead I just wanted to know, "What happened? With the David situation?"

"I kneed him in the nuts, and then I grabbed his windpipe in my hand and said if he didn't get off me, I was going to ruin the way he breathed for the rest of his life."

I could picture this scenario in my head, Grillings controlling her attacker, slowly leading him to the driver's seat.

"And then I walked home. I'd rather walk three miles in the cold than let a man abuse me the way he wanted to."

"Did you tell anyone about the star running back...?"

"Oh yes. And I was called a whore, and a slut, and a liar, and all of those things. Didn't bother me none. I knew I was in the right. But, you want to know how I got back at them all?"

"How?"

"I became a cop. I arrested some of them. I gave tickets to some of them. I patrol the high school football games, and I keep an eye out for the girls like me, who might need a little more protection from the guys like him." She patted my leg, just as I heard a man's voice in the hall asking where his daughter, Alex, was, and Max pointing in the room. "That's why," Grillings finished, "I can't wait to find the person who attacked you."

Neither can I... Dr. Watson growled, and I hugged my stomach, my little detective organ, my gut instinct to myself.

I smiled at Grillings as she got up and left the room just as two people who I had never seen before in my amnesiac life entered the room and hugged and kissed me. For what it's worth, they looked like very loving and caring people. I looked over their shoulders at Max as Ispy and Grillings left the room. He stood there, his arms folded in front of him, watching the group hug in the room. We locked eyes and I smiled.

He smiled back, nervously. Not like a star-running back, but an anxious smile just like a dweeb like me, or what I felt like. I'm someone who named their stomach after a nineteenth century English detective's partner, which means I couldn't be the coolest girl in the world, could I? And this boy who wore clothes that didn't really fit and drove a truck with rust and shocks that squeaked— we weren't the cool kids in the school, I'm guessing.

Now, I was the girl who tried to eat him.

He was the boy who tied me up and hospitalized me.

While I was being hugged by my strange parents, I felt like Max and I were the only two people in the world. All I wanted was to be alone with him.

Me too, Dr. Watson growled.

11

The ride home with my parents was as awkward as you might expect.

I rode in the backseat, looking out at the new world; the world I didn't remember.

The funny thing about not remembering your parents is that when you drive in a car with them, it's like driving in a car with two Uber drivers or something. Like a driver and a back-up driver. My parents seemed like they were fighting. Like, maybe they weren't the most loving parents anyone would ever have, and maybe their lives were tougher than I gave them credit for or had ever noticed. I looked at my Dad's right hand on the gear shift and wondered why my mother wasn't taking it in her own. And neither one was looking back at me, assuring themselves that I was okay. I wondered what our relationship was like before my "accident".

By the looks of it, it wasn't very 80's sitcom.

An 80's reference from someone born in the aughts....

My accident? Is that what I should call it? I thought to

myself, watching as the perpendicular streets counted down; Ninth Street, Eighth Street, Seventh Street. *Not "my attack"?* It wasn't my attack, though, was it? I was the attacked. *Maybe "my assault"?* But, that makes me purely the victim. And, who wants to think of themselves as a victim?

Despite what I was going to call my being-bitten-on-the-shoulder-and-left-for-dead moment, I was going to have to piece my life back together, try to be as normal as possible in the meantime, before anybody found out that I was not myself. That I was actually a crazy person who was slowly becoming a rabid cannibal, and that if anybody knew the real me—they wouldn't love me. No, they wouldn't take me to the hospital, they wouldn't pick me up from the hospital, and they definitely wouldn't be taking me home. I had found my way into the empty home, into the meat, to Max, to blood replacements, through the police interrogation, and now into the backseat of my parents car. I could find my way through this thing called life. I could hide the real me again, as I'm sure I did before, before my...

My *episode.*

My first chapter of the second part of my life....

"How did you know Max?" My father asks, cutting the silence with a knife *(is that a saying? It seems like a completely weird one, if it is)* and avoiding all small talk. His deep voice almost scared me because, without a radio on or any conversation, I was listening to the sounds of the car, and the way the wheels seemed to meet the road. The sound the car's body made when it went over a bump, creaking and cracking and resettling. My dad's dry hands and the way they let the steering move between his fingers, and the way he breathed deeply through his nostrils with breath, that I knew, smelled of cigarette smoke poorly hidden with mints. My mother's sounds were so minimal it was a pain to try and hear the way her tongue was moving in her mouth, surveying the insides of her cheeks and lips, looking for a fresh place to bite and chew. If I had cinnamon gum, I would offer her a stick, wondering if I was right, that she should smell like it.

Perhaps we get our appetite from her, Dr. Watson theorized. My stomach's grumbling was very noticeable from this here back-seat area of leather, red-seat belt release buttons, and no lint whatsoever.

"From school," I answer in sort of a teenage mumble. "Same classes."

"You know him well?" He asks, not realizing he is just asking for lies.

In that awkward way, I meet his eyes in the rearview, and we have a small game of staring chicken. His gaze filled with the wisdom of a life lived and loves-trusted-before-they-broke-your-heart. I, of course, was living in a world they would never know or understand, and that was how I wanted it, really, so I felt the more we connected eyes, the more he could see, and I hated that. For some reason, I hated this feeling and just wanted to look away. But also, I knew my father was battling my resolve, and I also knew he had to look at the road at some point, so I held eye contact until something caught in his peripheral and he had to look back at where he was taking us at a high rate of speed.

I looked back out toward the town that never changes.

"I wanted to know him better," I say, wondering if that answer with a slight bit of intrigue would rile up my parents.

I missed Max. I did. I didn't know if it was a lie or not, if I didn't know him well before, or we were best friends at school and he had decided to make a move and take me out on a date which turned into a disaster. But now, the before-and-after-episode truth was I hardly knew him, and I wanted to know him better.

Was I in love?

What was that?

My parents seemed like good-looking, nice people.

I wanted to be with the boy who tied me up.

"I don't want you seeing him anymore," my father told me, demonstrating how fatherly he was going to father me.

I angrily connected eyes with him again in the rearview mirror. He tried to stare me down again in the reflection, but for some reason, tears began to cloud my vision, and so I had to look away first.

I felt a pain in my throat, Dr. Watson rumbled with emptiness, and now my eyes were leaking. My mother looked over at him, looking equally surprised at his statement, wondering if she should combat him in front of me. He gave her the "be quiet" glare. She ignored it, turning around to see what effect his words had on me. When she saw I was crying, she took a moment to let it sink in, opened her chewed mouth to speak to me, thought better of it, and turned back into her leathery-squishy-squeaky passenger seat.

You two have a strained relationship, Dr. Watson informed me. *Otherwise, she would have protected you from him or offered words of comfort. There's a past there.*

I put my hands on my stomach, letting my hungry

detective know I appreciated his thoughts on the matter.

You should rip out the soft flesh of her shoulder, he continued. I pressed into him as hard as I could, feeling my fingers push into my abdomen until I released more gas bubbles from somewhere in my intestines to rumble deeper inside of myself

"No," I voiced.

"What did you say?" Dad angrily said.

"I like Max," I scoffed. "He wasn't the one to attack me, if that is what you're thinking."

"He didn't prevent it either!" My dad shouted, starting before I finished, and showing just how much he liked my first boyfriend selection.

"He's a kid!" I screamed back. "What do you expect from him? You think his parents would appreciate you wanting him to get hurt when it was *me* who ran away from *him*?"

That got my dad. I could see the wheels turning in his head as he played out the scenario of having to meet Max's parents, and talk about how their kids were stupid but at least his daughter was safe and unharmed despite their son. The opposite seemed worse; it seemed like an awful scenario for a parent to go through to tell another parent "thanks".

"Thanks for raising the kid that would sacrifice himself for your own."

How would there be no resentment there?

"Besides," I continued, using the silence as an invitation to keep on arguing, "it's not like you can avoid anybody at school, classes being mandatory and all, hallways only being so wide."

Brattishness seemed to come easily to me.

"Are you on drugs?" My mom asked, speaking for the first time in the car. I had to laugh at how normal that sounded.

Despite me wanting to say *you wish* it came more as: "I wish." And my mother snapped around in her seat so fast I could almost feel her urge to hit me.

"What did you say?" she said, staring at me, and my father's eyes repeatedly darted to the rearview mirror as now parenting was just a spectator sport to him.

"I said, I wish." I stared back at her. I was now learning more and more how contentious this relationship was.

It wasn't not true. How relieving would it be to know my current situation was due to my own actions, and to not be messed up or in trouble just meant I would not touch any more illegal substances? I wish this was just a byproduct of my poor decision making and that tomorrow I would make better choices and my shoulder would heal, and my memory would come back, and I'd be standing behind Max's open locker door, and when he shut it, he would see me, and I would smile, and he would smile, and I would ask for a redo of our first date, and he'd say sure, and we'd make out that night, and he'd make sure to never pass by the shoulder scar that made us us, and he'd kiss it, and every time he did, the bad feelings of the night, the fear of being attacked again, would numb a little bit more.

That was what I meant by 'I wish.'

I wish I could keep daydreaming about normalcy and Max instead of coming right back to the backseat of the car and my mother's hateful stare.

"Don't—get—cute," she said, stressing every word as if she was holding back the undeniable urge to smack me across the face.

"I thought I already was."

My dad slammed on the brakes, forcing every one of us to test the resolve of our seatbelts. I felt the fabric dig into my neck, and my mother let out a curse, and his name, which I learned was Chuck. Or Jesus. Both of them sounded like a curse word in her mouth, but I was pretty sure my sandy blond-haired father was not carrying a Hispanic name. A car behind us with an elderly couple laid on their horns as they veered around us, continuing to travel down the road.

We sat there, awkwardly stopped in the middle of the lane until my father began driving again. I was relieved to find out that they didn't smack me when I pushed their buttons; they just get really close to wrecking their most expensive possessions.

I couldn't tell where these feelings of animosity were coming from. I completely understood that these were my parents and I should love them unconditionally, but the thoughts that they didn't know me, didn't understand where I was coming from, and didn't seem to care to get to know me were very plausible thoughts going through my head and gut. When they showed up at the hospital it was all hugs and "glad you are okays!" And now that we are alone in the car, it was all accusations and new rules and accusatory questions. This was a blatant two-sided attack, and I had to wonder if they were only teaming up against me because they forgot what it was like to be a team themselves. If I had memories, would I remember a time when the three of us were a team taking on the world together? Tossing a frisbee in the park? Making s'mores in the microwave?

Gurgle, gurgle, goes my stomach, and I send a mental

synapse down that reminds him that we would only throw up the delicious s'more if we were able to eat one.

I looked over at the empty seat beside me, and instead of Max, wished that I had a sibling, someone to take some of this antipathy from me. I could almost picture what this sibling would look like: a boy, young, with very hurt eyes who didn't like when our parents fought. I sighed and looked back at my mother, who decided turning around was the best option.

"You will see Dr. Martinez tomorrow," she said in such a way I knew that I should know what she was talking about. "Maybe she can talk some sense into you."

"I was thinking of scheduling an appointment with Dr. Braunt as well," my father said, fully jumping on my mother's ship that was sailing to medication land for me.

"I would like to call Dr. Schmidt, too," I say from the backseat, waiting for them to ask me who that was. And when my Dad took the bait, I responded: "He's a family counselor. He might be able to discern when you two screwed up with me."

The hateful silence in the vehicle was palpable.

You could cut it with a knife, Dr. Watson sneered.

And no, there was no Dr. Schmidt. I made him up.

12

Home wasn't too far away after that, thank the Lord that I may or may not believe in.

It wasn't like all the other homes, and it wasn't on a street that seemed like the rest of the island either. Our home was on a street that dead-ended into a body of water. Raised on large columns of wood, perhaps to avoid any chance of island flooding, the home was two stories of safety. White siding, dark green shutters, and an old-fashioned wind vane on top with a rooster showing you which way the wind was blowing, and more importantly, which way the storm was coming.

When we pulled into the driveway, I made a conscious decision to take a second longer getting out of the car than necessary, to test my parents and see how much they were paying attention to their daughter who had just been attacked. As soon as the car was fully stopped, my father whipped the gear shift into park, my mom's car door opened, the keys were removed from the ignition and my father hopped out, and it was like the two of them were racing to see who could close their door first. My mother won, but as soon as both doors were closed, the overhead light shut off, and I was immersed in darkness. Just me, myself, and Dr. Watson sitting in the backseat, our seatbelt still strapping us in, hearing my parents walk away from the warm car and the cold responsibility of raising me.

My mom, for her credit, realized I wasn't following, and with her arms crossed defensively across her chest, leaned down over the hood, and lovingly demanded: "What are you doing?! Let's go, Alex!"

I sighed, unbuckled, and followed them out into the driveway and toward the house.

"What has gotten into you?" my mom asked as I passed.

"I was attacked tonight," I reminded her.

"That's what you get for dating before you are eighteen," my father paternally said.

"It's my fault," I laughed, feeling colder by the second as I was flanked by them approaching the stairs, which took us to the front door. My father lead, my mother corralled me, and I wanted nothing more than to just will my atoms to disperse; for me to disappear into the air.

My father sighed, turned around, and ignored the fact that while he seemed warm, both of the women in his life were negatively reacting to the cold, night air.

"It's not your fault," he said, actually disarming his previous comment. He stood above me, and I realized that while he wasn't as tall as Officer Ispy, I still felt protected in the shadow he was laying over me, blocking out the security light that we tripped when we approached the door. I could feel the heat of his coat, even standing three feet from him, and he looked down at my face. "I didn't mean to say that. I'm angry," he said, and I felt my mom shivering behind me. "I'm angry that you got attacked. I'm angry that I wasn't there to protect you. And I wish you would tell us or the police more so we could find the person, and I can personally rip their freaking arms off for touching you."

I looked at my Dad. He seemed to care, but it seemed his vengeance outweighed his concern.

"I know you think I'm lying or protecting myself or someone when I say I don't know who attacked me...." *You're lying about how you feel inside.... The hunger...* "But I'm not. I don't remember it."

"I'll get the police report tomorrow," he says, turning to put the key in the lock. "But I'm serious. You suddenly remember who it is, and you can tell me, or the cops, and we'll make sure they never touch a little girl again. This island isn't big enough to hide on." He opens the door, and I try to step past him into this strange house, knowing full well my bedroom is somewhere in there, and that bedrooms come with a door that I can just shut and end this day, but before I can fully get out of his reach, I stupidly let my anger talk for me.

"I'm not a little girl," I say, and he grabs me, his hand like a vice, but not hurting me. Still, I squirm in his grasp as if it does. He immediately lets go.

"You're so cold," he says, and I wonder if he means my attitude or my skin, but before we can dive further into the topic, my mother interrupts.

"It's freezing out, Chuck," she says, and closes the door behind her.

We're home.

I dawdle in each room, pretending to look around and

feel the feeling of home, but really, I'm getting the lay of the land. Some people might suffer a traumatic event and just immerse themselves in the safety of their house, but I don't remember this place, and so I have to figure out where everything is. I have to go slowly as if not to look lost. Once I discover there is no possibility of my bedroom being on the first floor, I ascend the stairs, and use the pictures hung in the hallway to pause and peruse.

My parents go left in the upstairs hallway where there are two doors. I glance to the right at two more doors. Half the doors are closed, and the adults enter the open one at the end, which must be their bedroom. I can see from where I stand that the other open door is a bathroom, and so my bedroom must be one of the remaining two closed doors. I will have a fifty-fifty shot of being right when I go off to select one.

I see the boy I had a faint vision of in the backseat in one of the framed photographs hung up on the wall. I don't know what I was more surprised about: the fact that I had a brother that I actually remembered, one person, one face, that seemed to stick with me despite my amnesia, or the fact that despite having a brother, he didn't seem to exist. Judging by his age in the photos, he was too young to stay home by himself. I knew in my heart of hearts that one of these closed doors was his bedroom, but I also knew that he was not in it.

Another mystery for another day.

The bathroom was to the right, and because I appeared to be the oldest, I figured that I probably got the room closest to it.

I heard my parents begin to argue behind their closed bedroom door about me, about the hospital costs, about each other's attitudes on the drive home. I turned from their door and headed to mine, a slight cramp developing in my leg. It was an ache that made me almost want to drag my foot as I stepped forward. Whatever the hospital had given me was beginning to wear off, and I could feel myself regressing.

I opened the door and saw how messy the room was; clothes all over the place, jeans and t-shirts like a teenage girl panicking before one of her first dates. I wish I could remember such events. I wish I could go back in my memory to happier, safer times, instead of only remembering scary, alone, dark times which consume my memory bank.

I determined this was my room, and I laid down on the bed, and before I could wonder what position it was in which I liked to sleep, whether it was on my stomach, side, or back, if I had a nightly beauty care ritual, if I should brush my teeth, I was blinking awake in the morning light.

13

I woke up this morning like I woke up last night; hungry, and with my entire upper body making the sound of "Ugghhhh...".

I laid there, my face half-smashed into a pillow—a pillow where the fabric was wet from my open-mouth breathing while sleeping, and the saliva that decided to go out and explore the vast, fabricated field of cotton only to sink into its despair. My first thought was how blinding and warm the sun was, my second thought was that I was awake, my third thought was how I must not be a vampire because I was currently not engulfed in flames, and my fourth thought was *where did that sound come from?*

My fifth thought was *Oh my God, I have regressed.*

My sixth thought was *No, because that would mean I would have forgotten what regression was.*

That pretty much catches us up.

I didn't forget where I was, and I didn't forget that my name was Alex Jordan. I could still feel a slight pain in my shoulder which seemed to be stretching down and around my shoulder blade. But, as I laid there in my bed, one hand reaching up to grab the iron bars of my headboard, and one holding a pillow close to me where I rested my head on its top half, I could feel the familiar stiff pain of waking up the new me. It seemed, as I slept, that my body would tighten up and feel like it was drying out. I stretched out, sending one large cramp through every limb of my body, and, like a rubber band snapping back, folding in on myself.

The hunger was amazing. I felt that if I lifted up my shirt, I would actually see my stomach starting to digest through my skin, like one large whirlpool right below my ribcage, a swirling blackhole of skin and liquids, eating me from the inside. But, when I reached down and felt my tummy, it was solid, and the pressure of my hand sent a gurgle through my insides.

I'm up, Dr. Watson said. *Let's go find ourselves some meat.*

"Ehhhh-Gus," I replied, thinking that that was a breakfast item. I didn't know what my stomach monster meant by meat, but a breakfast menu item was eggs. Eggs, and toast, and sure—bacon, but bacon was burnt to a crisp and hardly resembled meat anymore.

Max, Dr. Watson said. *Let's ram our tongue in his throat.*

I admit, it was a bizarre morning-after thought. Not only was Max probably not my friend anymore, I exceptionally doubted that I would ever score another date with him, or with anyone in my high school life. By now, Max had told everyone how big of a freak I was; how he had given me one date (one date!), to prove how cool I was, and I ended up running away from him and getting bit by a psycho lawn-biter, and then I tried to eat him, and "long story short, stay away from that girl."

I still didn't know how cool I was in school, or who I was in general, but I knew I was in high school, and I knew it was Saturday morning, as someone in the hospital last night had mentioned it was a Friday night.

Hey! Your name is Alex and you were attacked on Friday because _____!

So, no school for me this morning, which was great, as I still felt horrible and like I was getting worse. I felt like I needed to figure out my situation before being surrounded by judgmentally jerk-ish teenagers... my peers. I needed to figure out why, all of a sudden, I'm just a carnivore and why, all of a sudden, I'm even more-ish a cannibal. I could satiate this hunger with whatever meat is inside canned meal products, but Dr. Watson always seemed to want to eat a person. And what kind of hormonal imbalance was my puberty?

Maybe this is nothing new, he suggested through gargles.

What? That I have been a cannibal my entire life, and I just so happened to be bitten and given amnesia so the only thing that remained was my penchant for dining on my neighbors?

Sure. Go with that.

Mercifully, there was a smell coming from downstairs. Finding some flannel pajama pants and a t-shirt with a kind-looking bear on it, either way—much better than my previous night's clothing of blood and mud. My achy feet carried me from this bedroom of boyband posters, white furniture, shelves upon shelves of books (confirming the fact that I was either a book collector or well-read), discarded clothes and pastel-stuffed animals into the hallway of photographs and memories. I wondered if I was going to see a brother downstairs. I wondered if I was going to see my parents, and then hoped I wouldn't. If I had to, I hoped I would only see one of them. Not necessarily desiring one over the other, I hoped that I would only have to deal with one at a time. My parents' seeming resentment toward all things in their lives was hard to take, two pills at a time. Bitter pills to swallow, and all of that.

If I had lost my memories, I certainly had not lost the instinctual feelings of what I had been through. I was afraid of being attacked, I had warm affection for Max, and I wanted to avoid my parents at all costs. This seemed like typical teenager behavior.

In the kitchen my father was half-cleaning, half-cooking. He had made a plate of bacon, which he put out on the kitchen island, and was diluting the bacon grease with water in the sink. The kitchen got fantastic morning sun, which made the steam from the faucet water hitting the pan look like he was performing a smoky magic trick. He danced to a tune in his head and popped the last corner piece of toast into his mouth, wiping his hands together to get the crumbs into the drain before turning the water off.

My feeling of wanting only one parent to deal with turned into a "well, not this one", but I wondered if it would have mattered. I was hungry and cranky and if my mother was standing in front of me, I would have wished it was my father. I felt like a brat, and I really didn't care to be honest. How I felt was how I felt, and if you didn't like it—go to your own room, because I was coming into this one.

On the island was a plate of steaming, pepper-spotted scrambled eggs, a plate of burnt bacon, and a plate of buttered toast which my father had done the most damage to, not realizing it was that product that was doing the most damage to his waistline.

I stole a piece of bacon before he even realized I was in the room. The crunch of the food was loud enough to make him turn around.

"Alex!" He yelped. "You startled me."

I grunted. My mouth was dry and the bacon was so burnt, and equally as dry, that I felt like I was chewing glass. I breathed through it, never closing my mouth, and had pieces falling to my feet. The crunching didn't hurt, but the sensation was so horrible that I closed my eyes tightly, and let my father watch me eat his burnt bacon like a dog trying to lick the peanut butter off the roof of his mouth.

"Ayyyerooow," I said intelligently.

He looked at me, as one should, I guess, as if I had just begun peeling back the skin of my face to reveal I was an alien. And then his face formed back into the face of a warm and loving parental figure who had seen a zany side of me before.

"I know it's burnt, but that's how you like it."

I continued to chew and let the pieces fall as if I had forgotten which side of my mouth my throat was on.

"It's not that bad."

I tried to speak, "Gar-gar-gar," between all of the chewing and chomping, I wondered what had happened to my sweet voice. What happened to the conversationalist I was last night? I'm back to the same annoying, mouth-breathing, non-consonant-sounding person. Was it the blood replacement that allowed me to talk?

Suddenly, Dr. Watson was in control, and I was walking across the room toward my dad, my hands outstretched, ready to grab. My stomach was on fire, burning with hunger. It didn't get any sustenance from the tree bark bacon my father called food. He looked at me, almost recoiling at the thought that I would actually want a hug. But I knew I didn't want a hug. I knew that my thoughts up in my bedroom, in the privacy of my own space, were of taking my teeth, using them to pierce the skin of the only kid I knew, and ripping a chunk from living flesh; ignoring my victim's screams as I chewed the fatty tissue, my molars trying to masticate rubbery chunks of human.

I was a lion. And here was my poor dad thinking I wanted a hug. If Darwin was still alive and practicing, he would view this situation as a teachable moment:

"You should never try to hug predators," he would say. "Survival of the fittest puts the predators above the prey, the fighters above the flee-ers, the huggers underneath it all."

And Freud would view this as a "told you so" moment.

Naming these famous researchers reassured me that I was, at least, somewhat intelligent. Which is good to know considering how homicidal I am.

Just as I thought I was about to end my father's appreciation for my existence, I side-stepped him and went right to the opened package of raw bacon, and grabbed a peel. I hungrily stuffed a slice into my mouth, chewing on the delicious, cold piece of fat that almost seemed to bounce back into place after my teeth stopped sinking into it. Raw bacon was so delicious to me that I almost choked on my first piece, wishing to swallow large chunks in order to fill my stomach as fast as possible, in order to calm Dr. Watson, and have him stop thinking horrible thoughts for me.

I didn't want to eat Max; I wanted to meet him again.

I wanted to form words again.

Before turning around to see what my father thought of this situation, I took another piece of bacon, and with my genetically-evolved incisors, ripped off a piece of the meat. My stomach felt better, which allowed me to chew slowly, getting the large piece to a more manageable throat-sized bite and swallowing the lump down. I turned slowly, seeing my father's mouth collecting dust and drying out as he looked at his little princess chewing the flesh of a mud-wrestling animal. His face was completely white.

"You're going to throw up," he said finally. "Then how funny will this joke be?"

But I knew I wasn't going to throw up. I threw up beans. I would throw up bread. I didn't know about the eggs, but I knew eggs carried with them a certain smell, a certain rancid odor of sulfur that I didn't want to try and get down, and if I threw them up—I definitely didn't want to have to deal with it *again*. Bacon was fine for now, even if it wasn't bloody. Even if it wasn't, now, quenching my thirst. I knew he was wrong, but I didn't know if my voice worked, so I stood there, chewing loudly, my lips covered in some kind of grease. He stared back.

"When did—," he stammered. "When did you find out you liked raw bacon?"

I didn't answer.

I chewed and stared.

I ripped off another bite, chewed, and stared.

"I mean, it's not completely unnatural," he said, turning to clean more things up. "When your mother and I went on our honeymoon," he stopped, the thought changing his mood from being freaked out by me to depressed at how his life had gone. I felt like I normally wouldn't have noticed this, but Dr. Watson was on full alert for any type of meat so I was staring at my dad, at this piece of vulnerable, hundred-and-seventy pound flesh, seeing if there was a possibility of taking a bite without being overpowered and killed.

With every bite of bacon put into my gullet, I felt more and more awake.

"When we went to Europe, we stopped in this restaurant that served 'American Bacon'. That's what the sign said. We were starved for a plate of something we recognized, something like home, so we stopped in, and the bacon wasn't any more cooked than what you are eating now. Well," he stopped and turned to watch me. "I guess it was warmer. They had, at least, warmed it."

This meat lacks blood, Dr. Watson critiqued.

I was no longer as hungry, but thirsty.

I moved toward the refrigerator, not knowing what I was precisely hoping for. I felt orange juice would burn my throat, as would tomato juice. Water might be my only option.

I opened the fridge and looked in, feeling the wonderful cold on my skin.

I closed my eyes and took in the cool, artificial breeze; felt my stomach twist and turn with the pig flesh inside of it; felt the motor turn on to blast more cold air as the fridge temperature went up due to the open door. The fridge was half-full with no real food, just jars of stuff. It seemed this was a house of ingredients, which meant either they never sat down for real food, or someone was a cook here. Could it be my father? And where was my mother?

Drinking options:

Orange Juice

Apple Juice

Filtered Water

Two different kinds of Beer

Half Drunk Bottle of White Wine

Water it was, and I reached in to grab the Brita pitcher. When I turned around, my Dad was gone. The faucet was off, and the pan sat in the sink, half-cleaned. I hadn't noticed he had left, but I wondered what sent him off so quickly. How long was I standing in front of the fridge with it open?

I poured myself a glass of water and without closing the fridge doors, without putting the water pitcher back, I sat at the kitchen island and stared at the water. I remember how horrible it felt to just let the half-chewed beans waterfall from my mouth. Perhaps I had the flu, and I just couldn't keep anything down. This was common, right? Not being able to eat. And maybe this has been going on for a while, so when I was attacked, I was already weak. Doesn't explain why I would go on a date with Max, though, unless I was so starved for a date, I didn't let a little thing like mononucleosis, streptococcus, or seasonal influenza hold me back.

Holy moly, Alex, knowing all of these fancy terms....

Doesn't explain why you're so cold to the touch, though.

I took the glass of water to my lips, and slowly

upturned it until I felt the cool liquid trickle into my mouth, cooling my tongue and teeth alike. And then I opened up my throat and let it drip down, gulping as I went. It felt good. This combination of one part hydrogen and two parts oxygen felt like it was greasing my wheels, making everything work a little smoother. As quickly as it seems, as soon as the water was hitting my stomach, I could feel it being absorbed all throughout my body.

One glass became two, and two became three. Soon, I had to refill the pitcher in the sink. I watched as the water poured from the faucet into the top vestibule, then trickled out through the filter into the bottom part of the container....

I threw up. All of that water poured back out of me into the sink, mixed with a dark black substance that looked like dark fish food flakes. Whether or not it was dried pieces of my stomach, I did not know. Whether I had done too much water at once, or whether water was not going to be my friend, I also did not know. I waited until my tailbone stopped lurching up to push everything from my butt to my heart out through my mouth into the sink; then I stood there and whimpered.

It hurt.

I went from feeling greased to feeling wrung.

I poured one more glass of water, and took the pitcher back to the fridge which had warmed up considerably in that short amount of time; warmed up to the point where I smelled something I didn't smell before, and it made me look closer than I did before. A pound of ground meat had been thawing on the second shelf, probably pulled from the freezer yesterday for some kind of dinner today, some family dinner. The thought of sitting down with those two adult humans made me shudder, but I couldn't take my eyes off the brainy-strands of beef, the way it all looked pink from the red food dye, and more importantly, the blood collecting on the white styrofoam below it.

I reached in and grabbed the ground beef, feeling the weight and the texture of the saran wrap as my thumb pushed into the top. Quickly, not wanting anyone to know, I slammed the fridge shut, and stumbled to the living room where I slumped down to the hardwood floor between the coffee table and the couch, and I reached my fingernail into the plastic, broke through, and peeled it off.

I could see what I was doing, I was disgusted with myself even, but I couldn't resist the smell, the urge, to take a handful of this raw, bloody meat and put it into my mouth.

It was so soft.

Like Mint Chocolate Chip ice cream.

No... softer....

I chewed it, but I could break it down with my tongue as well. I used my talking muscle to jam it against the roof of my mouth and squeeze out as much of the blood and fat as I could, to drink the elixir of life, and calm down Dr. Watson, who was so angry with me for trying to drown him with water. This, he loved. This dead cow from who knows how long ago who had his brain shot out with an air gun, who had his head chopped off, and his body slit from neck to groin, and then was systematically eviscerated. This flesh that had gone through a grinder so that meat and bone, flesh and fat, were all the same texture to me.

In five minutes, the pound of meat was gone, and I was left with blood dripping down my chin, a styrofoam bottom, and ripped up plastic. And, for the first time since I woke up last night, I felt full. I felt great.

I felt completely disgusted with myself.

I slid the container under the sofa, reminding myself to grab it later and throw it out. I was going to have to come up with a lie of why there was no ground meat in the fridge anymore. Perhaps, if it was Dad accusing me, I could just shrug and say the word "mom" and some deep-seeded feelings would come to his surface and he would stop accusing me. Likewise, with her. Crumbling marriages with kids in the picture worked both ways, no? If they could use me as a pawn, I could use them as one of the castle ones, or the horsies.

Okay, so I don't play chess....

I stood up, feeling some power in my shoulders. As I walked, I could feel my ankles strengthen, and when I opened the door, and stepped outside, I saw Max turning up my walkway with a purse in one hand, and a pair of sandals in the other. Without thinking that I might sound like a deaf person who never had heard her own voice, I pushed my lips together, and then aired out a sound.

"Max!"

Oh yeah, my voice was working again.

I hoped he didn't smell the blood on my breath.

14

Max stopped dead in his tracks. He had been looking down at the ground, at where he was stepping, maybe counting his steps, maybe making sure he was not going to trip over a crack, or maybe he wasn't planning on seeing me. Maybe he was planning on putting the purse and the sandals on the porch or something, ringing the doorbell, and running away. Maybe this kid, this boy, who I had unceremoniously planned in my head to be my best friend in the whole wide world, was a kind of coward who would provide no security or even reliability and I was setting up my new, amnesiac life on a course for disaster. Isn't it funny how many thoughts one can think in a second? For I had not only devised this relationship with Max in the time that I saw him and called his name, to planning its eventual doom by the time our eyes met.

And that doom quickly receded for when he saw me, his first reaction was surprise, and then it changed in an instant to a smile of relief that he didn't have to do anything in order to bring the purse to me. By now, obviously, I assumed the purse was mine, since I didn't think Max, the eyes-on-his-shoes guy, would be confident enough to try to start a trend of men carrying burgundy purses.

Men, Dr. Watson scoffed. *Why, the kid is so young, he'd constitute as veal. Sweet, tender veal....*

It was easier to not think about now, easier to calm my urges with a stomach full of bloody cow. This was not the time to think about eating my only friend. If that time ever came, I would have to sit down and have a conversation with him. Until then, "hi" would do just fine.

"Hi," I said, tucking my hair behind my ear. I would have to shower again this morning since my hair was still embarrassingly greasy.

"Hey, Alex," Max said, and I thought about how both of our nicknames ended with an X, and how we would probably have to find more names that ended with X so we could pass the tradition onto our kids. Nicknames, because Max was probably short for Maximilian or Malcolm. Alex was short for Alexandra (as evidenced by a pillow in my room.)

Jax... could be short for Jacqueline or Jackson.

Dax... could be short Daxson or... am I just making this up?

Something to discuss later, I suppose, along with the fact of "hey, do you like me?" and also, "remember how our first date almost ended in our deaths?"

"How are you feeling?" He asked, like a gentleman.

"Better," I say, and I am sure he is referring to rest or something, but I am thinking about the carpet picnic I had with 1.07lb. of ground meat at $3.99 a pound.

Then I also think about how my ankles don't feel

perfect, and how my neck is stiff, and how there's an ache in almost every single one of my joints. That, and the fact that I do not have any of my memory back, and there's still a bite wound on my shoulder.... I am sure I could have given him a whole list of items that I was dealing with at the moment, but I am positive that is not why he came over this morning, purse and sandals in hand, wearing faded jeans and a T-shirt that did not have a kid's cartoon from the 80's on it. Rather, his shirt was a band named Def Leppard, and all I could think about was how did a deaf leopard hunt?

"How are you?"

"I'm good. I, uh—" he stammered, looking at the sandals. "I couldn't sleep last night, so I drove around the dark end, and... found these...."

The dark end must be the side of the island that was open to timeshare people on our little vacation island; the side of the island with empty houses, lit streetlights, and humans that tried to eat teenage girls—attractive teenage girls, I should say, if I don't float my own boat, toot my own horn, and the like.

"Are they mine?" I asked, stupidly.

"Do you still not remember things?" He asked, matching my stupidity, and I wondered if this was how teenagers really did communicate with each other, asking inane questions and stammering out horrible responses.

"Let's just say that I am glad it is Saturday, and I don't have to try and find my desk in every class that I believe that I am in. I mean, I don't even know where the school is, let alone my locker."

"I can help you with that stuff."

Dear God, my face felt on fire with the amount of blood

rushing to its cheeks.

"Thanks...." I pathetically tucked nonexistent hair behind my ear again, bit my lip to try and hide a smile that would not be hidden, and rocked on my heels, completing the look of a girl who was absolutely and grossly smitten with the boy in front of her.

"What do your parents think about all of this?"

"They still don't know. I don't want to tell them. They seem to have a lot of issues of their own they aren't dealing with, and I'm sure if I tell them mine, they would just use my amnesia as an excuse to not face their own problems."

I put some tally marks in the scoreboard of my mind on how smart that sounded. I was a regular B.F. Skinner over here, coming up with excuses to not have awkward conversations with my parents, which might lead to more awkward conversations with police and doctors about my amnesia and attack and proclivity for cannibalism. This way, keeping all these very important and serious things secret, I could stand on this porch with this stranger who was a first date who I have now elected as my best-friend-soon-to-be-life-partner, and just discuss unimportant things like school and the future and maybe the weather and how I seem to debilitate unless I eat raw meat.

"Oh...." Max said, still looking down at the sandals.

"Can I have those?" I ask, stretching out my hand, and then indicating the purse. "And that?"

"Oh yeah, oh sure," he stammered, handing it over. "This was in my truck. On the floor boards."

It was heavy.

Full of clues... Watson growled.

But, I was still reluctant to open it. Who knew what was in it, and I didn't want to be whipping out tampons in front of the boy who made me blush merely by smiling at me. Of course, I didn't know if I was getting my period, yet. Of course, I probably was since I was sixteen. Of course, blood is blood and he saw me covered in my own last night. Of course, all blood isn't *just* blood in the case of a woman's body, is it?

Right. Let's keep the period stuff shelved, shall we?

"Did you go through it?" I asked.

"Oh no," he said, continuing to start every thought with "Oh" in a very cute way. "Oh, I don't go through other women's bags, or any women's bags, oh no. I don't. Not since I thought I was going through my mom's purse at a department store one time? I thought she had gum. I knew she had gum, and I was like five, and I wanted some, but I couldn't find any in her purse. Turns out it was another woman's purse I was going through, and she screamed bloody murder at me. Stuff like that stays with a kid, you know?"

He jammed his hands in his pockets and shrugged his shoulders. I wanted him to keep talking, so I blurted out—

"My dad hates you, you know."

I know, it doesn't make much sense to me either, but that's the kind of stupid crap that comes out of my mouth when I'm not thinking.

"Oh yeah? That's not good," said my boyfriend of one day.

"No. He believes you didn't properly protect me last night when I was attacked."

"I guess that's true. You did get attacked. And he had told me to have you home safe by midnight. And you were actually in a hospital at midnight. Yeah, I guess that's true. I failed on my part...." He thought about it as my mind raced with the fact that he knew so much about last night, that he alluded to a conversation with my father at the time of picking me up on our date, that I realized I could talk to him about how it all went down last night, and maybe just live my sixteen years in reverse with stories. Max could tell me about last night, my parents about yesterday morning, and then who would tell me about Thursday night? "But, you did run off," he concluded.

"So you say," I said.

"So you did!" he said, defending himself with a shout. Not one that was attacking, but one that seemed to mean he was about to duck back into his shell and roll back home.

"You realize, with my forgetfulness and all, that you are the only person I really know. And that I forget our date, and everything that happened before it...." I didn't really have a plan of where I was going with this, but I thought that if I just kept talking, a truth would come out of my mouth that I hadn't thought of, yet, and then maybe Max could help me with that truth, and I wouldn't feel so alone and afraid deep down, past Dr. Watson, somewhere. "I woke up in that lawn last night, not knowing, even, the word for grass at first, almost forgetting how to breathe. I was soaked from the lawn, and I thought the streetlight was the sun, and I was lost." Max looked down, and I thought *oh my gosh, I'm making him feel bad! Pivot! Change course! You're going the wrong way and saying the wrong things.* "I mean, I didn't feel abandoned, or anything. I didn't feel anything! I mean, there were ants feasting on my shoulder and I didn't even feel them!"

Max couldn't help himself, and before he could stop, he scrunched up his face in disgust at my revelation that last night, on our date, insects were eating me, and not like mosquitos as we made out in the park, but real insects that take chunks of you back to their larvae to grow more insects.

What do mosquitos do with the blood? Syringe into their eggs? I'm getting off track.

"I went into the house where I was, my family's that we... rent out, and I got some food," Quick thought of throwing up all over myself while sitting down, "I took a shower, washed my clothes, went back out in the world, and found you by the... darkness....

"I was looking out at the bay—"

I stopped short, thinking that I shouldn't bring up the fact that I tried to attack him, but I instead brought up:

"I found you because I smelled you."

Which... is probably not the most normal thing to say, either.

"You smelled me?" He asked, as any normal person would. And then, like a normal person would, he smelled himself, starting with his collar, and then his arm pits, as if the only smells that radiate off a person are those two areas. I realized in that moment that I didn't smell Max now like I had last night. He didn't smell like a McDonald's hamburger, or a Sicilian meatball, or Chorizo sizzling in a skillet. All I could smell were the flowers in the garden, and the sea salt in the air.

"Were you wearing cologne?" I covered, not wanting to get into my hunger for him. "Maybe I remembered it from before the attack?"

"I did wear a lot of it. It being my first date and all, I sprayed it on my wrists and neck, and then, my brother told me... in his way... I was supposed to spray it in the air and walk into it. But I was already running late so I just came to get you, probably reeking."

"That was probably it then," I said, and we both shared a scoff and a smile.

"Oh well, I just wanted to get these back to you, and see how you are doing. I'm sure you were missing it, and maybe it will help you remember something...."

He turned around, hands still in pockets, and began to walk away.

"Max?" I called after him.

He turned in the exact same way he turned before, using his toes on one foot to push around on his other heel, like a dance move of sorts. I could watch him all morning long if he let me, and I wondered how creepy of a thought that was.

"Yeah?" he asked.

"Maybe you could come back at noon? You can tell me how the beginning of our date went last night?"

"Your dad hates me," he reminded me.

"Pick me up down the street? I'll meet you at the stop sign."

"It's a date," he said, smiling, and turned around to walk back to his truck, which I was just now noticing parallel parked a couple houses down.

He never looked back, which was a good thing, since the tightness in my ankles made it impossible for me to properly walk back to the door. I had to step, sliding the other foot forward, as if dragging a dead leg behind me. The lumbering motion made it impossible to tell how excited I was to run up to my room, empty out my purse on my bed for any clue as to who I was and who attacked me.

15

I wish I had my memory back so I could ask my old self why I had so much random junk in my purse. It almost appeared like I was still five years old with one of my mother's hand-me-downs, putting whatever item I found around the house into the purse to make me look more adult. But, instead of an ashtray and a candle, my purse held a curling iron, and a mister. No, not a gentleman, but one of those mini spray bottles with a battery-operated fan attached that would cool me off should I ever get too hot from curling my hair in a random bathroom somewhere (I guess). My trendiness for five stick packs of gum was quickly shot down as I had a purse filled with half-full packs of all different kinds of gum. I must be a junkie for the shelves at the cash registers as it seems I can't stop getting my hands on all different kinds of flavors and shapes of chewing gum.

Three tampons, two kinds of lipstick ("Devil's Tail" which was a light red, and "Mermaid's Bruise" which was a shimmery purple), napkins, coin change, eyeliner, eyeshadow, an iPhone that needed charging, a charger for the iPhone which I promptly put to use, and a wallet.

Inside the wallet was my temporary driving ID. I was apparently attempting to get my license for several months now, and I have to wonder what is holding me back. A school identification card letting me know that I was a junior at Ocean City High School and that I did like to add some curls to my hair, at least, when taking school photos. But, let's be honest, a girl who carries a curling iron likes to curl her hair, a lot. I also was carrying around a library card to the Ocean City Public Library, and a membership card to the Ocean City Recreation Center. According to an American Red Cross card, I was CPR certified, which expired next summer. There were two pictures, one of me looking super young, my little brother and parents, all smiling happily for the camera. My mom looked rested, and my father looked skinnier in the picture as well. The other picture was a little more recent and showed me with two friends who seemed nice, although where are they now?

Regardless, these two girls were cute. The picture was probably two years old, and so I bet the one girl got her braces off. The other girl had already started wearing make-up, and had done a really good job plucking and shaping her eyebrows. It didn't seem like we would need much help putting ourselves together. So, based on this picture, I would say that I would be okay come Monday should I go to school. I didn't need to be friends with everyone, but rather have two girls that I could lean on, and just get me through the day with a little bit of socialization. Maybe they would call on the charging iPhone before the weekend was done, and I could share my secret, and they'd laugh at how crazy my life is sometimes, *"Oh, Alex, you'll do anything to not kiss a boy, haha, even getting half-eaten! You're so silly..."* and we would go out for burgers and a milkshake, and talk about Max, and the date, and boys, and the slutty girl who smokes, and we'd cackle at how much better we'd pretend to be than everyone else...

...and then we'd drive them into a ditch and eat their triceps... Dr. Watson grumbled, getting hungrier. The raw meat was only enough for a couple hours of reprieve from the homicidal thoughts. It would take a while to thaw any more meat, and I already was trying to figure out how to cover up the first pound that I ate.

So, the phone was going to be the most rewarding item in the purse, along with my parents picking me up from the hospital, and Max, telling me my name and where I lived. If I was going down my list of questions I had when I first came to:

Who are you? Alex Jordan.

Where were you? The lawn of my family's rental property, then I was at Ocean City Hospital, and now I am home.

Why were you there? I was on a date. I ran away from the guy, presumably, to use the bathroom, (or was that just a lie?) and got attacked.

What's your favorite TV Show? I don't know that, yet.

What happened to your purse? Cell phone? Wallet? Identification? Max found it in his truck. Or on the side of the road? I think he said both things.

Lastly, I have to find out who bit me.

As soon as I gave my phone a nice five-minute head start, I pushed the Home key and began to boot it up. The same photo of myself and the two girls appeared on the screen and I was quick to figure out that these two girls meant more to me than my family. But wasn't that the way of things? You grew up in the house, loving your family, and when you got to be about my age, or a little younger, when the more instinctual, medieval human race would ship off their children to work or marriage, you began to rebel. Parents back in the day were smart to ship off their kids before they got chippy.

Of course, the first screen that comes up on my phone is asking for a password. Twelve buttons in four rows, three columns, which either said it was a numerical password, or I used the three letters on top of each of the buttons to come up with a clever phrase. But, how would I know my password when I didn't even know my middle name?

New Question: What is my iPhone password?

So, I let it charge, and I drag my dead foot out into the hallway, gripping the wall as I go because I feel like I might fall over at any second. Whatever is deteriorating me is doing it fast. All I have found that slows up the process is meat, and all I have found that has completely aided me is the blood replacement. If I want to get back to where I'm best, I would have to steal some of it from the hospital—

—or eat someone—

—and I wonder just how smitten Max is with me if he would aide in such an adventure. Could I trust Max with my secret appetite? He has already seen the worst of it, perhaps. So has the medical staff at Ocean City Hospital, and they probably have seen worse from people needing a different kind of drug fix. All I need is something the common person does not get addicted to, which should make it readily available, no? I should be allowed bags of the solution, much like sugar addicts can buy Ice cream or Reddi-Whip.

In the hallway, with all the pictures and closed doors, I examine my brother's image again. The way he seemed to age like any other normal boy, and then I begin to notice something else. His door is still shut from last night. And these pictures on the wall—while everyone seems to get older, he seems to have stopped at the age of eleven or so. Even pictures with him and I, or him with our parents, he never seems to get past that age. Then, two things click:

My little brother is probably dead.

He had lived and died, and I have forgotten every moment of it.

I stood there as a warm tear moistened my cheek.

Funny, I had not cried for myself, yet. For being attacked, for being... whatever I am now. Closest to it was being tied down in the hospital bed, and that was just from sheer frustration and the very real fear of *merinthophobia*. I had been so tired last night that I went to sleep without thinking too much, or I might have cried then. But this little boy, with his dark hair and awkward teeth, who seemed to hold so much joy in the world, as pictures prominently displayed usually hold, this boy is dead. My brother is dead.

"You okay, dear?" My father asked from his doorway, startling me. I didn't realize anyone was there, and the sudden voice almost knocked me to the ground. I clumsily wipe at my cheeks, my hands not working really well, and also noticed my nose was running, too. I must have looked like a mess, which was confirmed when my Dad found it hard to look at me, and rather—studied the carpet on the ground.

"Yeah, Da—" I said, wanting to say Dad, but not able to finish the last syllable. "Juh sad."

My voice... it was going. Are you kidding me? A pound of raw meat and I only got a couple of hours out of it?

"I understand. I do the same sometimes, too," he said, and came out to look at the pictures with me. He put his arm around me, and when I almost fell with the dead leg, he looked down at my foot. "Your foot okay?"

I knew I only had one word in me, and that to make it sound okay, I would have to really focus, so I did.

"Ah-sleep."

He took the answer in stride and nodded. He gave me a weak smile, and just like that, with his arm around my shoulders, holding me up, we turned back to the pictures on the wall. My father and me, a strange old man and me, looking at a life I knew I had, but couldn't remember one tiny detail of. Except, I remembered the smell. The smell of the hallway, mixed with that old person breath my father had coming out of his nostrils, and the somewhat stale meat aroma that emanated off of him. Not the delicious smell of Max, but a kind of smell where, if I was starving, might have made me salivate, but since I was just so-so hungry, almost made me lose my appetite.

Almost.

"I miss him, Alex," my father said, his shoulders shaking with emotion. "I miss him so much. Your mother doesn't like to talk about it, would probably yell at me if she saw me blubbering to you, but I just thought he had so much potential. He played sports, got good grades, had so many friends. He could carry on a conversation with the adults so well...."

Him talking about how great this human being was almost got me to cry again.

"...One of those kids that make you feel like you actually might be a good parent, you know?"

I didn't feel his hand leave my shoulder, or his presence leave my side. I actually don't know how long I stood in that hallway, his last sentence floating through my mind. I said the sentence twenty times, normally, and then putting emphasis on each word, trying to see if I had heard him wrong, or put the wrong connotations to it. But, every time I did, I heard the same disappointment in his inflection. I heard the same judgement and came to the same conclusion: I was not the apple of my parents' eyes. This kid was. This boy kid. This dead boy kid. And even though I survived and he died, however he died, I could not replace him on that throne. And since he died while being perfect, I would never be able to eclipse him.

So, whatever. I'll just hop in my new boyfriend's ride and sail into the sunset. The fact they don't like him makes Max all the sweeter as a proposition.

The fact that he honked from the street instead of coming to the door made him Prince Charming in my eyes. I gathered myself and limped downstairs and out of the door before my father even came to his bedroom door again to see what was going on. And I still never got a fair thought of where my mom was in all that time. She didn't seem to be home.

I don't remember when my father left me alone in the hallway, or when my mother left the house. I don't know what I looked like as I ambled to Max's car, or when I struggled so much with the handle that he had to lean over to open the car door for me. I can't tell you what the car smelled like, or what he looked like, or what the seat felt like.

All I can say is that I cried.

I cried and nobody comforted me.

16

"Ah neeee suh-eeem," I said to Max, completely embarrassing myself, and also putting him on alert that I was, once again, becoming the weird girl.

I was able to get my seatbelt on, but it was only with sheer luck. I grabbed the buckle, and simply aimed right, sliding the buckle right in. There I sat, with tears streaming down my face, staring straight forward, knowing Max was just looking at me, watching me. Maybe he was trying to figure out what I said, or maybe he was regretting the decision to come over, regretting that he was now stuck with me. Deciding whether he should either kick me out of his truck or painfully get through the next couple hours.

What was the point of all of this? What was the point of trying to figure out who my parents were, and how I could make their lives better by being more like the Alex that they knew? The Alex they knew who wasn't as good as the boy they lost? What was the point of trying to become better, healthier? Why not just let the hunger whisk me away to my death, and then I wouldn't be hungry for anyone? I wouldn't bother anyone. I would quietly be that girl that once was there and now is not. Much like my brother. Someone to mourn, but nobody to worry about.

In the meantime, as I was dealing with the sorrow of a broken home, Max's unearthly, unhealthy smell was filling the cab. The entire truck smelled of him, and his skin, and a certain spice he just reeked of. He was sweet, like the cranberry sauce over Thanksgiving white meat. He smelled sugary and woody, like a rosemary and brie chicken sandwich. The kind of meat you wanted to snip off a piece of and chew slowly with your back teeth, pushing it from side to side in your mouth, letting your cheeks soak in the fluids as much as your tongue. That's what Max smelled like—white meat, berries, and a melty, French cheese. And if you were as flipping starving as I was, tell me that wouldn't make your stomach-detective gurgle.

"Did the purse not help?" He asked.

I turned to him and the tendons and bones in my neck snapped, crackled, popped as I did so. My throat had become so dry from the crying or from my present condition, my rabies or whatever this was, that I couldn't swallow, and so I felt my mouth gathering a large pool of spit underneath the tongue and back behind the last teeth. I could play with the saliva if my nose wasn't blocked up with snot, and my mouth wasn't the preferred way to breathe at the moment.

My purse? I thought to myself, *my purse couldn't cure me from this disease, it couldn't bring back my little brother, it couldn't bring my parents to love each other and me. No, my purse didn't help. Not one bit. It gave me more gum, which would probably just fall out of my mouth if I tried to chew it currently, and a locked phone.*

"Mead," I said, not pronouncing my "T" correctly.

"Mead? Isn't that, like, beer?" Max asked, and I wondered if the only way I could get a date with a boy was if he was a raging moron.

"Mead," I said again. And then I focused, and not caring if my entire chin got soaked in escaping drool, I connected my tongue to the roof of my mouth. "Teh."

"You want food? Let's get food."

He put the truck in drive, and we were off. For the second time in two days I was in Max's truck, only this time I had been elevated to the cab, instead of tied to the back. If I played my cards right, I could stay here, and not be shoved out of the door to the side of the road or returned back to my house of dueling adults.

"I was thinking," he said, focused on the road, "of just driving around, you know, see what we could see, trace our path of last night. I'll show you where I found your purse. Do you remember where we met last night? For the second time? When you tried to... uh..."

He looked at me, and I slowly shook my head.

"That's okay. It was dark. I will show you that. You can see if you remember how you walked there from your family's rental. Maybe there's clues as to who attacked you? Although, the cops were out in small-town force this morning, studying the lawn. To be honest, you know what I think? I think small town cops can't solve crimes like the big city cops in all of those cop shows." The way he said "cop" so many times in one sentence annoyed me, and I sat there waiting for another "cop" to come out of his mouth to boil my blood, "because the big city cops have all of the equipment and people and lab technicians and such, and the small city cops just, kind of, rely on the fact that we all know each other, you know? That us small town folk look out for each other, and we know who each other are, and such. They rely on us being like, 'Oh, yeah, a girl got attacked? I saw Harry Samsonite, drunk as a skunk, ranting at the moon again last night, walking in that same area.' And they go to Harry's house and find him, blood on his chin from biting ya, and slap the cuffs on him, haul him to jail, and voila! Small town cops nab another—"

I wanted to say, 'Stop saying the word cop!' All I wanted to do was bark at him that he was talking too much, and I was hungry, and I didn't want a tour of the island, or whatever he was considering; I wanted meat. I wanted raw, bleeding meat. My stomach felt so empty, I thought it was going to fall out of me onto my jeans, because for whatever reason stomachs feel heaviest when they are empty. It was almost painful how starving I was, and how good he smelled, and how much his conversation annoyed me. These three things together made me lash out. And instead of saying "shut up!" or whatever raging thing was on my mind, I turned quickly and yelled nonsense from the passenger seat and reached out to grab him with both arms and clasping hands.

In a stroke of luck for Max, my seatbelt held in that way that locks one's back to their seat. I could feel it cutting into me as I growled, and drooled, and gnashed my teeth, reaching out to grab him. I wanted to pull him to me, maybe remove just as much of him as was removed from me last night.

He shouted "Whoa!" and swerved the car in a reactionary move, as if he'd just discovered a demon in his car. He swerved across the double yellow line, and before an oncoming car could end both of our lives, he swerved back, almost side swiping the line of cars parked on the side of the street.

I was trying to eat him. Dr. Watson, alive and well, was urging me on. *Get him! Devour him! Leave no juicy morsel behind!* and behind my eyes flashed images of little girl me eating a large slice of watermelon, the juices all over my cheeks, when all of a sudden, the watermelon is replaced with the crook of an elbow, my cheeks caked in red. Little me pulling a slice of cheesy pizza from the whole pie, the cheese so melty and gooey it doesn't want to let go of the rest, to zombie me, pulling off a shoulder, the tendons and muscles stretching painfully away.

He had pulled over into a parking lot, which was the safest move. He opened up his door, and put one foot out of the truck, giving himself an escape should I get free from the seatbelt that I wasn't even trying to unbuckle. I wasn't thinking about the seatbelt. I was thinking about him, and the joy of eating him. I stretched out my arms as if I could suggestively will him into them, my shirt soaked with drool, my tongue pressed firmly against the roof of my mouth in order to make sure I didn't bite it off. I gnashed my teeth and made a snarling sound.

Was I in control of myself? Or was Dr. Watson?

I didn't feel like I could stop.

Even when I saw Max watching me, his brow furrowed, his one hand on the door handle, his other hand on the back of his seat, I couldn't stop. He just stood there, looking at how crazy I must look, and even though I noticed I was making quite the spectacle of myself, I couldn't stop. A new pain came to me. A pain of shame which was the hardest pain to deal with, and I felt more tears coming. As I sat there, as much as I wanted Max to come to me so I could chew on his cheek, I also wanted him to slam the door and walk away from me, to leave me to die of starvation here in the truck. I didn't feel worthy of his attention.

That was what he did. After he looked off for a moment and saw something, he looked back at me, and then back off, and pushed himself from the cab, and closed the door. I think he mumbled "be right back" but I couldn't be sure over my own growls and useless intimidation. I watched him through the windshield, still careening for him, my fingertips dancing and sliding across the dashboard. I watched him walk away in the daylight, his worn jeans looking mighty good, and the final bit of my drool fell into my lap.

Max walked through the automatic doors of a grocery store. Without his smell next to me, I slowly started to calm down my motions, letting my shoulders sag and my hands fall into my lap. I still jawed, trying to keep the spit in my mouth.

What felt like two minutes later, Max walked back out with two blue doubled-plastic-bags of something. I must have fallen asleep, because there was no way the bags were just waiting for him at the door, but there he was, coming back to the truck, noticeably peering in at his psychotic, cannibal date for the afternoon; looking at me like I was a strange Rottweiler who happened to break into his car.

At first, I was behaved. I just watched him through the glass, coming back to his truck. When he knocked on the window, I looked over at him, tired and feeling used up. I wondered if he locked himself out, and then wondered if I would be able to unlock the doors with my limited capabilities. But, it appears he was just checking me. He opened his car door, and I smelled that late November meal off of him, and I was back at straining against the belt across my chest. Only this time, it didn't lock, and I was able to get a good reach out to him.

This must have been what Max was afraid of, because he threw the bags at me, and slammed the door shut again, and my hand was in the door's way, and the force of it shutting, jammed the middle finger on my right hand. The knuckle really smarting in on itself. His smell remained, infuriating and invigorating me and as I clawed for him, I pushed myself up from the seat, straining against the strap across my waist. If I just unbuckled myself, I would be free of this, but even knowing this, I still just tried to rip myself out of it, thinking it would just be quicker this way, when it wasn't.

My hands moved across the bags he had thrown in, and I began to rip into them, not noticing what I was doing. I had other things on my mind, the murder of my date being a high priority on my list, and he stood outside the truck, looking in, watching me, like a kid who threw a piece of bread onto an ant hill to see how it was handled. The sight of red inside the blue caught my eye, and I peeled away some of the plastic to see what he had bought; pounds and pounds of different cuts of steak.

Max was amazing.

Don't ask me how I deserved a friend like him, but as I finally slowed down, as I ran a delicate finger across the protective piece of saran wrap film over the fajita-cut meat, as my mouth found new drool to embarrass me, I suddenly felt an arm around me from within my body, and Dr. Watson said:

I love him. He's a provider. Maybe we should keep him alive....

I agreed, feeling Max's eyes on me as I pondered the meat before me, reading its label like a romantic card bought on one of those gushy holidays. Some men bring roses, some men bring chocolate, mine brings a center cut.

...For now, Watson finished.

I ripped into the top package of raw stew meat, and began.

17

Eating is eating, we have all done it. We know the process of ripping, chewing, swallowing, and enjoying, filling our stomachs, and returning back to true form; able to control our tempers. Back to energetic, able to focus, us. Able to not want to viciously rip the skin from a boy we are somewhat attracted to and run our tongues over his shivering muscle fibers. This may be just me (and, if my detective skills are correct, one other person out there who bit me to turn me into the new me) but I want to say that after getting through two pounds of the several pounds of red deliciousness before me, I was back to talking regularly, had a full stomach, and the ability to move without feeling like everything was dry rotting inside of me.

Max, at first, watched curiously from outside of the driver's window, then found a nice cozy spot leaning against the hood of his truck, looking out on the grocery store parking lot. At first, I thought he was so disgusted and revolted by seeing me eat that he had to just turn away, but then I realized he was keeping a look out. He would keep his eyes on cars that would pass by slowly, almost daring them to stop, not realizing that everyone driving through the parking lot was actually going slowly to find a spot. Who knows what would have happened if either of the cars next to us pulled out of their spot, and a new suitor had to pull in. I could see Max having some very aggressive altercation with them, marking his territory with his scrawny biceps, and his bravado, and making sure nobody saw his lady friend in the cab of his truck, watery blood dripping down off of her chin. We apparently parked in a spot next to two slow shoppers or employees, so we didn't have to worry about that.

While I was chewing the last bite I had decided to take, I easily unbuckled my seat belt, and let my binding recoil back behind my right shoulder. I used one of the blue bags as a trash bag, placing the empty, bloody Styrofoam containers into it, tying it up, and placing it on the floor by my feet. What was it about the blood replacement last night, and the red meat today, that has me so... me? Every time I get dim-witted, get thick-tongued, am I going to have to go into the meat aisle and slobber all over some raw T-bone?

Well, regardless of what is happening to me, it's over, and before I start sinking into another moment of absolute embarrassment, I pull the inside handle to my door, and gently step out of the car. The sunlight hits the wind, which hits my face first, and even though it feels too warm for comfort, it still, somehow, feels good. I look over to Max as I shut the door, and squint in the brightness toward him, wondering what should be my first words after such a demoralizing display of character. It isn't until I see him, just looking at me, that I realize he doesn't need some awe-inspiring speech from me; he just needs one word to know that I am okay, that I am not some mindless, alien-possessed being that will tear apart his body looking for his soul.

So, I say the first word that comes to mind:

"Antidisestablishmentarianism," I say, like a dip.

"Nice," he responds. "Kind of like supercalifragilistic-expialadocious."

"Something you say when you don't have the words to say?" I respond, still kicking myself for saying my twenty-eight letter word as if just to prove the fact that not only can I speak clearly, but I knew big words.

"Right," Max says, the smile glued to his face weakening.

"Sorry about..." I started, and finished, "the eating..."

"You seemed hungry," he deflected.

"How did you know I needed raw meat?"

Max looked at me and thought about his answer. Then, he looked off at the grocery store, at the clouds in the sky that looked like it might rain even though it most certainly was not going to, and then back at me, at the wound on my shoulder that was hidden, but he knew was there. And suddenly, as if remembering who he was a minute ago, he glued the smile back on his face, and made eye contact.

"You up for the drive?"

"Wait," I said, "you didn't answer my question."

"It's a long answer."

"Great. I feel longer answers answer more of the question, no?"

I walk around to where he is, and lean my back against the grill, crossing my arms to mirror his stance. He looked at me and smiled, chuckling even, and I couldn't help but to smile too, even though, deep down, I was getting a little impatient.

"You really want to have this conversation here? Now? In an Acme parking lot?"

"I don't know what Acme is, but sure. Good enough place as any."

"Acme is the only grocery store on the island. You don't remember it at all?" I shook my head, so he continued. "Man, no memory whatsoever. That's crazy."

"You calling me crazy now?" I said, instantly defensive, and then I immediately regretted it because what have I done in the last twenty-four hours that wouldn't be considered crazy?

"No," Max lied. "Just the fact that you have no memory, at all. You haven't told your parents still?"

"I was kind of hoping... it would just come back, you know? Like I would see something, and boom—it would all just click."

"I kind of have that hope, too," he said, nodding, looking down at his shoes and kicking the tiniest piece of parking lot pebble asphalt a couple feet away from us.

"Why?" I asked. Because, obviously, I knew why I wanted to remember who I was, but why did he?

"Because," he started. "I kind of like you. And I think you kind of liked me."

He didn't look at me as he said it. And by the way he intentionally didn't look at me as he said it, I could tell that he was embarrassed to actually be admitting it. And whether or not I would ever remember having a crush on this boy for, like, all the years we were in school together or whatever, I looked at him now, as he consciously didn't look at me, and I felt my face get flushed, and my stomach turn into knots, and I felt a warmth shoot all throughout my body. And this warmth, this flood of good feelings, made it impossible not to smile.

"I don't need my memory back to know I kind of like you, too," I said. And he looked at me with a little boy smile plastered across his face, and surprise in his eyes, and I laughed. For the first time in my new life, I heard what my laugh sounded like, and it sounded so... uncontrollable that I turned away and hid it with my hands, but I laughed some more as I angled my way toward the passenger seat. Not that being stuck in a cab with this boy I just professed my liking to was going to be any more comfortable, but I wanted to get out of this parking lot, I wanted to ride wherever he wanted to go, and I wanted to begin this life of red meat and memories.

Bring them on.

18

Max drove around, and I felt so brainless at the fact that it finally clicked that Ocean City would be a city by the ocean (the Atlantic Ocean, as he would tell me.) On one side was a bay, littered with sporadic islands of tall grass or reeds, and the other side was the expansive ocean that filled the air with the smell of salt water and a calming noise like the world was breathing.

I felt so bad for Max, who drove around with me by his side, thinking that any of this would even remotely spark some memory of my past life. Soon, I felt, he would start to lose hope he would grow tired of this adventure. He would go back to school, and hang with his friends again, and I would go back to school, and people would start giving me the cold shoulder, not realizing that I was only doing it to them because I didn't recognize them. Max and I would pass each other in the halls, him on his way up and out of this town, and me on the way down and out of my mind. That is what my future looked like.

Why are you always so glum? Dr. Watson asks,

impatiently, licking his fingers from the meal Max provided.

Teenage hormones make me moody! I shout back, not necessarily knowing if that was the case.

"Do you know about my brother?" I ask Max, breaking the silence from the last time I told him 'no, that ice cream shop means nothing to me.'

"Ben?" He asks, and I shrug, and he remembers that I have amnesia. "Yeah, Ben's his name. I don't know what his middle name is, was, or is."

"Was, right? He died?"

Max nodded, clearly uncomfortable that after one date, he was going to be the one to have to tell me how my brother died. "I know about him."

"What happened to him?"

Max thought about it, chewing his lip, and making sure the roads were clear before he got into such a serious topic. I turned away from him, looking at the world passing by, not wishing to see his face as he had to go into a story which would, ultimately, make me sad. I tried to focus on the houses, on the way the sun reflected off the windows of them, the churches on random street corners. This island seemed so small, and it felt that after ten minutes of driving, we were already coming to the end of it. How could I, a girl who lived in this town for her whole life, not recognize one single aspect of it? Especially with a place so small, I am almost certain I passed the same things, the same sights, every single day.

When one gets amnesia, do all of their brain cells die?

Do brain cells really store the information like little bubbles of memories, or am I just making that imagery up in my head?

Max, thankfully, broke my train of thought before it completely derailed to a place that completely didn't matter.

"He was killed," he said, and I felt the truck slow down, even though he didn't brake. No, the world slowed down. "They found his body, uh, floating against the pier down at 55th Street. It being such a small island, the whole town had heard that he drowned, probably just a mistake, some... he was, like, twelve or so, and the boy goes out into the ocean.... Your brother liked to surf, but he wasn't too good at it yet, and so people just figured he hopped on a board, went out, and a current got him or something."

"But, he was killed?"

"He... yeah. You know... ugh, man, I wish I wasn't the one telling you this, but you know how when people die in the ocean, or, anywhere I guess, deserts, rainforests, that if they are not found right away, the wildlife get them? Well, your brother had a lot of wounds on him, and people saw that when they pulled him out, but really, everyone just kinda thought the fish got him."

I wanted to throw up in my mouth. Sure, I thought about eating people, but this was my brother, and the thought of little fish mouths nipping away at his dead body made me want to roll down the window, lean out, and let the raw meat and stomach acid paint the side of Max's truck. But, the thought of throwing up the soft tissue of my lunch made me equally more sick, and more willing to try and contain it within myself.

"They took him to the coroner, who is really just a cop with another degree here, Officer Winslow, that's his name, and the coroner said that they weren't just fish bites. Some of them were, but he felt that some of the wounds were made before your brother died."

"Bites? Like mine?" I felt my shoulder, feeling a pang of pain, but knowing it was just in my head.

"No. But, pieces missing. I don't really know what it was, or how it happened, but they just suspected foul play, or that's what they reported, and then we all caught wind of a portion of the truth. That your brother didn't drown.... They knew that because of his lungs and the lack of liquid there. He died from, like, shock or something. And that there was chunks of him missing, but they were... ah, I don't know a better way to say this, but they were more than likely, um... carved out, is what they said."

"Carved?"

"You know, like a turkey, or whatever, when you remove pieces of the bird, because nobody is going to pick up a turkey, and just, like put their whole faces in it, and tear off a piece, you know?"

I thought about what he was saying, trying to picture the boy in the photos, bloated from the water, and death; white, but covered in blue veins, grey eyes, with pieces missing from his shoulder, his hips, his ankles.

"But, what you are saying," I continued, letting my focus be on his death, and not his being dead, which let me keep my emotions in check. "That he was eaten by something or someone. They had used a knife and fork and not just locked their jaws on him like they did me?"

"No, no. That's not at all—we don't know how it happened. We just know that—okay, I see how you are seeing that, but... no, I mean, carved out could mean, like, a sculpture out of ice, a canoe out of a tree trunk. Just because I said carved, doesn't mean it was an eating thing."

"You said carved like a turkey," I reminded him. "Carved like a thanksgiving turkey."

Max shook his head. "That's not what I meant. I just meant they knew he was murdered because of his lungs, and the pieces removed from his body."

"Do you know which pieces were removed?"

Max sat there. We were stuck at a light, and he looked as if he was thinking of the question, absent-mindedly nodding his head. The light turned green and he continued on driving, continued on nodding until he realized that I was looking at him.

"Oh, what? No. No, I don't. Why would I?"

Sure, I thought to myself, *why would he?*

I tried my hardest to think about my brother, to try to remember a time when he absolutely annoyed me for something as stupid as just existing, perhaps being in the same room as me, or watching the television when I wanted to watch the television, or suggesting to Mom we have hamburgers one night when I felt we were having them too much, and was it too hard to ask for a taco night every once and awhile?! But, no, none of that came. Not even a vision of my parents when bringing up cooking dinner, or what would be on the television that Ben would want to watch, or what I would want to watch. My brother was going to be the ghost in the room that I could never see.

Apparently, I was already done crying tears for him. As I sat in the truck, Max wound it around a cul-de-sac, which marked the end of the island, and began to loop his truck back to where we came. The island kept going, to a place with no streets. A lighthouse rose out in the distance, and there was a path through some shrubs, with a red sign that had a lifeguard's white cross on it. This was not where we were going. The turning truck put it all behind us, and we started going north again on the island.

This put the ocean on my side of the truck, and as we passed 55th Street, I looked out the side window and saw the pier he had mentioned for a flash before it was hidden again behind a row of houses.

"Stop," I said, without thinking about it.

"You recognize something?" He asked, the excitement in his voice.

"Stop the truck!" I hollered at him.

"Let me find parking, please," he said calmly, almost too much like a father would.

"Let me out of the truck!" I said, grabbing for the handle, finding it, and trying it. But the door was locked when the car was in motion, unless I reached for the lock and manually unlocked it. By now, Max had seen my desperation and was slowing the car, so by the time I got the car door unlocked and open, my seatbelt undone, the truck was barely crawling when my feet hit the asphalt.

He was not running behind me. I heard him reach over, yell my name, shut the door I left open, and heard him drive on. But I had to see it. I had to touch it. I had to come face-to-face with the pier, knowing one thing for sure about my life. That this pier was the site of where my life went to Hell the first time.

I came upon a sign, very new looking, stuck into the sand that read:

THE BENJAMIN JORDAN PIER
Fishing Hours - Dawn to Dusk
Do Not:
Jump from Pier
Throw Fish Entrails into Water
Leave Rods Unattended
Leave Kids Unattended

I thought it funny that it seemed they valued the unattended rods more than the kids, and then I wondered if not leaving your kids unattended was a reminder of just why the pier was renamed for my brother anyway. But, he didn't fall off the pier, did he? His body was just found bobbing in the water next to it. If someone found me dead in the yard last night, would there someday be a plaque in the yard that read:

THE ALEXANDRA JORDAN LAWN
Visiting Hours
10am - 9pm
Do Not:
Leave Your Kids Unattended
Let Your Dogs Poop Here

Probably not. But a boy found at a pier made that pier special. And why not use the boy's death as a way to remind the other sons and daughters that this was a cruel world which showed little mercy for someone's age or innocence when selecting them to die. I mean, I almost died last night, which would have left my parents childless, and even though they were a pain to be in the same room with together, they certainly didn't deserve the death of both their children.

And if we call children "orphans" when both of their parents die, what do you call parents whose children die, leaving them childless?

And why, did it seem, were their children the ones being attacked? Being left for dead? Having chunks removed from them?

I think our mystery is deepening, Dr. Watson said, completely on my side of things because he wasn't hungry and looking to get us into trouble.

So, my brother was killed, and I was attacked. *Do you think it was by the same person?* I ask my stomach.

Could be. Could be a coincidence.

Do we believe in coincidences?

If we want to.

I decided I didn't. Whatever had attacked my brother had also attacked me. Some man out there was obsessed with my family. Or woman, I guess it could be. Perhaps it was whoever one of my parents were having an affair with. Perhaps that is why they hated each other, because there was infidelity, and now, the mister or mistress was trying to off the children because that was the only thing connecting the one spouse to the other. I began to think, with all of this murder mystery business and the fact that my stomach was named Dr. Watson, if I didn't have a predilection for Sherlock Holmes novels, or Agatha Christie. I needed to go through my book collection at home to confirm this theory, but as I sat down in the sand, hugging my knees close to my chest, quietly staring at the way the waves broke on the wooden supports of the pier, and envisioning my brother's body in the water there, I thought to myself how I would have to solve the mystery of my attacker. Quite possibly, before the attacker came back and finished the job. In fact, as the sun began cresting toward the bayside horizon, there was a very real possibility the person would come back tonight, and where should I go to make sure they didn't find me?

Max scared me as he sat down next to me. I, at first, thought it was a stranger, or my attacker, who still could be a stranger, but no, it was the guy I just ran away from. He must have known I had come to see the pier he had just talked about. He didn't say anything, anyway, but just sat there, wiping the sand from his hands, resting his elbows on his knees to look out at the never-ending ocean before us.

"My brother and I would come here to fish," Max said, breaking the silence. Well, not silence, as the waves crashing was the loudest sound around us, the seagulls squawking in the air was second loudest, and there were people and kids on the pier up above laughing and joking around, despite the fact that it was the off season.

"Did my brother and I get along?" I ask, feeling the hard peach pit of emotion settle right in the middle of my throat.

"Um, to be honest, Alex. You and I didn't talk much. I assume you did, in the old, sibling love-hate kind of way...."

"Why do you assume that?"

Max thought about it. "Because it seems you wanted me to answer you. I don't really know."

"Then, just say you don't know," I say, letting my anger and frustration with my life get the better of me. "I'm unsure of everything in this world, and the last thing I need is answers that aren't necessarily correct. Am I right?"

Max nods, and I can see it in my peripheral but I am still so fired up that I decide to twist the knife deeper.

"Can you answer me?"

"Sorry, I was nodding. Yes. I understand. I... I sometimes always feel like I need an answer to things, and so... it's not you, or us, or anything, but I sometimes just make things up on the spot to make people feel better."

"That's an awful trait."

Max shrugs. "So is amnesia and trying to eat people."

Are you kidding me? I think as I turn to face him. *How dare you!* I want to shout, but it stays within my throat.

Actually, I chuckle. I express joy at this humor from this boy who I have been attacking, who defended himself by making fun of me, and I appreciate it. I like the fact he's willing to cut me down, in the same way that I cut myself down, and the smile on my face, and my shaking shoulders seem to remove some kind of weight from me. The world is what it is, and whether I approach it spitting fire or sulking with my head down makes no difference.

I might as well go into my battle with a sense of humor because there's no reason to face the worst with sorrowful expectations.

"I think my parents should get divorced," I say, moving to a different topic than my brother.

"Because they blame each other for your brother?" Max asks, bringing the conversation right back.

"Oh... maybe..." I wish I could remember the happier times, the times where the bad things, and bad memories, hadn't touched our household.

"The death of a child usually has negative ram... rami... what's the word?"

"Ramifications?" I say, happy to know I might be

smarter, albeit more clueless, than him.

"Yes. Thank you. Negative ramifications on families. Some use it as a way to come together but, from what I remember reading, they usually fail. There's a blame that happens."

"Are your parents still together?" I ask, hoping for hope.

A sort of dull look passes over his eyes, as if he has already explored the depths of his soul to answer this question once, and how dare I forget his answer and make him answer it again. I scold myself for forgetting this piece of my friend's history.

"My father left us," Max finally said. "We don't know where he is."

"Sorry..."

I think about how, maybe, if I could just remember my parents before my brother's death, I could find the things that they loved about one another, and maybe use it to bring them back together, and since I couldn't remember being such a snot beforehand, maybe I could become a better me, a kid they needed.

Maybe I should tell them the truth about me, I think to myself.

The freak that you are, Dr. Watson responds.

"How did you..." I started, Dr. Watson's observation opening another can of worms. Max saw me at my freakiest and still hung out in the cab of his truck with me, drove me around, and chased me down after I ran away again. What kind of freak must Max be to even want to continue to be in my presence? "How did you know that meat... that I needed meat?"

"You said it," he reminded me.

"Yeah, but... do you know of anyone else that eats raw meat fresh from the butcher?"

"Isn't there, like, a French dish? Tarter or something?"

I thought about it, and even though my memory, somehow, remembered random things like pop culture references and such, I had absolutely no idea what he was talking about. Especially because tarter was something the dentist scraped off your teeth, right? Or was it a type of sauce people dipped fried fish in when they weren't eating meat on Fridays during that religious holiday where people lent each other things... right? Or am I getting totally confused? Was I that religion? Would I just have to starve on Fridays? What happens if you eat meat? You go to Hell? Am I such a cannibalistic freak that I'm going to Hell anyway?

"I don't think you think it's normal... what I ate today."

Max shrugs. And I realize what has been gnawing on me this whole time. The thought behind the thoughts that I would try and laugh off as if they were silly to even think about, the avenue to explore. All of this time, my thoughts were on what had happened to me: the attack, the hunger, the hospital visit, the missing memory, the somewhat-talking stomach, but there was something really upsetting with it all, wasn't there? I didn't just have amnesia, but there was a serious illness that I needed to figure out, something that attacked my speech, my mobility, my entire identity. I pictured my dad shuttering in the kitchen, and my mom wrapping her arms tighter around herself outside of the car. The only person who didn't really shy away was Max, and maybe that meant he was the only person I could trust.

"I think something's wrong with me."

He looks over at me, and I instantly regret saying anything. Especially something so unrehearsed. I realize that trust to not judge, and trust to care are two different things and while I didn't think he would judge me, if he didn't care about my confession, I would just die all the same. I feel my eyes stinging with tears and look away toward the pier, remembering my brother. I look to the ocean, its endlessness more inviting than this thought spiral I am about to go down because I want to be anywhere, mentally and physically, than sitting here next to a boy who can destroy me with a laugh-off or any other reaction that didn't feel perfect to me.

I think I can just walk into the waters, swim away until I can't swim any further, and then just sink. I think about the fish eating me, my brother, and my parents hearing their second child died, this time with an actual bite missing, and I look down at the sand, and think about how there are infinite grains of it, and how if you looked closely enough, this sand was made up of several different kinds of rocks, and I felt how many thoughts I had racing through my head. So I looked up and back at Max, whose mouth curled into a smile, which faded, and came back, as if he was trying to hide it.

"I think you're Alex Jordan," he said. "And the rest, we'll find out together."

And my stomach drops and I can't breathe and I almost feel like I can't move, like I have no strength in my shoulders, and my legs feel gone, and it's a good thing I'm sitting. I can literally feel the earth get heavier under us as Max puts all of his weight down on his hand and leans toward me, and just like some poet said at some time or another, I felt some type of magnetism in the air. I felt the stars align and the moon catch fire and the tides change and gravity adjust and all I knew was that this boy wanted to kiss me and I couldn't want anything more than to kiss him back.

I meet him. Not halfway, because he had a head start, but definitely before he started getting curious if I wanted to kiss as well. I had no memory of ever doing it before, but I pressed my lips together, and then to his, and he did the same back, and it felt weird, and dry, and okay, but I stopped focusing on the nerves in my lips and focused on the tingles throughout my body. He made a move, almost to go away, but I put my hand to his cheek, which he shuttered at from how cold I am, and he stayed put so I could kiss him again, relishing in the feeling of his hot lips on mine.

As first kisses go, I'm incredibly self-conscious. Even though he seems to be no expert, I do believe I'm fumbling a little bit more. That I am a little too aware of the breath through my right nostril as the left is still plugged. I feel saliva on the corner of my mouth, not knowing whether it is his or mine or if I should be grossed out about this. If it feels good, and boy does this, it's an okay kiss, right? I wonder, letting my thoughts get away from me, so I use my other hand and now I have his face between my two hands as the kissing gets hotter, more fiery, and I feel his hands encircle my lower back, bringing my body closer to his.

His mouth opens up, and I feel his tongue, and an urge surges deep within me, and I open my mouth, thinking about how I should meet his tongue with my own.

And I bite.

19

"Oh my gosh!" I say as he gets himself away from me as quickly as he can. I see the blood before I know where I got him, and he looks back at me, anger more than fear, in his eyes. I see blood on his bottom lip, dripping onto his chin, as if he himself just ate raw meat.

"You bit my lip," he said, his tongue swimming in blood and spit.

"Your lip? I thought I got your tongue," I respond.

"You were going for my tongue?!" he spits, blood and spit congealing a clump of sand. "Dammit, Alex, why would you do that?!"

"I don't know!" I say, going full-on truth mode.

Smell his blood, Dr. Watson said, rumbling. And I could, even with the misty ocean breeze, layering the air with the smell of salt water and fish. I could smell the iron seeping from his lip, that metallic smell mixed with berries, and to me, and my stomach, it smelled delicious. I didn't know whether all I wanted to do was grab Max and kiss him again because I liked him so much, or because I was hungry.

Either way, Max was over it, over the moment, and me, and he stood up, wiped the sand from his pants, and began to walk away. I continued to sit there alone, hating myself for being so emotional and impulsive to the point that it seemed I couldn't do anything right. I looked at the pier, at where my dead brother was found, and I wished the roles were reversed. I wished he was dealing with this life, and I was the one sleeping soundly somewhere, skipping merrily through the clouds with one of our dogs who died when we were children that I, also, don't remember or know if they actually existed.

I wiped a tear away, just as I felt sand being kicked up next to me from someone walking too close. When I look up, I see Max again, hands on his hips, looking down at me.

"Are you coming?" he asked impatiently.

"You want me to come with you?" I ask. His lip is still bleeding, and he knows his lip is still bleeding by the way he keeps tucking it into his mouth and sucking the new blood coming out. Oh... to be him... satiating me.

"Yeah. I mean, I can't just leave you here, can I?" In a very backwards way, Max was telling me he wanted me to come with him, that he was worried about me, and at the same time, making it sound like it was the biggest chore in the world to care for me. Either way, I agreed. I didn't want our time together to end, so I picked myself off the sand, shook as much off as I could and slapped my hands together. Turning to the pier, I say one last goodbye to my brother, Benjamin, and blow a kiss to the one support beam, I felt, was the one where his body was bumping up against when it was discovered, and I turned to Max to let him lead me back to his car.

The truck ride was incredibly awkward. He continually sucked on his lip, and I continually smelled his lip from over in the passenger seat, one hand wrapped around my stomach, trying to keep Dr. Watson from rumbling, the other out the window, angling it so the wind whipping by would hit me in the face, decreasing my chances of sinking my teeth into my driver.

I reached down past my knees, and find the blue plastic grocery bag containing the meat. Less self-conscious, and not really all that hungry, I feel it's something for me to do while ignoring the boy trying to ignore me. Maybe if he saw me eat more meat, if he saw that I was trying to quench my hunger, he also might try to kiss me again. Of course, the second thought is that he would watch me put bloody cow muscle in my mouth, and then decide that he didn't want to touch tongues with someone who ate like that. Which, I mean, I couldn't really blame him.

It took a couple of blocks for me to notice that I was sitting there, the skirt steak still packaged in my lap, my middle fingertip lightly caressing the saran wrap, feeling the ridges in the... food.... Is it still considered food if it's uncooked? Unsafe for human consumption? Should I be considering tapeworms?

Can I not remember tapeworms, and instead remember something useful, please?

I decide to start a conversation.

"You have a brother?" I ask.

"Why?" He immediately fires back. I wonder if it is the question that rattled him, or if he was just waiting for me to make a noise so he could snap at me.

"Just making conversation," I say, and watch the same

houses pass by the car.

Max swallowed his thoughts, his pupils darting back and forth as I continually played with the plastic, letting the sound comfort me until he reached over and pulled the red meat from my lap, putting it on the middle seat next to us. "Yeah," he said. "An older brother. Greg."

"How much older is this Greg?"

"Four years. He's in college. Or was. He's home now."

"Graduate?"

Max looked where he was driving, lost in thought. "Something like that."

"He's alive, though?" I ask, and I don't know why I ask, perhaps looking for something in common with him, like, Oh my Gosh! Your brother died, too! And I realize how horrible that all sounds, and so does Max.

"Jesus, Alex..."

I want to ask about Greg, about his interests, about where he likes to hang out around town, or who he hangs out with, or if he has a girlfriend or not, but I realize that any of the answers would probably sound foreign to me in the grand scheme of things.

He points wildly with his finger at nothing in particular, as if just aiming his attention at specific parts of an overall, general world. "So, none of this looks familiar? Nothing striking any bells?"

And I look around. It all looks familiar, from last night, and today. It all looks like the same house, the same construction company, the same two levels, both with porches, and the same pastels painted on the exteriors. The same count of houses between every perpendicular street, the same beach view or bay view at every street, depending on which way one was looking. The same streets lined with the same parked cars, and the same double yellows telling Max not to pass, painted in the middle of them. Everything looked the same, but none of it brought up any memories as to where I was last week.

"No." I said.

And that was it, that was the end of the conversation that I started, that I tried to steer as adeptly as Max was driving me home, and for which I didn't feel like pulling teeth any more. Max had a brother who was still alive, and I did not. Max wanted to kiss me because he thought I was beautiful, and I tried to store his lips in my stomach. Max tried to date me for whatever reason, and I ran away and became a completely different person. And now, Max was dropping me off at home where my parents were waiting on the front porch, eyes wide with suspicion and anger. This time, it was directed at me. Both of them, working together, to be disappointed in me.

At least I could do some good today.

Mom came to get me from the passenger seat as if she was pulling me from a burning building, while my dad headed straight to Max's driver side window and put his finger directly in the boy's face.

"How dare you, you hear me?" was the first thing I could intelligibly make out from the vitriol. My mom was in my ear asking me questions, making sure I was okay, that I wasn't hurt, trying to understand my thought process of just running out. "My daughter was attacked last night, while under your care, and you think the smartest thing for you to do is to come in and take her out?"

"She asked me to drive her around, see if she..." But he stopped. He remembered me telling him that I didn't want my parents to know about my amnesia. He quickly stopped talking, and just looked up at my father who, if a truck door wasn't in his way, would be chest to chest with the boy I just bit.

"Is that blood on your lip?" Dad asked, prompting Max to tuck in his bottom lip and hide his wound. "Did she have to hit you for some reason?"

"No, sir," and both of the males looked at me, tucked under my mom's shoulder, being almost shoved toward our house while trying to walk sideways and see what was going on between them.

"He bit his own lip," I suggested, and Max, a twinge of pain on his face from reliving the moment, turned back toward my Dad.

"Her purse, her keys, her cell phone were at the house. You don't think that seems suspicious?" My dad kept on, playing detective.

"I returned the purse this morning, sir," Max stammered, trying to remain respectful. "I didn't notice she didn't bring them out with her."

Dad's finger points to his chest with each word, "that—didn't—answer—my—question."

Max, getting so frustrated that I could see tears coming to his eyes, bit his lip, squeezing more blood into his mouth. "I understand how that could alarm you."

My father's hands clenched, and unclenched. He squeezed his jaw shut so tightly, I wouldn't have been surprised if his teeth started cracking apart and shattered into dust so that he was only left with a mouth full of gums. Max's statement that he understood where my father was coming from seemed to do the most to disarm the middle-aged man. So, my father backed away from the truck as a sign of 'I give,' and allowed Max to put the truck in drive, and continue on his path down the street.

My mother's arm grew more tense around my shoulder, and she ushered me into the house I had only come to know yesterday.

I couldn't remember what a break-up felt like, or if I had ever experienced one before, but that was what it seemed like, watching Max drive off. I was sure I would see him again at school, but it felt like, with a pain in my chest, he would never again truly see me.

20

"I forbid you to see that boy again," my father laid into me as I sat at the kitchen table. My mother was next to me, so we both looked up at this man on a tirade.

"I underst—" I started, trying to use the same disarming tactic of my ex-boyfriend, but not being able to get the words out before my father—

"I didn't say you can speak!" he shouted.

My mother cast her mother hen gaze at my father, and for once, in the short span that I'd known both of them, he stopped his posturing and stood down. My mother's hand moved back and forth over my arm, blazing a trail there in comfort, but really, it felt like she was rubbing off layers of skin. She gently shushed no one in particular and, by the way she was acting, I wondered if I was crying uncontrollably and just didn't know it. My father, now with nothing to say, walked around in circles, hands on his hips, breathing so hard from his nostrils it was like he was trying to start a fire on his upper lip.

"You are so cold," my mother said, and I moved my

arm away from her, closer to my chest, wanting to complain about how hot her touch was to see how she felt about criticism, but I kept that thought buried inside. She watched as I took my body part back, and for the briefest moments stuck out her bottom lip in a kind of pout, which just seemed silly. "Why did you leave the house like that?"

"I didn't even know you were home," I countered.

"Of course I was. I was in the basement, working out," she said, as if even if I had my memory, I should know that if my mother was not in my vision that she was downstairs working out. That's where she would be. Always.

"I asked Max to pick me up and drive me around so we could talk about last night."

"For five hours?!" my father shouted, giving both of us a jump scare, which he tried to dispel before my mother glared at him again. "Sorry. For five hours?" he said, calmer.

Had it been that long?

We just drove around.

"You missed your doctor's appointm—" Mother started.

"Then why are you covered in sand?" said the man who, presumably, bought a house in a town on a beach.

"We stopped at the pier," I said, forgetting exactly which street the pier was at, and not wanting to sound like a complete fool for not knowing it off the top of my head.

The mention of the pier saddened the room, and both of my parents began to shut down, not looking at each other. Only my mother periodically glanced up at me, her eyes getting wetter and wetter with each look until finally the tears escaped down her face, collecting mascara as they streaked for the jawline finish line. She finally got up to get herself a tissue, and in a small moment of embarrassment, my father reached out, thinking she wanted to be held. But she passed right by him, so he put his hands back to his hips. I saw it all, even if they really didn't.

"How often do you guys go to the pier?" I ask.

"Why would we go to that stupid pier?" My mother asked, not turning from the sink, probably wishing she could just throw me in the disposal and be done with me, with him, with this life she was thrust into.

"Ben," I say, and she turns, and lashes—

"I know!"

It's my turn to cry and even though I just relearned how to do it, I already freaking hate it. I do believe my mother is a beautiful lady, and I believe that she had gotten a horrible end of the stick (is that the saying?) by having one child murdered and another child, who is me. I believe the working out is doing her good, but the sunbathing is aging her. She must be pretty smart, the way she carries her face high, and the way I can tell that her mind is constantly working behind that furrowed brow. Even when she's lost in thought, she seems to be taking in her surroundings like an arachnid. I believe these things about my mother, because I do not know.

What I know is that when my mother yells at me, my rib cage feels like it shatters, and I'm five years old again, which I'm sure I was at some point, and all I can do to stop from exploding from the chest out is to release the pent-up emotional steam through the liquid of my eyes. I mourn for my brother, for my parents, because it seems their pain turns to anger when they see me, or when I bring him up.

My dad goes in to hug my mom, to comfort her instead

of me, and she lets him for the briefest of seconds, before she comes back to her senses. She pushes him off her, and turns on me, angry that I would get such an emotional reaction out of her.

"What's the point of going to that pier? It's where he floated up to. It's not where he... it's not where he died, it's not where he was taken, it's not where he's buried, and it's not... it's not where he lived." She looks around at the kitchen, up toward the ceiling, the house, as if Ben was all around her, like a tornado of memories, and maybe he was. Maybe she was drowning in the constant reminders of a dead son.

"That pier... that pier with their stupid declaration of him... where everyone likes to pretend we learned something that day when my son washed ashore for some... bluefish fisherman to spot.... We didn't learn anything. What's the point, knowing that someone out there kills kids? Killed my son and got away with it? You don't see the police come by anymore. The news stopped running the story. Everyone goes on with their days, and I still don't have my son. But, let's name a pier after him so we can pretend like we're not trying to forget the horror. This horror I live with every day. This horror you seem to be chasing after by leaving the house with some strange boy with not so much as a note to say where you are!"

"I'm sorry, Mom—" I start.

"Don't, Alex! I'm sick of it. You never talk to your father and I anymore. You think this is just a hotel where you can come and go as you please. I went to the rental this morning, and it's trashed. Throw up on the ground, blood in the upstairs bathroom. I don't know what kind of party you threw, or when, but you're gonna get your butt over there and clean it up."

I look down at my hands, at the cut there from the can, at the dried blood from the meat that Max bought and remember that I forgot to grab it. I left it in his truck. And I wonder if my parents found their pound of thawing meat missing, and the wrapper under the couch, and if that was just another thing I was going to have to deal with today.

"I'll help—" my dad suggests, but Mom is running the show now.

"No, you won't. She needs to learn that actions have consequences. She will clean it up. Heaven knows we need that rental money, and we can't rent it looking like that. Answer me, Alexandra Madison Jordan!"

I get so excited to actually hear my middle name, I almost smile, but then to hide the smile almost makes my brain hurt. Remembering the tone in which my full name was said, like my heart was an echo chamber, made my tear factory start churning double time behind my eyes. "Yes, Mom. I'll clean it."

"When are you going to do it?"

"Right now?"

She nods, satisfied with that. In all honesty, I wanted to clean it up last night, but felt there were other things more pressing. Being forced to do a chore didn't bother me—the yelling about it was the worst part.

My dad looks over to my mom, and carefully asks.

"Can I, at least, drive her over?"

21

The man in the car was different than the man I had known. My father drove the car, turning on the radio to some oldies station I, of course, didn't recognize, and he tapped his fingers on the steering wheel as if he was helping the percussionist keep the beat. When I looked over at him just to wonder who he thought he was, he looked back at me and smiled; smiling as if we weren't just put into our places by the other woman in the house. I wondered if he thought that there was some type of battle going on, and because she yelled at me, is forcing me to clean, that I, somehow, had come onto his side of it. Which, I had not. If there was a battle between my parents, I was going to be on my side, and my side only.

The other concerning thing about this car ride was not that I was going back to the house where I was attacked, but that Dr. Watson was stirring again. My hunger pains had returned, and with them, my penchant for smelling everything as if it was food. My father's smell, however, was sort of rancid, and completely unappealing to me.

Knowing what I knew about my new self, and health, and how things generally disintegrated, I could probably be in my new house for an hour, cleaning, before every limb started falling asleep, I started drooling, started growling like a person with no lips, and worst of all, started thinking about eating my fellow human beings.

Why is all of this such a bad thing? Dr. Watson asked from within. *You got a fraction of a taste from Max, and you can't deny that more wouldn't be the most amazing meal you have ever known.*

And I can deny it, and I will, for as long as I am able to, I tell myself, knowing full well that internally, clearly vocalizing your thoughts is somewhat outside of what people typically do. Or is it?

Your father smells rancid because he's old. Max smelt like buttermilk pancakes and bacon because he's young, sweet, tender, and has lean muscles, my stomach and appetite told me. *What you smell in the air is the people around you, and what you crave is what they are carrying on their bones. You can't eat prepackaged meat forever. You're going to have to take a larger bite than a snip from the lip eventually.*

What if I surround myself with old, rancid people and do not crave eating humans at all? I ask.

That's like someone saying they are going on a diet by hanging out in a dumpster.

"So..." my father started, breaking my conversation. "Did you have a party in the rental?"

I, at first, tried to think about whether I did or not; a habit, I guess, of forgetting that you have forgotten everything. Knowing what I did know about myself, I didn't figure I was a girl to throw wild parties at places without her parents there. Knowing what I did know about me, I remembered that the person who trashed the home was myself while alone, last night. The blood was mine, the puke was mine, the mess was mine, I whole-heartedly admit that. But, not out loud

"I won't yell at you or anything if you just want to tell me. I just... didn't think you were the type."

"What type would that be?" I ask, begging for more information.

"Come on... we have to yell at you for reading too much. You could be a straight-A student if you focused on your studies more. You sit in your room, on the beach, at the parks with a book in your hand, and instead of enjoying what's around you, you're glued to the page. I don't even remember the last friend you had over. It must have been either Amelia or Gianna, but I don't think I have seen either of them in the past year. What happened between the three of you?"

Bingo, names of the two girls in the picture. Which one had the braces? I now knew two things, the names of my pretty female friends, who might not be my friends anymore, which was probably my fault, and the reason why I carry their picture around still. The second fact being that I'm a bookworm with no life. Bookworms are usually smart, right? They say feeding the brain with the written word is the fastest track to intelligence.

"My grades are fine," I mumble, not really knowing, but still feeling the need to defend myself.

"They could be better," came the standard parent response.

"I don't know what happened with Amelia and Gianna and me," I say, sighing this absolute truth out the window, realizing my breath didn't show up on the glass despite being so close to it. "And before we get too off track, no, I did not have a party at the house."

"Maybe it was last night? Things got out of hand? You don't want to tell us the truth about it all, so you make up some story that someone attacked you, thinking it would help you get out of trouble, because we would believe it, because of what happened with Ben?"

He had been rambling, knowing the point he wanted to make but not knowing how to get to it. But, once he did, I could see the sense he was trying to come to, feeling better about the world if his daughter was some kind of pathological liar instead of someone who, through no fault of her own, was attacked by someone in her own front yard. I felt the emotion welling up in me, and at the same time I felt a stab of pain in my foot, wrapping around the protruding ankle bone. I could feel my deterioration start to speed up with the emotions I was trying to bury.

I know I don't remember, don't know much, but I know that my own father should believe me when I say—

"There was no party! It was me! I trashed the house on my own after I was attacked last night in the front yard! Why don't you frickin' believe me?!"

"I don't want to know any of the details but, what happened last night between you and Max?"

"Nothing."

"I know that's not true. I was your age once. I went out on dates. I took girls out in my car, and you know... things happen. It's nothing to be embarr—"

"Ew! You're my dad!" I said, feeling something inside.

Hunger, Dr. Watson tries to distract me.

No, I feel it. I feel a feeling I felt once before. Something from before the re-beginning. I feel it now while looking at my dad, who is having a hard time looking at me. I wonder if I forgot the word for it, or if there is no word for it, or if it's just a feeling that people can't really describe. A feeling like attachment to this man. Attachment? Like him and I were entwined someway, and even when I was embarrassed by him, or disgusted (as I was currently), or when he cried on my shoulder in the hallway, or yelled at me in the kitchen, that no matter what— he was my Dad. He was my father. Whether I remembered our past or not, I could feel it with him now. This was the man who raised me. I smiled at myself that I now felt something from the past, for someone, other than lust or hunger.

I felt... love.

"Why are you smiling?"

A lie on the spot: "You thought I would actually throw a party. With what friends? Amelia and Gianna? And Max? Not much of a party. We decided to trash the place in the midst of all our reading?"

My father chuckled. "I don't think your friends do much reading, dear."

And I laughed with him, slightly getting the joke, and not knowing whether it was true or not. Should I defend them anyway, because they were my friends? Or were they really my friends? The barrage of at-the-moment unknowables made me reflect back to what my mom was talking about in the kitchen. The pier was just a place, but it wasn't where Ben died, was attacked, was buried... so, where were all those places?

Adding it to my list, Dr. Watson said. *Find out all these things... after dinner....*

We pull up to the house, and I still see my imprint from

where I laid the previous night on the lawn. There is no driveway, so my father skillfully pulls up along the curb, putting the car in park and turning in his seat to see me looking at the grass, and how the blades never got back up again, and how I knew, somehow I knew, that there was an ant hill somewhere amongst all that lawn wilderness, and them ants knew what humans tasted like, and maybe, just maybe, because of my stupid error in judgement the night before, I had irresponsibly started a battle between human beings and insects, and didn't I read somewhere that there are two million ants for every human? Couldn't two million ants take down a human?

Would humanity blame me?

"What are you thinking about?" my father asked, not realizing the depth to that question. "Do you want me to... you know what? I'm coming in with you."

"No," I said, convincingly.

"I would feel better if I—"

"It's our rental, Dad. I shouldn't be scared to go in, should I?"

"But this is where you were attacked last night; I better come in just to be safe."

"If you want to."

He checked for traffic coming down the road his way before opening up his door, and I stepped out of my own onto the grass. It was actually a good thing he came with me, because once I walked up the front steps, my knees started clicking like I was an age I did not possess but I have felt since the previous night. I suddenly felt nervous to enter the house alone. I took the key out of my pocket, one of my only possessions I actually remember obtaining, and hand it over to him so he can unlock the deadbolt.

Whoever attacked me probably doesn't have the amnesia I have, and therefore would know exactly where I was when they jumped out at me. So maybe, just maybe, they were watching me as I waited at the front door to enter with my father, this big(ish) man who would probably rip someone to pieces if they tried to hurt me. Max was just trying to drive me around and my father pounded his finger into his chest. What would the big man do if he caught someone actually causing me harm?

Inside, he surveyed the damage my mother described, saying that he had not seen it for himself. The kitchen, to both him and I, smelled horrible from the drying vomit and the opened cans of food. The upstairs bathroom, the one I thought I cleaned, did not look like I attempted much at all except smearing blood around with my hand. In fact, I was almost thinking someone had come back after I left and was murdered there with how much I didn't recognize the carnage in the little room. Of course, the fact that the bathroom was almost purely white made the red splotches everywhere stand out even more.

My father looked at all of the blood, his mouth wide open.

"Well, I can see why your mother was so upset by this. What did we tell you about this place?"

I looked at him as if I forgot, which was kind of the truth.

"This place here puts food on our table. What we get during the summer helps us get through the winter. We have to treat it with respect. We're not like some people that have a bunch of these. Part of the reason your mom might be stressed. Definitely can't rent out a place where the bathroom looks like the set from *Psycho*."

Psycho... that was the film's name with the stabbing scene....

"Perhap not," I say, feeling my tongue getting heavy, my neck weakening.

"Are you okay, kiddo? This seems like a lot of blood."

"I went to the ho-pital, remember?" I reply, realizing that I had lost the ability to say my "S"s.

"You know what? I'll help you clean this."

"I'm fine."

"Honestly, this seems like a lot and I don't think—"

"I'm fine, Dad."

"Are you sure?"

"Yeth- yeah... go. I got thith... I can clean," and as my speech got worse, my head got heavier, and my neck felt like I was straining to keep my head up. I thought back to the meat in Max's car, to his bloody lip, and knew that I was going to have to settle for what was in some of the cans downstairs in order to get through the cleaning. Perhaps there was more SPAM. No offense to the makers of SPAM... but once you had a bite of boy, SPAM was just pork in a can....

My dad opened his mouth to say something, but then closed it, breathing heavily out of his nostrils. Finally, he decided to just let it out—

"It's not drugs, is it? You're not on drugs? To deal with... some kind of pain in life?"

I looked at him, trying to make sense of this, and for the first time I wanted to tell him everything, and I mean everything. But I didn't want to see the same face I can now remember when I let dry bacon fall from my mouth. I wanted him to love me like his little girl again, because I could somewhat remember what that felt like.

"I won't love you less," he continued, as if reading my mind.

"No, Dad," I said, staring into his eyes. "I promi-eh-s you, it not drugth."

"Okay..." he said, looking at me funny. "What's wrong with your mouth?"

It's a homicidal maniac with no empathy, Dr. Watson growls.

"I bit my tongue," I say, and actually think of doing it. Biting it clean off, chewing, enjoying.

"Okay," Dad said, sighing with relief and smiling. "I'm going to go to the store then. Anything in particular you want for dinner?"

Yes, said Dr. Watson. *But not if you insist on cooking it....*

I sigh, struggling to maintain an upright head, wrestling to keep my eyes on him. "No."

"Okay, I'll leave you to it. Cleaning supplies are in the hallway closet. Be safe, and I'll be back. I love you."

He leans in and kisses my temple. Pausing.

"Love you," I respond, and for once, it's not just a scripted reply. I know I mean it.

I barely heard the door close behind my father before I crumpled to the ground. I had used up all my strength to just lean against the door frame, to appear like a normal, healthy teenage girl. When I was finally able to not do it anymore, I couldn't do anything else but relish in the feeling of the itchy carpet fibers digging into my cheek and stretch out on the upstairs floor hallway. There was a good chance that sand was falling off my skin, making it so that I would have to add vacuuming to my list of things to do, but at the moment, I couldn't get up. The world I was currently languishing in was clearly laying down, not moving, and above all things—not cleaning.

I hadn't planned it, I hadn't even thought about it, but as I was laying belly-down on the ground, looking down the hallway with the same perspective as a rodent, I suddenly found myself absolutely, and utterly, aslee...

22

At first, it felt like a massage. Truly.

I kept my eyes closed, feeling whatever was going on; trying to make out what it was, and what it was of mine that the masseuse, currently straddling my lower back with their legs, was working on. One shoulder, as if I was only tense in one shoulder, the opposite of the one that had the bite wound, the stitches, the gauze. New sensations started to permeate what was happening which added to the confusion. For instance, it became apparent to me that it wasn't hands and fingers working on my shoulder. I came to this conclusion by counting the amount of hands on my arms—two, one on each arm, holding me in place as...

What was running down my neck? I thought to myself.

Granted, my thinking was cloudy, because I had not eaten in a while. I remembered how weak I must be to fall to the ground in the first place.

I opened my eyes to get a visual. The sun had gone down, the hallway was dark, and my world had gone black.

Whatever was running down both sides of my neck was warm, and thicker than water, and starting from where something was clasping onto my shoulder. It was collecting at the front of my throat and falling to the carpet under me, which was slowly growing in warmth and wet. I began to stir, lifting my arms to put under me, to push myself up, and suddenly I felt the weight of whatever was behind me, pushing me down into the damp fibers, keeping me in place. That's when the fear hit me like the floor hit my face.

Something was on top of me. Something heavy.

A person. And they were pinning me down.

As I felt the sharp stabs of pain in my neck, where I previously thought it was fingers opening, and closing, and squeezing, and rubbing, I now understood that it wasn't a hand lined with needles that was causing me pain—it was a mouth. A mouth, opening and closing. Someone's jaws lined with teeth currently pressed against my shoulder where my shoulder met my neck, spit flowing from it over the wound that it was creating, mixing with my blood that was pouring down my front. Just as soon as I figured all of this out, I made a noise that was somewhere between a growl and a squeak.

I was both angry and afraid in the same instant, filling with an emotion that was eliminating my thoughts of anything but survival.

"No!" I said as forcefully as I could, and whatever was on me returned my vocalization with a grunt of its own but continued to chew and gnaw on me. Fear gave way to anger, which gave way to strength, and I put my hands under myself and pushed up only to feel the weight weigh down on me again. *No, dammit,* I shout in my mind, and Dr. Watson is silent, because he's just a stomach, but I feel him clench as my body does, and suddenly every synapse I have is firing together in anger and self-preservation. I shove harder, only to feel no progress to my getting up. My hands clench and unclench, grabbing at the carpet fibers uselessly and letting go. My situation feeling like it was getting more desperate as whatever was using me as a meal now felt it was on a time crunch because now I was alert. I wasn't just laying down to be dinner.

"Geh-off!" I shout, my voice sounding scared, scaring me ever more, and all of it, the weight, the chewing, the smell of my blood, the grunting, my voice, my desperation fills me with horror. "Geh-off me!"

I didn't know if this thing and I were alone. For all I knew, there was a line of hungry eaters out the door, each waiting to get a bite. Each viewing us, hoping that I would just settle down so they could put a piece of me in their empty stomachs, so they could feed and move on with their existences, and leave me here, covered in holes like my dead brother, and soaking into a carpet that would eventually have to be replaced so vacationers could rent out the house.

Get up, Alex! Dr. Watson urges. *We are not the ones that should be eaten!*

It hurts, everything hurts, and the more I struggle, the more it hurts, but struggle I do to try and get whatever this is off me. I understand the feeling of hunger, of losing your mind to feed as I had done with Max in the truck, which terrifies me even more that this thing might not be able to control itself at the taste of me.

Finally, I'm able to unbalance it by pushing up on only

one arm. The beast, as we'll call it, moves, adjusts its body weight so I quickly push up with the other arm, fully knocking its weight off-kilter to allow myself to turn over onto my back.

Success!

I look up.

I don't see him clearly, but I can tell it's a male: a human male. Brown hair that hangs down, covering his eyes. There are craters all over his face, and now that my nose isn't in the carpet anymore, I can smell him, and he smells like road kill; like the kind of road kill that has been simmering in the sun, and is just about to burst from the gases collecting within itself. His mouth is glistening with his spit and my blood, and I can't tell whether it's the night or his skin, but he looks darker. Not ethnically darker, but rather, like his blood is black and it shows on the surface of his skin. He looks in the moonlight or the streetlight or whatever light is coming in through the foyer window, like some shade between blue and purple from what I can tell, and the oddest thing about it all is that his clothes are new.

Us being face-to-face surprises him for a spell, but only so long as to realize he's still hungry, and I'm still food, and he comes back in for more. This time, his mouth closes on the front of my neck, and it feels so much more personal, so much closer. Maybe it was the fact that his rancid scent filled and burned my nostrils, or the fact that I can now witness his mouth feeding, and that my dread and anger completely dissipated into disgust and fear and sadness. I felt myself cry as I grabbed at his hair and pulled. I pulled so hard that large clumps of it, still attached to skin, came out in my hands, and his head didn't budge an inch, his mouth still chowing down on my clavicle. I felt the roughness of the skin of his face, grossly cold and not smooth due to his inverted pimples or whatever kind of rot his face was going through, rubbing against my cheek. This was all keeping me from calming down and assessing the best way out of this.

"Dhop!" I shouted, but to no avail. I kicked and flailed my legs, but his body weight was between them so when I kicked them up, I was wrapping mine around his body, and if ripping off his scalp wasn't going to get a reaction, I doubt squeezing him to death between my thighs would get his attention, either. Besides, I didn't want to be wrapping my legs around this beast in some type of intimate way, like I saw in a movie once before my mother put her hand over my face....

A memory! I scream in my head!

Not now, Alex! said my jealous stomach who hated when my brain worked. *Fight!*

I reach my hands up and I put them on either side of his face, roaming with my thumbs, feeling his craters, or his acne, or whatever bumps and crevices are making him more hideous than anyone absolutely should be, and suddenly I find his nose, and I let that cartilage appendage lead me to his eyes. With everything in me, and the realization that I won't survive if I continue to be his meal, I push my thumbs into his eye sockets as hard as I can. I feel his grape-ish eyeballs push back into his skull until they can't be pushed back anymore. Just as I feel like I might end up pushing through something, popping them back into his brain with blood pouring down over my wrists, the pressure I am putting through his eye sockets is enough for him to pull back and up from me. Using his head like a bowling ball, I use my leverage to guide him to sitting up, and when I feel he is properly off-balance, I shove his head to the side, into the wall, and I roll over.

He bounces off the drywall, not really concerned with his eyes, and grabs out for me, finding an ankle as I try to push back with my hands and feet away from him. There's something deep inside of me, a forgotten recollection of sorts, about another time I was attacked, and suddenly the air I'm pulling into my lungs feels devoid of oxygen. I can't breathe, my heart races and I hear the drumbeat of pulsing blood in my ears. *What is happening?* I scream inside of myself, trying to get my organs to work again, to focus, as even my eyes seem to be vibrating from what I can only assume, yes, is either a panic attack or I'm going to drop dead on the spot. I feel the bite wound on my neck, that back and front, but not the pain of it, only as if my skin isn't going to close anymore.

The steps downstairs are an arm's length away, just far enough for me to reach out and grab one of the wooden bannisters as I choke out sobs. He tries to pull me back toward him. I kick, several times, only finding his face once, hearing a sickening crack that brilliantly brought me focus. My other kick scraped his fingers off my shoes, so I planned to stand up and run my little butt out of the house, forgetting, of course, that I was in my weakened state. So, standing up was extremely shaky, and running down the stairs and out of the house ended up being me just throwing myself down the stairs, hitting every hard edge.

I crumpled to the floor at the bottom. Nothing hurt, but everything was in pain. My heart was calming just when I felt I needed it to show some fight. I turned my head to look back up from whence I came, and saw that I had taken a size-able chunk out of the stairway drywall with some body part of mine, and that my attacker, refreshed and re-blooded, stood, seething at the top of the stairs.

He looked down at me, as he had through our whole meeting together. He looked... familiar? Was that possible when I couldn't remember anybody? I was almost sure that this was the person that attacked me last night. Rather, I was hoping it was the same person and there weren't two of these weirdos out there. Maybe Ocean City was just a place where weirdos collected, and this was as common as vampires in Transylvania or Bigfoots in the Northwest Woods or...

You are a weirdo like them, says Dr. Watson. *And if you don't move, weirdo, you're gonna be a dead weirdo.*

I try to lift myself up, but I only get so far as a leg underneath me when the front door opens.

Bursting through it, like an emo hero, is Max, a knight in all black clothing, coming in to save me from the beast, who—

I turn to look back up the stairs, and there is no sign of the guy. Max kneels by me, checking to see if I'm okay, and probably, discerning the fact that I fell down the stairs, making sure that there are no bones protruding from my skin in any compound fractures. Seeing as how it didn't seem like anything was broken, he gently turned me over, putting me face to face with him. Whether it was my pain, my fear, or him, I was suddenly breathless.

Once settled, he began to look at the wounds on my shoulder, but before looking too closely at them, I noticed him looking around the house, up the stairs to where the thing was moments ago, and then down each hallway. Only upon knowing we were alone did he look closer at my bite wounds, which brought his face closer to mine, and I had a thought to just reach out and kiss him, and another thought to just reach out and bite him, becoming the thing I had just escaped from.

"What happened?" he asked.

"Ah-dat!" I said, trying to say the word "attacked" and failing horribly.

At the sound of my voice, Max knew what he was dealing with, what I was dealing with, and he properly responded by backing away from my face a couple feet. I could see the dried blood on his lip, I could remember the smell of it, and despite my uncontrollable hunger for it, I kept myself on my back, on the ground, laying under him, which was a healthy alternative to eating him. Our eyes met, and he seemed distant, perhaps also thinking about the meat in his truck.

I smile, trying to convince him I won't eat him.

He smiles back, "Hi."

"Argh."

Lord, take me now, I thought to myself, completely embarrassed.

"Hungry?" Max asks in that same tone, as if we just got up from a nap, and I don't have another gaping bite wound that is soaking my shirt in blood

I nod, refusing to sound like a moron again.

I feel the piece of wood hit the side of my face before I hear the door frame break. The door opens and Max leaves my side before I could see what looked like a bear tackle him to the side. It took a moment for me to realize it wasn't an animal, but Officer Ispy's large body pinning Max to the stairs. Officer Grillings flashlight lands on me, and my weakened condition.

"Ow!" Max shouts, and it's almost so pained it sounds like a cry. When I look over, I see Ispy putting most of his weight on the boy, and I could certainly see why the boy would be in pain. "Get off of me! I didn't do anything! I found her at the bottom of the stairs!"

"Neighbors said they heard a struggle. A girl saying "No!" and "Stop!"" Officer Grillings said.

"That's what I heard, too! That's why I'm here."

"You heard her shouting all the way from your house on the other side of the island?"

"What are you, Daredevil?" Ispy asks.

As Ispy crushes the boy underneath him, Grillings kneels down next to me, and my mind wonders just where did the man go who had attacked me, and how to communicate this to the officers in front of me. For sure, they could go upstairs with their guns, and remove the scum from the face of the earth. Ispy himself could probably put a fist through the guy's head, pushing his face through his skull, much like I tried to push his eyes down his throat. I smelled Grillings flower-de-cologne, and felt her burning hand on my face, feeling her fingernails as they grabbed the collar of my shirt, lifting it away to inspect my wound. I saw her mouth downturn at the corners as she saw how bad it was.

"Jesus, sweetpea, what is the deal with you and people biting you?" she asked.

"Uh-stahs," I say, as drool leaves my mouth and runs back down toward my earlobe in, what I'm sure is, a very sorry display of character.

"This boy attack you?"

I shake my head, and try to utter my word again, "Uh-stahs!" and she is clueless until Max pipes in from under the hulking man.

"Upstairs!" he shouts. "She is saying upstairs! The person must still be here!"

Grillings took out her gun, and, in full professional mode, locked eyes on the top of the steps, and began advancing up. As she passed Ispy, the man put his arm out to block her path, and mumbled, "Want me to do it?" Grillings shook her head no and continued up. I watched her go until I couldn't anymore. Either the pain or the blood loss was too much, but either way, I went back into my world of dark, hearing Max grunt from the weight on him, and Ispy grunt from the struggling under him, and Grillings' footsteps on the carpet.

My last thought was of my attacker, the way his hair hung down, the way he looked... familiar...

Hey! Your name is Alex and you were attacked on Friday because there's a beast who eats people on the island.

And then my world went black....

23

For the second time in two days, I awoke in the hospital, this time with a whole lot more concern surrounding me. I heard my parents yelling before I opened my eyes, and before I took in the sight I could smell the sanitized environment of the hospital, and knew where I was. The sounds of the machines beeping away with some kind of measurements, the smell of medicine trying to mask the smell of sickness, the feeling of warmth from heaters and blankets hiding the coldness of the steel and the staff. I wasn't in my own room like last time, I knew, because it was too loud, and I heard more than just my parents and a nurse who was fiercely trying to defend herself and the actions of the hospital. I could hear curtains opening and shutting much like shower curtains on shower rods.

When I opened my eyes, all I saw was light. Fluorescent light from the ceiling, blinding me, but after a couple of blinks, my pupils focus and I'm back. Back looking at the white ceiling tiles pockmarked with black spots, with the framework that is older, off-white, yellowing with age. Back to the curtains around me, separating me from the rest of the world with a thin piece of privacy fabric and the same three monitors telling the doctors and nurses something about me that I would never be able to read myself.

This time was different. This time, waking up, I felt so much more alert, aware. The IV still dug into my arm, but I felt the tape as well, pulling at my skin. I felt the bandage on my other shoulder now, and my first thought was how uncomfortable it was going to be to wear a bra, with the straps digging right where things kept trying to devour me. *And not only a bra, but you are going to have to find a new way to carry your schoolbooks as a book bag is just not going to cut it,* I said to myself. With the clear solution being pumped into my arm, Dr. Watson was somewhere inside, curled up like a kitten, purring softly with delight. If there was anywhere I felt like home in the past two days, it was at the hospital, and I was almost relieved to be back.

And then the curtain opens with a flourish, and Dr. Patel stands there, his cinnamon skin a shade of umber under his eyes, but still carrying himself well despite how tired he is. His lips are pursed past the point of pouting, and as he looks down at me his glasses slide down his nose to position themselves right where it's possible that he can read the tiny print on his clipboard. The delicious-smelling nurse swoops in behind him as he departs, and I feel her fingernails as she grips my hospital bracelet to scan it into her machine. She looks up to read the far away monitors. I wonder if she even notices I'm awake, but once she squeeze-checks my IV, I hear her begin to talk and I wonder if she's addressing me or just talking out loud.

"What a day," she sighs, and without windows, I can't confirm whether it is day or not.

"Hmmph," I reply, not necessarily an award-winning conversationalist, but realizing I have nothing in my vernacular, yet, to counter adult-defeatism.

"How are you feeling, Ms. Jordan?"

"Chewed up and swallowed," I answer.

Immediately, I break through her. At first it's just a small laugh that escapes through her teeth, as if she has never heard a response like that before. And then as my joke bounces off her insides like a pinball veers off the rubber bands, she laughs. She can't help but to laugh, and it makes me feel so good that I can get such a joyous response out of it. She calms herself down, her curly hair bouncing on the side of her face as she nods and begins to mark something down on the clipboard as she gets control of herself.

"Yep, yep," she says. "I imagine so. Yessir."

"Jokes are probably in poor taste, huh?"

"Hey, I think if you going to be put in the situation you are in, and you are going to put on that brave face 'bout it? I say good for you. Keep it up. Something doctors and hospitals don't tell you because it's free? Good attitudes slow disease, prevents sickness, and cures bad days. So, you keep it right up. If a girl like you can keep smiling, ain't no reason why I can't persevere through my next couple hours before I get to put my feet up."

"If you ever want," I tell her, knowing she's wrapping up her check on me, "you can always pull up a hospital bed and chill out with me. I won't tell anyone."

"Why don't I just move you off yours, and you can do my rounds for me?" she jokes.

"Sure!" I say, wondering if maybe I could just become a regular human being if I had an endless supply of whatever was in my IV. "Can't promise all your patients will be alive when I'm done, but I'm willing to give it a try!"

She bursts out in her infectious laughter again, "Oh yeah? Well, I'll let you in on another little secret. Neither can I." And she laughs again at the odd joke that is so dark that I can't stop from joining her.

She reaches out for the curtain, but before she can grab and pull, it is done for her, and my father stands there, computer-technician-turned-war-general, first seeing his daughter awake and laughing, and then turning toward the short nurse laughing with me, and his blood boils. I have never seen my father so angry before, but there he stood, in his dorky khakis, and a plaid shirt tucked in so the wrinkles didn't show, with a belt buckle shining. Working on computers had damaged his posture, but tonight he stood tall, he stood protective.

"What's funny?" he asked, and both the nurse and I stopped laughing. We could tell him the joke that I said earlier, but he probably won't find it amusing; boys eating his daughter and such. Or we could tell him the joke the nurse said, which probably only doctors and nurses and good-humored/dark-hearted patients would find amusing about the fact that, perhaps, the same amount of patients would die whether it was a sixteen-year-old girl looking after them or this studied, but tired, underpaid nurse. Nope, Dad wasn't our audience for our comedy bit, and so we kept it to ourselves.

"Hi, Dad," I said, taking the attention off the nurse so she could scurry past him to do her job, hoping he didn't ruin the joy I had just given her with his persnickety attitude.

She tried to shut the curtain behind her, but my mom was next, right on my father's heels and she kept the curtain open.

Both of my parents were by my side quicker than they have ever been, and I stared back at two sets of eyes filled with worry and anger. But not anger toward me, I don't think. Not by the way they both apologized profusely in their roles of not protecting me, or of putting me into a dangerous situation by forcing me to clean up my own mess in the rental. Which, I mean, I totally get as, yes, I should be responsible for the mess, but I let them apologize a little more because truthfully, the apologies between them and me had been a little one-sided for too long.

"I'm so sorry I made you go over and clean that house—" my mother began.

"Oh no, dear, I'm sorry I left you alone—" my dad continued.

"But, you, at least took her! I was thinking she should walk. I was so angry when I saw it—" my mom went on.

"Yes, but I was there. I was there, and I thought going to pick up spaghetti sauce was more important than making sure my daughter was safe."

They both rubbed at my arms, and for once the touch of another person didn't feel like fire. The touch felt... dare I say, normal. And I didn't know whether that was because they had actually cooled off, or I had warmed up, but it felt... weird. I couldn't tell whether I liked it or not. Were they touching me too much? Was that what was annoying me? Would I have preferred if they just sat back and looked at me? Or maybe I was annoyed because I actually was thinking about—

"How's Max?" I asked, thinking back to the small boy who was being pinned by the large man on the steps.

My father's face sunk into himself, his chin hitting his chest as he inhaled a big calming breath, but my mom didn't miss a beat.

"Max is here. He's downstairs in the waiting room. He didn't want to come up, because of your father, so he's down there. The police talked with him—"

"We have to ask, though, Alex," my father barged in. "He attack you?"

"No, Daddy," I respond, not knowing where the "-dy" suffix (Is that technically a suffix?) came from, but realizing that it quickly tempers his mood, and I log that as another tactic I can use with my parents. "Max saved me. I was attacked upstairs, and fell down the stairs, and the beast—" as I like to call him "—was going to come down the stairs, and Max ran in, scared him off, and was checking on me when the two cops came in."

There was silence as my mom and dad looked at each other, and then my mom whispered, "That's exactly what he said," and I couldn't tell whether that made them skeptical of the story or if it confirmed in their minds what happened as well. Either way, it was the truth, and it was all I had.

"I still don't like him," my father chimed in.

"Oh, Dad... you're not going to like any boy," I say, with a light voice that even I don't recognize. Something like placating my father while reducing myself to a ten-year-old. Perhaps he had more in common with adolescent me. Maybe he wasn't so scared that I would make bad decisions back then. I remember a time when my father took me fishing and relished the fact I didn't squirm when baiting the worm on the hook. We were fishing at the beach, on the pier. I thought about my brother's body floating on the pier below.

Memories...

"Call it father's intuition," he retorted.

"There's no such thing," my mother said, making sure she didn't look at him, and just kept her eyes on me, her molars attacking a piece of cinnamon gum. When my mother made a biting comment like that, she said it out of the corner of her mouth, which had to be some trait she picked up from a small screen actress, I feel. Someone who talks to the audience, not expecting anyone to hear. But, what my mom didn't realize, or didn't care about, was that we all did.

"What is wrong with you?" My dad says, not backing down.

"What do you mean?" My mom plays clueless.

"Ever since Benjamin—"

"Don't you bring up his name at this hospital—"

"Ever since, you have had this chip on your shoulder, this disdain for me that just is completely.... It's miserable, honey. It's miserable to be around. Alex agrees."

"Don't talk for her. You're no picnic either, dear."

"Get a divorce already," I shout over both of them, not being able to stop myself. There was something so deflating, so depressing about watching your parents, the two adults that are supposed to guide you through life, bicker and argue and appear as mature as a high school relationship. Especially when they had entered into said arguement with no reserve, and didn't even realize the volume of their voices in a place with no walls, no doors, and other very sick people who probably had more things to worry about than my parents inability to get along.

They look at me, they look at each other, and then they look back at me, their breath caught in their throats. I'm confused about their surprise as if they never themselves thought about the notion of ending this contentious relationship. *Divorces happened all the time*, I thought. *They were so common that successful marriages were the new weird, no? Was I born into a family that believed, under no circumstances, one should ever get divorced? Were we Amish or something?*

"What is going on here?" Came the authoritative voice behind my parents. Before I saw Officer Grillings, I could see the giant Officer Ispy walk up, and look down at everyone, including my father. When my father took a step to the side to allow Grillings entry in my little curtained area, my dad took a step closer to my mom.

"Just talking with our daughter, officer," my mom answered what I thought was a rhetorical question.

"Were you two talking with her, or at each other? Whole hospital floor thinks you both need a break. Go get some coffee. It's been a long night."

My father looks at Ispy's hulking size, and then back at the smaller officer. "Can you legally talk to my daughter alone?"

"With your permission," she replies. "Unless you have a lawyer you want to call to make sure she doesn't say anything that might incriminate herself. Do you think your daughter has anything incriminating to say?"

My father shakes his head and I am relieved because I can barely count on two hands how many times I have wanted to attack someone in the last couple days, and I would think that probably wasn't completely legal behavior. *But thoughts aren't illegal,* Dr. Watson says.

No, but when I tried to attack Max the first night, and then in the car today, I reply. *Or yesterday,* I thought as I caught a glimpse at the heart rate monitor which let me know it was a new day, the third day of my new life: a Sunday.

"You two go cool off. Let us sit with our girl here," she smiled at the both of them, watching as my father lead my mother out of the room, and I felt so horrible watching them go after saying that I thought we should break up our home, and that they should not be my parents anymore, but remarried, remastered human beings that only saw me part-time. After that, my mom and dad had completely shut down. I loved them and missed them the second they were out my eyesight.

In all, I felt like a horrible daughter. I wondered if that was typical of my age.

"How you doing?" Ispy asked as tears came to my eyes.

I couldn't answer; just shook my head.

The big man laid his big mitt on my shoulder, and held it there as I cried, probably thinking that it had something to do with my being attacked. But only me and Dr. Watson knew it had absolutely nothing to do with that, and had everything to do with the fact that I was utterly confused about life, about the bigger picture, about who I was and who I was supposed to be, and how I was supposed to act, and how I was supposed to get through tomorrow just to get to the next day, and where does it all lead from there? I was crying because every move I made seemed to make things worse, and now I just crumbled my parents. Like, what kind of girl am I? What kind of daughter? Who would even like someone like this?

"Well, look," Grillings said, trying her best to be calming. "Normally, there would be a detective or two here to try to ask you some questions, get your story, but Ocean City only has one detective, okay? One detective and five police officers and one captain. And that one detective is off on assignment right now, as there was something found in the bay before you woke up."

"What?" I asked, my curiosity up.

Grillings looks at me and sighs, perhaps hoping I wouldn't ask.

"A body," she says, and I tense up. "Now, look, don't do that. Don't get all worked up. I know 'body' sounds like this ominous word, but you know how many people live here in Ocean City? Ten thousand. Number spikes to a hundred and thirty thousand during tourist season, but... you know how many of that ten thousand are just a bunch of old farts who grew up here, and will one day...?"

She leaves the sentence unfinished, looking at me, wanting me to do it, perhaps to get more comfortable with the word, the idea, "become bodies?" I ask, and she sits back and smiles.

"Exactly. That's all it is. We are born, we live, we stop living and we leave our bodies behind."

Except we are trapped in this one, Dr. Watson argues.

We're not dead, I counter.

Yet.

"Body in the bay, could just be a person who had a heart attack and fell in. We don't know. People hear body, they think killer, but nine times out of ten, no, I'd say, ninety-nine times out of a hundred—"

"Less than that, even," Ispy argues.

"Ninety-nine point nine, nine, nine, nine percent of the time? It's not a killer, it's human hardware that fails—"

"My brother was killed," I say, realizing the last time I had these two in front of me, I did not have the information about my brother. "Was he just an exception?"

Grillings face dropped as she looked at me, clearly forgetting who I was or what my family's past history was, or just realizing that she knew these things, but she misspoke as she let her tongue get away from her. Either way, she quickly sat up, put her hands together in front of her like she was praying and stared into my eyes.

"Your brother's death was a horrible tragedy, and that is why we want you to be safe."

I didn't want to talk about my brother, though. I didn't want to stop her from talking about the body in the bay, because as much as she wants to say it has nothing to do with anything, the way Dr. Watson was getting up and listening more, and the way shivers travelled down my spine when she mentioned it, I knew it could have a little more connection than what we previously believed. I wanted to meet this overworked detective and tell him everything I knew, but first, I wanted to see one last person.

"Can you get me Max?" I ask Ispy, because I'm afraid Grillings will try and talk me out of seeing him.

"What do you need with Max?" Grillings asks before letting Ispy go.

"He saved me," I say to her, looking into her eyes. "I would like to thank him."

24

When he came in, he looked smaller than I remembered, thinner and frail. His clothes hung off him like he hadn't eaten for days, and his hair was as greasy as ever, as he continually used his hand to get the bangs out of his eyes. He was dressed in jeans, an open button down over a grey shirt and a jacket that seemed out of place for the not-so-cold weather, but perhaps when one is just skin and bones, they need a little more protection against the elements.

He followed Ispy in, which didn't help how tiny he looked to me now as Ispy was still the largest man I have ever laid eyes on, and his mere presence with Max made it seem like he was watching the boy, making sure the kid didn't make any false moves. Grillings herself kept an eye on the person who saved me tonight, and I had to wonder, after my father's intuition and now these two police officers, if anyone really trusted Max. The way he looked down at the floor after making eye contact with me confirmed that he knew everyone suspected him of wrong-doing.

"Can we be alone?" I ask the officers.

"We'll be right outside," Ispy says to Max, and only to Max. The boy nods, slowly, knowing full well he is under a microscope.

Once they were gone, and the curtain was closed, we heard their footsteps go off into the distance until we couldn't hear them anymore.

"I got you something," Max said, barely getting the words past his bitten bottom lip.

"Flowers?" I ask, knowing full well there was nowhere to hide flowers on his person. "I don't think you can bring flowers onto a floor like this, in case someone has allergies."

"No, I—" Max stammers, and he opens up his jacket to reveal an inside pocket, and inside the pocket—

"Is that one of these?!" I ask, pointing to my own IV bag of delicious, Alex-feeling-normal serum.

"Saline," he says as if he invented it. "I googled it, and it's just like salt water. Has chloride in it. It's used to keep people hydrated, keep the blood flowing, treat blood loss..."

None of it was making sense to me on how it was able to cure my thick tongue, how it kept my mind sharp. What disease would I have where I was constantly dehydrated? Since Dr. Watson didn't offer any theories, I wondered the question out loud to see what Max came up with. He had an answer.

"Well, chronic dehydration," he started, and Dr. Watson *of course, so simple, so elementary. You said constant dehydration and the medical term would be "chronic" dehydration. Of course, it is...* "The disease says you would have dark-colored urine—"

"I haven't peed... for awhile...." I say, now realizing how bizarre that is.

"Okay, well," Max says, getting out his phone. "WebMD says you would also have dizziness—"

"Yep."

"Muscle fatigue—"

"Absolutely," I say, remembering pounding on the front door with my forearms because I was leaning against it, barely able to even straighten my wrists to knock.

"And extreme thirst," he finishes.

"Is extreme hunger part of it?" I ask, but also thinking back to how the dry bacon was horrible to me, but the juicy bacon, the one I can suck the fat out of, was perfect. Which makes sense if I need the liquid. *What happens when you eat an apple?* Dr. Watson passively-aggressively asks, knowing full well that I throw up anything not meat, but that was a question for another time.

"Well, yes, because a lot of people who overeat do so because they are thirsty. They don't drink enough water, and so they crave salty foods which will keep water in their system."

"So, I suffer from chronic dehydration?" I ask, kind of disappointed that that is all this is. I felt like I had a somewhat cooler, and more unique disease. But, perhaps I should just be grateful that my sudden mania is brought on by the fact that I need to carry a water bottle around, but then I think about throwing up the water in the sink, and—

"Well, you also have amnesia, and that's not part of this," Max reminds me.

"Oh yeah," I say, and the real reason I wanted to see

Max comes to the forefront of the conversation.

As I had laid there in bed, I didn't have a eureka moment. It wasn't as if the clouds had parted, but just by the fact that when I saw my Dad, I could remember his occupation, that I knew what my book bag would feel like around my shoulders... some of my memory has returned. Not all of it. Not even close. But, I have enough of it where I wanted Max to come into my little space, and I wanted to see his face when I told him what I knew. But first I wanted the saline solution, so I reached out for it, and Max put it in my hand. I felt the plastic bag of liquid in my hand, felt the weight of it, felt the liquid slosh in its prison and I wondered how I was going to use it if I didn't have an IV needle at home.

A problem to solve, Dr. Watson said.

And then I turned to Max, and I didn't take my eyes off of him, even though his eyes darted all around the room.

"Max," I said. "Look at me."

And he did.

"I know who attacked me."

Max's face dropped, like I knew it would.

25

The plan was in motion. Not a very specific plan, per se, but one that I had somewhat come up with while lying in the hospital bed, as the doctor came in, the nurse, then my parents, and then the two officers. I felt like none of them were expecting much out of me, so I sat there, staring at the white ceiling tiles with the black marks on them, and I considered what I knew, what I remembered. I still couldn't think of which one of my friends was Amelia and which one was Gianna. I could remember what the school hallways looked like, but I had no idea which rooms I was supposed to go into for which classes. I, of course, did not remember the password to my phone, but did remember that I was going to have to take it to an Apple store in order for them to reset it and open it for me. I remember enjoying my father's cooking, and the fact that he burned things for me because I enjoyed the taste of charcoal back in the day. My mother and I would explore together. That was our thing. And I remember being on a kayak behind her in the bay, watching as the sun was either setting or rising, and us really pounding away at the water with our paddles, battling a current.

I don't remember Ben, but I remember his hands. How small they were when I was smaller as well. When he was practically a baby, I would pretend to be asleep, and he would want me awake so he'd come over and knock at me with his little hands, and I would try not to smile; try not to alert him that I was awake. Perhaps that is where I became so adept at pretending I was asleep in hospital beds, in upstairs floor hallways when someone was trying to eat me from the shoulders down....

I remember the boy, the man, the man-boy that was on top of me. I remember him from the night I was trying to go into the rental home to use the bathroom, and I remember that is all it was. I told Max I would be right back, we had been laying in the bed of his truck, staring up at the stars, and I loved it even though I realized how cliche it was that this boy, on our first date, had me on my back in the truck, looking up at the stars and trying to figure out what was a constellation, and trying to remember what the story was behind the constellations, and he struggled with it all. I had always been fascinated by the mythology behind astrology and so I let him stammer and stutter until I finally said something like: "Well, I heard somewhere that Sagittarius was a centaur who gave his immortality to someone else because he was tired of suffering from a poisoned arrow...." And Max would look at me, and go, "yeah, that's right. I forgot that part...." And on and on we'd go.

We had seen a movie that night as well, after the pizza shop with the really greasy pizza. This I remember now, and I was so nervous for my first date that I didn't eat much of anything, not until the popcorn. The lightness of the popcorn, mixed with the carbonation in the soda, performed a sort of science experiment in my empty stomach, before the days of Dr. Watson (and maybe this helped create him) but suddenly I was having "trapped air" pains.

What was a girl to do?

Where was a girl to go?

Laying with this boy I had a crush on, staring up at the stars, and suddenly my stomach is rumbling something fierce, and I feel the gas inside start working its way downward, and I know I need a break from this moment, this place and time, before I can return to it, and really enjoy it for what it is. But, I'm beside myself with discomfort, and perhaps Max would like to kiss me by the end of the night, and I didn't want to be bent over at the waist, holding my guts in, trying not to, excuse me, fart in one of the most important moments of a young girl's life.

So, I did the math. We were five blocks from my parent's rental. There was a hide-a-key outside. If I gently excused myself for a moment, leave my sandals in the bed of the truck to move faster, and ran the five blocks (perhaps passing wind as I did so, as it was common for the jogging to jostle things loose inside) I could get inside, go to the bathroom, get back out before Max got too distracted by my weird departure to really care about letting it ruin the evening. But, I didn't run.

This was the reason I was at the rental, but I couldn't remember getting there. How did I get there? Memory is a tricky thing....

Nothing... darkness. Did I run to the house or did Max walk me? In any rate, the beast attacked me and I ended up in the...

Grass.

But, the hunger was real, and controlling. And if the beast attacked me on the front lawn with no one around, why wouldn't it kill me? Surely it would take more than one bite. Perhaps he'd thought he killed me. Maybe a car came to scare him off. Who knows why he did it, but the next time I would return to my family's rental, he would be there again for me. This time, he wouldn't stop. Not until I fought back, and I got myself away by throwing myself down the stairs. And Max came in at the perfect moment, right on cue, as if he knew I was going to be there, or if he knew this person was going to be there, and...

You know that feeling you get when you first see someone you like? At first, there's just a curious attraction to them. You catch a glimpse, and they check all of your first look boxes, which are so general that even a good head of dark hair could be the box to check, which gives you pause for a second glance. And then you see other boxes to check, their style of clothes, perhaps how clean they are, perhaps how white and straight their teeth are, the smoothness of their skin, how they laugh, their confidence level, and pretty soon you're not just looking, but following with your eyes, and you see them interact with the world, and if nothing about them turns you off to this point, you are growing an infatuation, and your observations about their interactions start to grow an envy in you because you begin to want them to interact with you, and so you start to see who they interact with, and how they interact with them, and you begin to formulate in your mind how you will interact with them so that they will want to continue to interact with you. That's how all this mess starts; this... messy in-like, in-love, love stuff.

That is how I know the person who attacked me.

Not because I had a crush on him, but because I had a crush on Max, and I was following Max with my eyes, and yes, okay, a little bit with my feet, as I wondered where he went after school as everyone took off for the beach, or the arcades, and he took off the other way like he was either too cool for everyone else or everyone else was too cool for him. Either way, it was a mutual parting, and my friends went to the beach, and I followed this kid, this quiet kid named Max, to a gas station where he bought groceries, mainly meats, Gatorade, and licorice, and I bought a pack of gum, because I had to buy something or someone would be suspicious of this girl stalking this guy (as they should be, I guess) but my curiosity was just too precarious, just too strong.

Curiosity killed the cat, Dr. Watson would suggest, somewhat ironically.

But satisfaction brought him back, I'd counter.

Only eight times.

A park tucked away amongst the non-rental houses where the ten thousand year-round residents lived. What we all consider a secret park because we hid it in the backyards, we kept it from being placed on maps, we owned the park and we didn't want any boardwalk-crowding tourists coming to use it, bringing their colon-filled dogs to leave piles of poop, bringing their picnic baskets to escape the craziness of the beach, leaving their sandwiches baggies and Capri-Suns behind for us to clean up. No, this park was ours, with its pond, and its gazebo, and its benches dedicated to residents who have come and gone for residents who just come to feed the ducks (which, let's be honest, are the only things that can kick the seagulls butt when it comes to food).

And, in the gazebo, I had seen Max, washing licorice down with a gatorade, giving a man-boy the blue, plastic grocery bag of meat. This beast... with what is now my appetite.

It wasn't until I was being attacked and rolled over last night, and I looked up at the man-boy that I sensed something familiar about him. I had seen his pock-marked face from behind someone's backyard deck since I couldn't just walk out into the park without being seen. But, even being so far away, I knew how ugly this guy had become, as if he was rotting away in the sun, and I wondered if he was homeless. Was Max just such a sweet, gentle soul that he would go grocery shopping, perhaps with his lunch money, for this man who had fallen on hard times? This man who had teeth that seemed to protrude from his lip, or lips that seemed to recede back into his face, cheek-bones that could cut glass, and hands where the skin seemed tightly wrapped over the bones and tendons. The kind of person who just horrified you by how gangly he looked? It made me like Max even more. As he and this unfortunate one talked, I turned around, spitting out a piece of flavorless gum in someone's bushes and popping another piece in my mouth, and I happily strolled to the beach where I would find my friends.

I didn't remember all of this at the time, oh no. I remembered this when I was asleep. Somewhere between Grillings walking up the stairs, and the hospital fluorescent light, it was like someone, perhaps my dear old Dr. Watson, flipped a switch on my subconscious, and flashes of memories began to piece themselves together. The bite of last night reminded me of the bite of two nights ago reminded me of the teeth I saw in the gazebo reminded me of following Max, reminded me of the first time I saw Max, to the time Max and I were in his truck looking at the stars and I was trying to hold in the fart that would probably smell like the man who was biting me last night. This was how the old noggin worked, like circles of memories.

None of any of this had anything to do with my iPhone password, though, unfortunately.

When I told Max I remembered who attacked me, he hung his head, and his bangs fell into his eyes, and his knee begin to shake, and we both became aware that somewhere, behind the curtain, two police officers were just itching to do me a solid and bring my attacker to justice, and the one person who could probably lead them to him was sitting right in front of me. Max, the provider of meat and saline, the kid with the shy smile and no knowledge of the stars, who loved the predator and the prey alike. My sweet Max who had no idea what he was involved in, or how to stop the avalanche he created.

"Who is it?" he asked, staring at his shoes.

I shrugged and smiled at him. He was so nervous.

I had a plan. I was going to yell at him, to accuse him of being a part of something, but I had no proof of that. It was me that he fed like this other guy. So, how involved was Max? Was he just the feeder of beasts? (Was I a beast, too?!) Perhaps he was just a peacekeeper of the creepy things on this island and I had suddenly become one of them, and if I was to survive not being a murderer, I would need a friend like Max. (Did Dracula have a Robin? Maybe he should have.) I remember he never answered my question as to how he knew I needed meat. I had at least gotten my answer to that.

Regardless, I couldn't just jump out of my skin at Max at the moment; not until I knew everything. And if I scared him off, maybe he would run the other person out of town. Maybe he would rat me out and it'd be a life of syringes, lab tests, and tabloid headlines like Bat Boy, but I would be Freak Girl!

Only survives off raw meat! Come see her in her train car circus cage!

"Upstairs!" Max's voice cuts into my thought spiral. I remember what he had shouted last night. "The person must still be here!"

He had pointed the people pointing guns to go after my attacker... Was he an ally or a foe? And, how much of a difference was there between the two?

"I don't know his name," I responded. "But I recognized him."

"Oh yeah?" he asked, slightly disbelieving because two days ago, I didn't recognize myself. "You recognizing things now?"

"Maybe... some things..."

"Maybe you just created this guy in your head. Creating memories instead of actually remembering them."

I couldn't understand why he was fighting me on this, which was putting him in more foe territory than anything else, but I had tried to eat him multiple times, so he could also be guarding himself against anything that might resemble excitement about future developments with me. And maybe he was right. In my mind's eye, I was remembering this boy that I had a crush on, deliver raw meat to a monster in a perfectly painted white gazebo next to a glass-calm duck pond on a brilliantly sunny day with simple, wispy clouds in the sky. Did such a place really exist on this island with the same dang houses lining the same dang streets or was I thinking of some ABC Family show?

The nurse whips the curtain open but is looking down at her clipboard, which gives me enough time to tuck the saline under my thigh before she looks up to address me. She's tired, and she asks the question, "Alex Jordan?" And I respond, "yes" and she asks, "birthday?" and she doesn't see me peek at my wristband, and squint at the numbers, and say, "April twenty-first" and she nods, and says: "Good news. You get to go home."

As if on cue, my parents show up behind her. My dad's arm was around my mother's shoulders, and her arm around his waist, with the same smile on their faces they used to wear as they watched five-year-old me dig a hole in the sand that they knew I would eventually be bored of in less than ten minutes. But we were a beach family, in a beach town, and digging holes was just something we did. In the same instant, those smiles looked dang fake for two people who I just told to get a divorce, and I knew why they were wearing them in front of me.

"Ready, honey? Officer Grillings said the detective will meet us at home," my mother said.

"Can Max ride with us?" I ask, realizing that Max has not turned around to face my father, and knowing that both men did not want to be in the same car together. Max's eyes went wide, pleading with me to take it back. My dad sighed, but my mother smiled.

"Of course," she responded, and just like that, it was a done deal.

"But I have my truck here," Max tried to use as a sensible excuse.

Oh no, you don't, Dr. Watson sneered.

"My dad can drive you back with his car," I said, putting on a puppy dog look into my eyes that I knew would work on my father occasionally. "Please? You saved me. I would feel better if you were with us...."

This last line did two things: one) it broke my father down, because he wasn't "man enough like this boy" to save his daughter from the attacker he kinda delivered/drove his daughter to, and two) saying no to accompanying a girl who had just been attacked would be a horrible look for Max, who was already the bane of my father's existence. Not that it looked like Max and I had a great relationship outlook for our future, but it still was a small island, and he most assuredly did not want to have to run into my father three times a week at an Acme with my father thinking Max was the reason his daughter almost died like his son.

"Come on, Max, help me get her into a wheelchair."

26

The ride home in my father's car was similar to the ride home in my father's car last night, except this morning, instead of the quietness, feeling like I had done something wrong and my parents feeling like strangers, I sat in the backseat and looked over to Max, who was doing his best to focus on the houses outside of the window. The sun was rising over the ocean, illuminating the sky blue before the oranges and reds mixed in, and I realized that the kayaking memory I had with my mom was more of a sunrise and less of a sunset, which made sense, because if memory serves me correctly, my mom liked to work out in the morning, and now I was almost sure that the kayaking trip was me trying to bond with her and not the other way around. Currently, she was snoring in the passenger seat.

My dad drove with no stereo on, letting us all wallow in the silence of four people who all had strained relationships. Every line of tar which was haphazardly laid on the road, wretchedly and unevenly, we felt and heard as the car drove over it.

This was all okay by me, though, as I did not want Max in the car for his conversation. I wanted him in the car to keep an eye on him.

When we arrived at our home, everyone was happy to be done with the ride, most of all me. I immediately opened the door to step out, almost giving my mother a heart attack as she quickly unbuckled her seatbelt to get out with me, thinking I would need her shoulder to lean on just like the other two times I had arrived home. But, with the saline in my system I was feeling quite all right, and knowing that I had another one tucked into my waistband (although I had no idea how I was going to administer it) made me feel like today was going to be a good day. Besides, out of the four of us, I was the only one to get any sleep, so I was expecting the majority of the people I knew and remembered currently to be passed out at any moment.

My mother was at my side instantly, and we both heard the doors slowly crack open as my father and my male friend both knew what the next stage of their morning was; a long, dismal ride back to the hospital, just the two of them. While I so wanted to be a fly on the back window, watching the two stew in their own discomfiture, I knew that I couldn't get away with it. Besides, it wasn't part of this half-baked plan I'd hatched.

"Thanks, Max, for coming back with us," I said demurely, my mother's arm around my shoulder, her hand grasping mine by my clavicle that was just recently Max's friend's chew toy.

He smiled in a smallish manner, locking quick eye contact with my father, who was also standing outside the open car door, watching the women make way toward the house. I turn around, wondering just what I could say to really light the fuse on the current situation. What would have Max's mind race with the possibilities of what I remember and what I don't? And so when I stop to face him, everyone looks at me, and I smile at the boy I went on one date with, and I say, "Thanks for showing me Sagittarius the other night."

My father's face is instantly angry as he probably thinks it's code for something else, but Max at first is confused, and then I see the recognition I wanted. He now believes, nay, knows, that I remember some things, and now he doesn't know which specifics. Let my dad think that the stars are code for sexual congress and Max believe greek mythology means I can bring the whole world down concerning his aiding and abetting island monsters.

Both of the men climbed into their respective seats in the front and closed their doors. The car's engine still rolling, they slowly backed out of the driveway, and I started a clock in my head.

"I can get to bed by myself," I told my mom at the base of the stairs after she'd put her purse down by the door, knowing that the boys had been gone for forty-five seconds.

"Are you sure?" my mom asked, one arm still around me, the other hand on my abdomen as if, any moment, I would topple over.

I stand straight up in a display of utter strength, and my mother looks at me, judges me, considers my athletic ability of balance to be perfect, and stands back from me. She rubs her palms on the thighs of her jeans, as if either I was dirty, or she was sweaty from holding me up and getting me into the front door. "Okay," she says, awkwardly saying bye to her daughter where we'd both be in the same house anyway. "It's morning, so I guess I'll go to the basement to get my work out in."

"Don't you want to go to sleep?" I say, thinking that's where she was going to go.

"Oh no," she responds. "If I sleep now, I'll be up all night. Mike Murdock says, 'The secret of your future is hidden in your daily routine.'"

"Who's Mike Murdock?" I ask, wondering if I should know this.

"A person who said that quote," she responds, not knowing herself. "Now, get up to bed, get some rest, and we'll talk about the upcoming week, and dinners, and everything when you get up, okay? Dad will be back... all that. We'll sit down, okay?"

"Okay," I reply, seeing her mood increasing the closer she got to her workout. I begin to ascend the stairs with no problem, and after a couple, she stops watching me, stops seeing whether I am going to fall or not, and she heads for the basement. I wonder if "all that" we will discuss includes their eventual dissolution of marriage and me having to pick which one I would rather live with. I hate myself for suggesting such a more confusing future than the one I have already been slotted for.

When I hear the basement door shut, I quietly creep down the stairs, putting my weight on them, hoping they don't creak-and-crack like the horror movie houses. But it seems like I have the grace of a ninja. I get to her purse, and take her car keys out.

She parks on the street, away from the house. Her car starts with a purr, and I put it in Drive. I begin to turn left out into the road, when another car, coming my way, blares his horn, and almost side swipes me. I slam on the brake, jolting myself to a stop, my heart racing.

"Come on, Alex," I say to myself. "Watch the road."

You're gonna kill us with your temps, Dr. Watson chastised from within. *Where are you even going?*

"Back to the hospital," I say out loud, checking my sideview mirrors, seeing two more cars coming, and then an empty space where I can pull out.

By my count, the boys have been gone for five minutes.

I was running out of time.

27

Driving was rough, but not impossible. I was able to figure out how delicate the steering wheel was, but also how to hold it to give the car's wheels room to shift if necessary. Driving straight meant keeping a good grip, keeping it slightly turned as the wheels didn't seem aligned. Turning down West was a challenge since the center of the road was elevated slightly, creating a dip on either side, making me turn the wheel slightly to the left just to keep going straight. If I did not think fast, and, I'm sure, if I did not have the saline in my system, I would have let the car veer to the right, and I would have either sideswiped or crashed into one of the many cars parked on the side of the road.

I couldn't see around the cars parked on the side of the roads when I came to intersections, so I feared I might suddenly get T-boned. *Mmmmmm, T-bone...* which just raised my anxiety even more, as I did not believe I had any business behind the wheel of a car. At sixteen, just with my temps and no memory of how I even got the temps, driving a car was kind of like hopping on a bike when never seeing one before. I had motor memory when it came to some things with this current adventure, but I also had a blind spot in my vision as to how quickly this could all go sour. One car driving forty-five miles per hour meets another car driving forty-five miles per hour and two people going on with their days are suddenly linked in twisted metal, shattered glass, and death. Who thought it was a good idea to invent cars anyway?

I had minimum time, as Max was probably nearing the hospital with my father, and if my mother finished her workout early to see her car missing, or my father returns home to see my mother there working out, but her car gone, or if anyone checks on me and realizes I'm gone, or, say, I get pulled over and arrested for not having, you know, a real license... all of these things could severely damage my plan, which was to get to the hospital, find Max, and trace him—no, *trail* him, as they say. To follow Max to his next destination, which I was almost sure I knew where it was.

Not where. But what it was.

I drove down West until I saw the familiar bridge taking the locals across the bay into the next part of the city, where the hospital, the liquor store, and the docks for out-of-season boat storage were. Once on the bridge, the familiar blue and white hospital signs directing me to where I needed to go to keep someone from dying were every half mile or so, so I carefully followed those until the big cement building loomed over me. I didn't know how many patients this particular hospital could hold, or how many it serviced on any given day, but the parking lot was quite spacious and very detrimental to finding one boy and one truck.

I went slowly, knowing that at any given turn my father would see my mother's car, and even though he would have no reason to look twice, he still would. And most assuredly, he'd see me, or the license plate, or something that would confirm to him that something weird was going on, and he would follow me. Same thing with Max, if he saw that I was suddenly in the area when I wasn't supposed to be. Man, even a parking lot enforcement officer might think I'm suspicious and put cuffs (or whatever they allow a parking lot enforcement officer to have) on me. I tried to calm myself, knowing that the faster my heart pumped, the faster my inner deterioration would be.

Why don't we just wait by the exit? If Max is in here, he will surely drive by it to leave, said my beautiful, happy-in-saline stomach. I rubbed my diaphragm in appreciation, thinking that if maybe my stomach was somewhat like a dog, it would appreciate the show of affection. Although who knows what kind of nerve endings stomachs actually have.

I had arrived at a parking spot at the exit just in time to see Max's truck drive by. I didn't know where my father was, so I waited around thirty seconds or so just in case, but he wasn't coming. I doubt very much he stayed in his car like a gentleman and waited for Max to get in his truck and start it up. I'm sure as soon as the door was closed behind Max, my father peeled out, anxious to get home, or, at least, anxious to get away from his daughter's... boy-that's-a-friend. Coast being clear, I put the car in Reverse, backed up, turned the wheel to the right, put the car in Drive, straightened out and found the exit behind my man;

following the leader to my beast.

We drove back across the bridge to the island, which slightly upset me, because I was hoping that my beast, my attacker, was actually situated out of town, and therefore, if this went sour or not, that Ocean City was safe from him. Knowing he was on our very small island made me believe that it was up to me to see this through to the end. Today.

If I had a phone, I might be tempted to call Grillings and Ispy, see if they believed I was being paranoid about Max, and see if they wanted to be my back-up on my current case. Although, they might catch me with saline, and I'm pretty sure robbing a hospital was a much more serious crime than robbing, say, the corner convenience store. Calling my parents was out of the question, because I could totally be wrong about everything, and they like to judge about anything, especially Max.

But he got us saline, Dr. Watson reasoned. *He can't be all bad.*

And that was true. If he was on the side of my attacker, why constantly be around? Why steal me something that would help heal me? Why scare off the attacker last night instead of holding me down, and letting the beast have his way with me? Was there something I was forgetting about life? About the reason people might try and play both sides of a situation? Was there something in human nature I was forgetting?

I allow two cars to get between me and Max's truck so that he doesn't notice I am following him. Snippets of movies where the evader notices he's being tailed and high-tails it out come to mind, weaving in and out through traffic, and I don't know much about me and life and driving, but I know slow and steady is my best course of action thus far. I'm the tortoise in that rabbit race story.

But I'm racing against time, against... what?

"Am I dying?" I say to no one in particular.

My stomach was silent. My all-knowing, all-smelling guru that drove me hour-to-hour, making sure I had motivation for something, even if it was just the next meal, buried itself somewhere between my pancreas, liver, and spleen and thought about my question. Or maybe it didn't think at all, because stomachs rarely have their own separate consciousness and this was all a part of my psychopathy. That was probably it. I was just on the fence between crazy and rational and this was me aware of just how nuts I was becoming.

A couple of years after puberty, everyone stops growing, stops developing, and essentially, we can determine that that is when we stop living, and start to die. So, yes, you stopped growing last year, when you were fifteen, and now you are dying.

Where was this voice in me? My head? My stomach? My Jiminy Cricket?

"I meant," I say, sighing, making sure to take the same turn as Max as he heads south on the island. I was happy it was morning turning into day so we would have sunlight for a while, because, at night, this side of the island would be pure darkness, and evil excelled in the dark. Although, the farther we got away from the north end, the farther we got away from my house, and the more likely it was I was going to get into more trouble by them finding out I had stolen the car and ran off... again.... I'm such a horrible child. No wonder they wanted to get a divorce. They couldn't protect one child, and they couldn't raise the other properly. Perhaps tagging in some step-parents would put me on a better path....

"Is this... appetite for meat, this chronic dehydration, the fact I get so tired so quickly.... Am I dying?"

You've been to a hospital twice in two days. Did they tell you you were dying?

"No. But, I feel different."

You're just being hard yourself. You thought you could trust Max, because he liked you, and he's the same age as you, and probably going through something similar, but what you need to realize is that your parents were once the same age as you, and they love you unconditionally, and this boy doesn't, and your parents are your greatest fans. You want to go with your gut? Tell your parents what happened to us, let the chips fall where they may.

"You're not really talking to me, are you?"

No. I am merely the voice in your head.

Max parks his truck on the side of the street where houses are being constructed for more island expansion on the southern tip of the island, for more tourists who are coming in a couple of months. I pull over my car a block away, finding a nice spot on a corner so I don't have to do that thing, what do they call it, where you back your car in and to the side between two parked cars? Whatever kind of parking that is called, I have no interest in trying it for the first time today. So, I find a corner spot, I pull over, and I watch.

This side of the island still has shrubs, and bushes, and isn't just paved and cleared and sand. To my left is the beach, the last lifeguard post for the block of 59th Street. Keep going south of there and you'll find yourself, in a mile, at the tip of the island. The only thing down here is a storage shed for the lifeguards and the lighthouse I saw yesterday that I don't remember if they still use or not. The pathway to both of them is one single sand trail through bushes with thorns that house a population of horseflies.

Just looking at the pathway, I remember the flies that bite. I remember it's only the females that do, that they do it to feed their eggs, that their mouths have a stabbing organ with two sharp blades, and then a sponge to lap up the blood of the victim.

Isn't it nice when God gives you the proper tools? Dr. Watson purrs and stretches out.

Max gets out of his car and I see three more pouches of the saline in his hand. I try to control my jealousy that he only gave me one, and this other person gets a handful, but I can't. I am reminded of the saline, though, and I take out the bag and inspect it. "0.9% Sodium Chloride" it reads with a lot more information that all goes down to the final line of "Distributed in Canada". There's a spout at the end with a blue cap where a tube would attach to a needle in my hand or arm. Would saline be as effective if I just drank it? Would I get sick drinking sodium chloride?

I watch as Max enters the shrub area trail, disappearing behind the first bush. He's either going for the lighthouse or the guardhouse. My bet would be the guardhouse, as a lighthouse is probably patrolled more, making sure no teenage kids like us are trying to use spray paint to become immortal.

Yes, dear. Let's not try it out. Find a needle.

"How much time do I have, do you think, before I start to lose my strength?"

An hour or so.

"Great." I say to myself and take the saline with me as I get out of the car.

I walk a little slower than the pace I saw Max setting since I don't want to catch up. I don't want him hearing me coming up behind him, and if for any reason he had to pause, I don't want to bump into him from behind. Max wasn't the goal here, but the goal was to... what? See the beast again, confirm it was him, and... what? Find a phone somewhere? Was there one in the guardhouse? The lighthouse? There were phones, probably, in all of these empty houses down here. Not the ones under construction, but the ones farther north, a couple more blocks. So, my overall hero-plan was to sneak up to the guardhouse, confirm my attacker was in there, and then run a few blocks toward a phone and call police, all before I'm either spotted by one of the boys, or my strength gives out and I fall into a heaping pile of Alex, and my cannibalistic beast attacker devours me alive?

Everybody good with this?

All set! Dr. Watson says. *And may I point out that if it comes to a fight, we already know how delicious Max is.*

I smile and bite my lip as I enter the shrubs, seeing the horseflies flying about, branch to branch—the boys collecting nectar and the females out for blood.

28

Funny enough, the guardhouse was called "The Lifehouse," which, I'm sure, was a play on words with the lighthouse, and the fact that it was where the lifeguards stored extra floats, their paint for their lifeguard stands, extra flags, life vests, tools for boat upkeep, and everything else guardsy. It was about the size of a log cabin, I would say, recalling pictures of them in our high school text book, or maybe I had seen one in person, or maybe I had imagined being in one as I sat in history class and daydreamed about being married to Abraham Lincoln while staring at the photo as my teacher prattled on about how dangerous it was in America when everyone showed up with a dream and no plan. The brick building had no windows and just two ways in or out. One way was large double barn doors, presumably big enough to carry their row boats in for repairs, and the other side was a simple door that could only be locked outside with a padlock, which hung open, very noticeably, from the latch.

I had been right so far.

As I walked up to the building, looking down at the sand, I tried to discern how many footprints had recently gone into it. Perhaps there was more than just my attacker in there. Perhaps Max had multiple saline bags because he was keeping a multitude of these things in this building, and I was about to just deliver myself into a crowd of gnashing teeth, lashing tongues, and slurping lips that would rather devour me than get to know me. But, as far as the sand was concerned, Max was the only recent visitor, and there were other people in and out of the Lifehouse all the time. It was storage for over two hundred lifeguards to point a fact.

Why do I know this? I thought to myself.

Because you probably want to be one, Dr. Watson answered. *It's a pretty sexy job. Much more flattering than wearing a pretzel hat on your head and rolling hot dog wieners in dough on the boardwalk....*

I nodded to myself with that rationalization, thanked my stomach, and shoved the saline IV in my waistband so I could use two hands to steady myself against the building right by the door. I couldn't hear any sounds other than the seagulls in the distance, the waves of the ocean, and a couple of kids somewhere out there, screaming in delight at something. Any sounds from inside the building were nonexistent, or at least, the walls of the building were very thick, and very good at keeping the conversation in. I pushed my ear up to the wooden door, knowing full well that if Max, or whoever, were to open it any time, I would be in a bad situation, but all I needed to hear was Max and someone else talking, and I would be off.

What if he's just talking to a lifeguard buddy of his?

Dammit, I thought.

I needed visual. I needed to see the pock-marked face, and the bangs, and the skin that looked like a drowning victim who'd actually drowned in fryer oil. If I called the cops on Max and his friend, I would be the looney. I would be the stalker. I would be the one who got in trouble for taking the car, driving it without a license, and by the time everyone sorted out everything, I would be fit to be tied, drooling and not making any sense, so you can chalk up a one-way trip to the mental hospital as well.

I needed a visual. And I couldn't wait outside the building for one if they were going to be in there all day. I didn't have all the time in the world.

I walked around the building, hoping fruitlessly that there would be just one random hole somewhere that would allow me to look in; one place in the brick or mortar that didn't take, that insects or birds had dug into, but the building was as solid as it should be. The double barn doors were locked with a chain and padlock, so there was no way I could, maybe, just whip open the door as if the wind caught it, and duck back into the shrubs, waiting to see who closed it. Those doors weren't opening. The only way in or out was the unlocked padlocked one Max had gone through, and I had no way of knowing what was on the other side.

I walked up to the door and closed my eyes. I knew I was going to have one second, one pristine moment to look into the building, and I figured Max and his partner would look back at me, and then I would take off running as fast as I could, back down the trail through the bushes and horseflies, past the block of houses under construction, and I would run up to the first person I saw, or the first house that I could break the front window to get into, and I would dial 9-1-1, and start shouting where I was. But, if Max and the beast were in there, in the dark, I would not be able to see them with my eyes adjusted to sunlight-pupil-size, so I closed them, let the pupils dilate, and reached out for the knob, finding it with the skill of a blind person.

I twisted the knob, which squeaked, and I shoved open the door, stepping up to see inside as I opened my eyes, and saw—

An empty storage shed with shelves lining the walls filled with supplies and two large row boats, overturned in the center, on stands that kept them a half foot from the floor, white with the words "Ocean City Lifeguards" painted in black on the sides. Curiously, and against my better judgement, I took a step inside, and another one, looking behind me to see if anyone was going to step into the doorframe and trap me in, but outside was the sunlight I remembered, and the door stayed open for my escape should I need it.

There was no sign of life or dying teenage boy in here. The cement ground was covered in sand from people's dirty shoes, and their footprints from walking around. The air smelled of salt water, wood rot, and perhaps the slightest bit of decay, like a rodent had come in to escape a storm and has been laying in the corner, unmoving, for a month or so, slowly devoured by ants and maggots.... *Ants....* The strange part of it all was there was really no place to hide because it was all just one large room. The shelves were pressed against the wall, the products on the shelves were neatly arranged, the ceiling was high and flat with just four fluorescent lights hanging from it.

That are on, Dr. Watson pointed out.

And just as my mind and my gut wrestled with the fact that maybe Max didn't come in here, that someone just forgot to lock the door and he had actually gone onto the Lighthouse, the door slammed shut behind me, scaring me, and making me jump to turn around to look at the boy I had a crush on. Max, who had been hiding behind the door. He looked at me, surprise on his face, seeing me out of bed, out of the house, across the island.

His surprise turned to confusion.

"Alex?" He asked, not quite happy to see me. "What are you doing here?"

"Hi, Max," I replied, trying to figure out what angle I wanted to play, whether flirt was the way to go, or damsel-in-distress, or mother-in-charge. So many psychological angles a girl can play, amiright?

"What are you doing here? Your parents know you're here?"

"Your parents know *you're* here?" I counter, wondering if I should better define parents as just "mom" as the subject of his father leaving seemed to still be a sore spot for him, but correcting myself seemed the worse way to go now, so I just remained silent.

"What are you doing here?" He asked for the third time, and this time, his tone clearly made it known he was over my stalling.

"You gave me a saline bag," I smile, taking it out of my waist band. "But I have no idea how I'm even supposed to use this."

I smile at him, but mainly myself for coming up with that reason so easily, and it made so much sense. So much sense, in fact, that Max looked down at the saline, at the blue tip, and smiled back up to me, buying it, as they say, "hook, line, and sinker". He stepped across the room to me, the sand crunching beneath his feet, and I look over his shoulder at the door, and wished it was open, and wished I could see the sunlight now that this boy was closing the distance between us, but I kept the smile on my face, because the reasoning was good, the reasoning was solid, and I heard something behind me, the wood of the lifeboats shaking, and I wanted to look, but I was afraid if I broke eye contact with Max that he wouldn't believe my lie about the saline pack, and needing an IV, so I kept my attention on him, but he looked behind me, and so I began to look behind me, but all I saw was that one of the life boats had shifted on its stand. It wasn't perfectly parallel to the other one, and I realized at that moment that an overturned lifeboat would be a good place to hide.

That's when I felt the Beast's arms wrap around me. I dropped the saline bag to the ground and couldn't move.

I was caught.

And all I could do was look at Max... who smiled.

29

"I'm glad you're here," Max says, and I barely hear him because I am loudly cursing myself out in my own head. The small, rotting rodent in the corner, the smell, was a teenage boy beneath the boat. How could I have missed such an obvious clue? Now with his arms around me I was almost dry gagging at the smell that was poisoning my nose and clouding my mind, and the air felt heavy, as if the smell had mass and was collecting at the back of my throat. The taste of the smell of body rot made one realize what licking the slime off of deli meat would taste like if you washed it down with chunky milk.

"Why?" I ask, tired of struggling against the strength of the Beast. Every time I tried to move, he would just lift me in the air. My kicks did nothing to his shins except tighten his arms, and I feared that any tighter and one of my delicate ribs would pop.

Besides, Dr. Watson informed me, *the more exertion you partake in, the less time you have to be you. The faster your heart pumps, the quicker you'll turn weak.*

So, to honor my stomach, I tried to relax. I tried to meditate. I put the tip of my tongue to the roof of my mouth, and I breathed in through my nose for a count of four seconds 1...2...3....4... and where I heard this, I have no idea, but I kept the breath in for a count of seven, and then I breathed out of my mouth for a count of eight. This helped me focus on what was going on, on what was around me, on Max, standing in front of the unlocked, slightly open door, the saline bag on the ground under my feet which might pop if Beast boy drops me. There were no weapons on the shelves, nothing to help me fight these two. There were also these arms around me, which were covered in dirt, hair, boils, and dry skin. When I passed by a bump with my fingers, it fell off, and I prayed to whatever was holy that it was a piece of dirt or dried mud, and not a piece of Beast.

I wondered if I threw up from all the things I was disgusted by around me, if that would make the floor slippery enough to trip my attackers, and then I could maybe dart for the door, and continue on with my plan; my plan now of running for a phone and calling someone better at dealing with this kind of conflict than me. I tried to ignore the smell, the arm around me which was falling apart, the fear that these two could do whatever they wanted to me, and perhaps rape was second to being eaten alive, but I didn't wish either upon myself. No amount of meditation would save me from that, and perhaps therapy couldn't touch it either.

If I scream, maybe one of those kids in the distance would hear and come running.

And then you deliver a kid to this man-eater, Dr. Watson theorized, and he was right. It was me versus them until I could figure out when to get away.

"Do you know what you are?" Max asked.

"A girl?" I asked dumbly. "The girl you wanted to take on a date to look at the stars. That you wanted to kiss on the beach." I tried to remind him of the times he liked me, hoping that would dispel his notion of doing whatever it was he was thinking of doing. "That you saved from being attacked."

"Twice, actually," Max countered. "Do you remember the first time? You had me drive you to your family's place—"

And I saw it in my head, clearly, just like that. I did have to go to the bathroom but had asked Max to drive me to my parent's timeshare, and he had. We had driven, and I had my barefeet dangling out of the passenger window as he drove. When we arrived, I hopped out, saying I would just be a second, and I looked at him, smiling, and his face lit up in fear, and—

Blackness.

"You were feeding me to him."

"How was I supposed to know you were going to want to go to your parents place? Bumping into him was totally random."

I didn't know if now was the appropriate time to bring up the fact that girls pass gas, too, and I wondered how the Beast would react if I did it this second. At this point in time, with how he smelled, it might freshen up the place a little to be honest. *I'm sorry,* Dr. Watson said from inside, *I got nothing in the arsenal for you.* I thanked him anyway.

"What am I, Max?" I asked. "To you?"

He stepped close to me, looking at me, into my eyes, the spit on my lips, my smooth skin. I tried to read his face, his eyes, the way his lips pursed together, the scab of dried blood still on his bottom one. He examined my face for something, but I couldn't determine what. This boy looked at me, gazed at me, not as if in love, but as if intrigued by what he saw, or what he didn't see. And I thought back to that first night, by the road, by the bay, in the hospital, when he was always looking at me curiously, and something clicked inside my brain. He wasn't surprised by what I was; he was surprised by how I was fighting my conversion into what the Beast had become.

"You're remarkable," he said, and for some reason, I didn't get the butterflies in my stomach like one would when a boy you wanted to date said it. In fact, it felt more like a line, a line to get me into the bed of the truck, to get me to open my mouth when he kissed me, to have me lay back as his hands wandered.

My back hurt from dangling in the air. I was really hoping I could throw up now with how close Max was, hoping that he would throw up as well, and we could cover the floor in oil and acid and I could slip and slide my way out of here, but Dr. Watson, again, was letting me down.

"Who's your friend?" I ask.

"You know who it is."

"Greg," I say. *Beast,* I seethe in my brain. "Your brother."

All the Beast does is grunt, and maybe chuckle a little. A fear balloon starts to expand in my chest, and I can feel it begin to bubble up in my throat. The civilized conversation was calming me a little bit, but to hear the Beast make sounds right behind me, in my ear, rushed the fear back into every one of my limbs.

"Can he talk?" I ask, hoping the answer was yes, and

we could sit down, discuss our lives and our hopes for the future, with two of us dealing with some kind of illness and the third being the only person to know about it.

"He ate his tongue," Max says matter-of-factly, as if it was something one had to fear at the family dinner table if someone didn't bring out the dessert fast enough. "Greg's been through a lot. Similar to what you have going on inside of you, but you are handling it remarkably well."

"Oh yeah?" I question, not feeling like anything has been going at all well the past three days. "How so?"

"Let her down, big guy," Max says to his brother, and I can tell the Beast is thinking about it, but finally his arms slowly lower, and within inches my feet are back on the floor. "Thank God for the hospital visits so I can figure out the saline. Greg would have ripped you apart. The tongue and everything, he was losing all self-control."

Sadly, I feel a familiar ache in my ankles, and know the timer has already started for me to just lay down and become Greg's breakfast. The fear balloon pushes past the back of my throat and wedges behind my tongue, and it's all I can do not to choke and cry from how horrible my final moments are going to be.

I feel Greg move off somewhere in the shed, and I lean back, feeling the overturned lifeboat under me, and I sit down, taking a load off my feet, hoping that by sitting I can control my heart rate, my breath, that I can slow the growth of the weakness inside of me. I focus on my breathing, knowing that the fear is increasing my pulse, increasing my adrenaline, and if I could nap, I would, just to wake up in the hospital and it would be Monday and the scariest thing I would face would be the school hallways and not knowing which friend was which.

Max sits next to me, which means there's a clear pathway to the door, but I am as sure that if I darted for it he would reach out and grab my wrist as I am sure about anything, so the best plan of action at the moment is to talk, to converse, build trust, and maybe learn something about myself.

"Well, for starters," he says, and I can smell him, the berries of the blood, the succulent meat and the gravy of the boy I liked. "You smell wonderful," he finished. "Your skin still looks pretty flawless. You aren't some..." he motions over to his brother, who is just standing in the corner, breathing through his mouth, his shoulders moving up and down with every breath, drool starting to fall from his lip, and we both try to pretend like we're not seeing it. "Some..."

I look over to Max, who is having trouble finding the words, and I see he has tears in his eyes as he looks at his brother. I look back to the boy named Greg, the boy I consider the Beast, and I don't see what Max sees. I see a monster. I see something that looks like a boy who grew past six feet, who then died, and is now walking around, and drooling, and who has taken multiple bites out of me. I see nothing to cry about. I see something to fear and hate, and I realize how different our perspectives are, and I realize that Max will always love this monster in front of us, and I will always hate it, and this is where Max and I could never work out. That no matter how many saline packs...

"Greg..." I begin, but I don't want to humanize it, so I restart. "Did he kill my brother?"

"No," Max says, sniffling away some snot, but rubbing his nose as well to make sure none was dripping out. I thought about being grossed out by how filthy his hand must be now, and then realized we were talking about the living rotting, and came to my senses that it probably wasn't the grossest thing happening in the room at the moment. "Greg only turned a little bit ago. I swear to you."

I feel an anger balloon now begin to well up in my stomach, attempting to chase the fear balloon away.

The Beast grunts in the corner, taking a step forward, and I know that if I begin to look like a threat to Max, I will have this hulk bearing down on me, and I wonder how strong my ankles would be if I tried to run now. But, to try and run is what I will have to do at some point. I have absolutely no confidence in my debate ability to get myself to stroll out of this shed and this situation, and so I look for my moment, my time to shine, to get away. It would have to be soon or all I'd be doing when I stood up from the lifeboat would be throwing myself back down to the ground.

"But, he's never too far from me. He hangs on the dead side of the island where he can walk around freely. He practically owns the dead side," Max says, and I want to argue the geography of the island, and the politics, and how one doesn't just get to choose sides, and if the tourists aren't here, it doesn't mean whoever is walking around owns the streets, but it's probably a dead-end argument so I let it go. "He saw our headlights; he was hungry. I was in the truck, he bit you, and I chased him away. End of story."

"I woke up alone."

"I was afraid. I thought you were dead. I went to the bay to think. I was trying to protect him by hiding him, and then he attacked you when I was the one responsible for you. Believe me, Greg doesn't come without his problems. Then I saw you, and you were alive! But you tried to eat me...."

"Why?" I ask. "Why did you take me to the hospital?" I say, and tears fill my eyes. I have been alive for two days, and I have felt the weight of more emotions barreling down on me to the point that I want to break. I wonder if letting the disease overtake me wouldn't be such a bad thing. The Beast in the corner who is collecting drool at his feet isn't crying, isn't doing much of anything but breathing and waiting, and here I am, fighting to keep my humanity, and all it seems to do is cause me pain.

"I like you," Max says, and I bury my face in my hands, just to get away from everything that is surrounding me, like an ostrich with its head in the sand, and I feel his finger tuck a piece of hair behind my ear, and I shiver. I'm somewhere between wanting him to hold me and wanting to rip his heart out. Not literally, though.

A little literally, Watson says, and shows me an image of how juicy the heart would be to take a bite out of, and I'm sorry to say that I agree, a little literally.

"I'm a monster," I admit, trying to control my sobs, which have a tint of laughter with my inside joke with Watson, and I feel snot on my upper lip, and I feel tears on my cheeks and palms, and I can't control my breathing or my shoulders shaking, *or your pulse*, and I know! I know I'm failing at keeping control, at keeping myself sane and human and time is not on my side, and I just want out.

"No, you're not," Max says, and laughs, and I hear Greg shuffle closer, and I tense. "You probably should be, but... you're Alex. I have liked you for a year now. I was excited when you said hi to me, and beside myself when you agreed to go out with me. I think you are one of the... most real people at our school, Alex Jordan. You don't buy into the popularity game, you don't dress to impress, you wear comfortable clothes, you get your studies done..."

"And now, I'm a freak," I say, and I can't help looking up and back at the Beast, at his rotting appearance, at my future. And I think about how having something in common with something isn't always, necessarily, a good thing.

"When I found Greg," Max starts, finding it hard to look at his brother. "He was on his dorm floor. Ya see, in college, they say the weekends start on Thursday nights, but Greg didn't want to get into too much trouble, so we had a standing date. Every Thursday night, we'd get online and play Xbox together. Except one Thursday, about two months ago, he doesn't get online. He doesn't pick up his cell phone. 'Okay,' I think. 'Big bro is in college, doesn't want to play this Thursday.' But Friday, I don't get a call or an apology from him. I wait the whole day, through school, band practice. I even went to the football game that night just to get my mind off of it. Nothing. Saturday, I drove up to his college. Took about two hours. Found him on his dorm floor. He lived alone. I thought he was dead until he moved.

"He had some leftovers in the fridge he ate at first, some tuna from cans. At this point, he still had his tongue, but he had already begun to disintegrate. The blackness that was around your shoulder? Spread across his skin, turning it grey. The doctors giving you antibiotics cleared it up. You see... it was too late for him, but I wanted to know. You know, how you were remaining you as he was becoming him....

"A girl had turned him, one he'd brought back to his

dorm on that Wednesday night. He didn't think anything was wrong with her, and as they were making out, getting hot and heavy, she bit his forearm."

I look over at the Beast, who rolls up his sleeve to show me his bite mark, one that looks like mine, that he gave me. In the same instant, I feel a bit of a camaraderie with him, and disappointment that he thought he could just take a bite out of me. As if passing on pain was the same as passing on an act of charity.

"Where is she?" I ask.

"Still at the school, I believe."

"So, she's probably infecting more people?"

"Look. I put Greg in the truck and brought him back here. He stayed with us, with my mom and I, but the hunger was driving him crazy so now he goes house to house, sometimes stays here."

"How many people has he bit?" I ask, looking at him. And the Beast raises a finger and points it at me.

"Just you. Alex, we don't know what we're dealing with. I left Greg alone for a weekend and by the time I got back, he had swallowed his own tongue and locked himself in a bedroom on Thirty-Eighth Street. He had forgotten how to open a door by turning the knob. The hunger doesn't just eat away at your body, it destroys your brain, and if you don't keep up with it, you're gonna be... I mean... I don't know what."

"A zombie," I say. "Right?"

"I don't know what this is. But the saline seemed to help you so I stole some to see how it would help Greg. We can maybe find a cure. Fix this before anybody has to know about it."

And there it was. I was just about to say I was enjoying

the conversation, to talk matter-of-factly about what was going on. To learn more about my situation, the past of it all, to realize I wasn't alone in this, that I was one of two on the island and who knows how many else in the world. That there had been some research done, even if it was only done by a high school boy who was failing miserably at keeping his brother together. This was my life now, my new life, and if I didn't act fast it was going to be my past life. And I had never wanted to tell anybody what was happening, that I was flawed, that I was dying inside, and I was craving meat, and I was scared, and I felt helpless and hopeless, and I just wanted everything to be normal, but I didn't know what normal was, and so I wanted everything to be over. I didn't know who I was, and now that I knew what I was, I felt knowing who I was before would probably kill me.

I had enjoyed the conversation until Max said to keep it secret until I was (maybe never) healed. And I had a problem with that.

I wasn't alone. No, there were others out there like me, and perhaps we could help each other if we just talked about it. If we opened up about our diseases we were trying to keep inside, keep hiding. *Maybe the best for—*

"—Greg would be if we just told people what was happening," I say out loud, not meaning to do it.

I look over to Max to gauge his reaction, and I see we both tipped our hands a little too early. Now we both knew we wanted different things and couldn't trust each other. We were on two very separate pages, and neither one of them fit in the same book. And so as Max stood tall, getting his mind back to the point where I was an enemy who stumbled across their little hideaway. I heard the Beast step forward behind me, and the smell of Max's berries gave way to the rancid smell of his brother. I knew it was now or never, and I put all my hopes, dreams, and strength into my ankles and I took off for the door.

I got two steps before I felt Max's grip on my wrist tug downwards, and I was thrown off my feet, and met the ground with my shoulder. The Beast stayed back as Max was instantly on me, his weight on my chest as he straddled me, his knees jammed up into my arm pits, his hands at my throat. He squeezed, cutting off my air, not allowing my anger balloon and my fear balloon to go back down, so they both were wedged in the back of my throat where I could no longer find room to breathe. I slapped at his hands, scratching them as best I could, but his grip was high-school-boy tight, and I slapped at his arms, which felt like rock even though I doubt he worked out much. My heels hurt from kicking them back down into the sandy cement, and I looked up at my boyfriend since Friday, and at the pain and fear in his eyes as he choked me, and I looked back toward his brother, who stood there and watched, and I felt the world start to go black.

"I'm sorry, Alex," Max seethed, sending spittle down to my face. "I'm so sorry. He's my brother."

Fight, Dr. Watson said, urging me from inside, feeling the two balloons I imagined inside my throat get popped by a joy needle.

I was about to die. The hunger, the rot, the unknowing of who I was to become was about to be a distant concern.

There was no reason to fight. He was too strong for me. I felt the veins bulge in my temples and on my forehead, I felt my tears clog in the corners of my eyes, and I wondered; if I was a zombie, why would I need breath?

Could one choke a zombie to death? No, a zombie was dead, already. Was I not dead already? Was Greg?

I wasn't a zombie. I was something else. And we all feared me, and Greg, and "it," and that's all Max was fighting, that's all he was trying to kill. Not just me, but the truth of me.

I reached up and put my hand to Max's cheek. This poor confused boy. I could not verbally communicate with him as he was crushing my windpipe, so my best bet was through touch. When he didn't move away from one hand, I reached up another and put it on his other cheek *just like when we kissed.* His eyes began to glaze over with tears, and his grip loosened just a tad, enough for me to cough, to expel some air, which meant that I could probably whisper.

"It's..." I say softly, feeling that my voice box has been damaged, and everything would be raspy. "Okay...."

Max begins to cry now, that same heart-throbbing sobbing that I was doing, and I see that he is just scared, that he doesn't know what to do so he is just lashing out. To protect his brother, he must kill me. To keep his name out of it all, he must make sure nobody knows, and that means not letting me leave this shed alive. But there's still some good in him. I know this by the way he is crying, the way he shakes in my hands, the way he lets me touch his face, the way he lets go of my neck, and I wrap my hands behind his head, my fingertips through his hair, and I bring him to me in a hug, to hold his shaking body close to me.

And then I clutch him tight and bury my teeth into his neck.

30

As I struggled to detach all the skin from the bite I just took, I wrap my arms and legs around him to hold him into place. Blood pours from the wound, and I can't tell what is more delicious, his flesh or his screaming and crying. Don't judge me, because I am taking care of myself, and my bestest friend in the whole world, the man who has been around since the beginning of my dead life, my good ol' gut detective, Dr. Watson, who is splashing around the blood I'm drinking like a five year old in the front yard water sprinkler. I hold on as Max tries to get away, like a farm girl with her prize pig, and I laugh, and I sink my face into his neck for more.

Dear God, thank You for this sweet nectar of a human being. Thank You for creating such a glorious meal. Thank You for using Your talents for good and creating a world that has over seven billion of these happy meals for me. Keep them crossing my path, and I will forever take care of the bad seeds, so as they may not grow into bad trees, and we shall have no more bad forests, bad groupings of these people in our future. I shall feast on the blood of the young and treacherous. I shall forever only devour the criminals. Amen.

And I bite more, and I eat more, and I chew more, and I suckle more at this wound that I am just making larger and larger. When I lick, I can get tongue-deep inside of this boy's neck. I am gripping him so tight, and he has struggled so mightily, that his shirt has come up, and I can feel my fingernails digging into the flesh on his back. I can feel his blood coursing through my blood, and my strength returning to an unprecedented level. Taking inventory of what has happened, I do not believe there is a dry spot on my face, I am covered in Max's blood, who is growing weak in my grip, and I would care if not for the fact he was just recently trying to squeeze the life out of me.

The Beast throws his brother off of me, and it doesn't seem like either of us care that Max bounces off a shelving unit and to the floor. I am back in the air again before I know it, ol' Gregory hoisting me up by the front of my shirt, and I bat at his strong fists and wonder if I should just slip out and go about this fight shirtless. Instead, I kick out, finding purchase right between his legs, and send the rot-boy to his knees.

"Alex," Max wheezes out, his blood and spit pooling on the ground as he struggles to crawl toward me; looking quite pathetic, looking like something I, in a million years, wouldn't have fallen in love with. But I wonder where this new ego of mine came from. I wonder if this was the difference between butcher meat and living flesh. I try to rationalize it, I try to control my feeling of euphoria, knowing full well if I let the feeling overtake me, that I will become addicted to it, and I will end up like the Beast here, this boy on his knees who had attacked me twice.

"Shut up, Max," I say, and circle around the real enemy in the room, this decaying abomination who lunges out and grabs me around the knees. He lifts up, sending me to my back, and as he crawls up me, I punch down with my hands, my palms, my fists, down onto the crown of his head, and then his face as he gets closer up my waist, up my ribcage. I grab at his ear, and tear at it, and tear it off, but it doesn't seem to faze him. His groans and yelling get louder, and I match him.

"Get off of me! No! Greg! Get off of me!" I struggle and kick, and I tear off the other ear for good measure, because I don't know what I'm doing, but if I dismantle him piece by piece, eventually he'll have nothing left. I tear out handfuls of his hair, digging my nails into his skin; I peel back a whole layer from the back of his neck to the top of his skull. By the time he gets up to my face, there's skin and hair everywhere, like a backyard catfight, and the smell brings a puddle of stomach acid to my throat.

"Kill her, Greg," Max chokes out, and Greg opens his mouth.

I see the lack of tongue. I see a black hole where there should be a red throat. I see rotted teeth that would chew me up, and swallow me down, and I know if he gets a taste of my flesh, he's going to be riding the wave of strength and positivity I am also currently on, and with all my might I grab the sides of his face, and push back, not allowing him to come any closer. He grabs at my wrists, but I move them quickly, my fingernails clawing and digging at his face, removing flesh in lashes. I remember the last time, when I shoved my thumbs into his eyes, but before I give it a second thought, he uses one of his hands to grab my forehead and slam the back of my head down into the concrete.

That does it. That dazes me. My hands fall limply to the floor, and I open myself up to my fate. Max has gone silent and I wonder if I killed him, and I believe this would be the proper justice for a murderer. Did I really want to live the rest of my life knowing I killed the first boy who even dared to take me out? The boy who knew I was attacked, and by whom, but tried to cover it up? How many emotional conflicts could one girl actually face?

But, if I gave up now, that would mean my attacker would win. I think about Grillings in the hospital room and her being attacked, about the power she found.

And didn't I feel great after drinking the blood? Didn't I feel like I had a strength to me I'd never felt before? Didn't my fist feel more compact than ever? Didn't my shoulder feel like the wind moved for it, not weighted down by fatigue and gravity? Didn't my elbow feel locked, and immovable? And when I reached up to throw a punch with my right hand, didn't my left side dig into the floor, making sure all my weight was behind it? And when I landed that punch across the bottom of Greg's left jawline, how rewarding was the crack I heard when I broke his jaw?

One punch stunned the Beast, another punch completely dislodged his mandible to the point it hung loose. The Beast was unable to close his mouth, oozing the darkest drool-mixed blood I have ever seen, past the bitten tongue, and I was petrified just seeing his upper skull and the hole that went back into his head, up into his sinuses and nasal cavity.

Greg sat there, staring down at me, so I did the only

thing I could think of, what I started with his ears. I reached up, grabbed the lower part of his face, my thumb digging under his chin, my fingers tucking over his back teeth, and I ripped at it. Some skin and muscle tried to keep it in place, but it was no match for my resolve, and pretty soon I was holding Max's brother's lower jaw in my hand. The Beast reached for it, so I threw it across the room under the lifeboat he was previously hiding under, and he began to crawl toward it.

I know I should have moved but I just laid there. I felt great, but tired. I felt like a winner who got second place, but the race was over. I looked over to Max who, if not dead, was not about to get up to sing show tunes anytime soon, and I heard his brother, the awful moaning of a guy with no tongue and now no jaw, who was scared about the condition of his brother, and probably the condition of his face, and I laid there thinking about the way my face was covered in someone else's blood, and the horror of it all, and how my life had gotten to this point. I felt the sand under me, the blood in it, the cold concrete, the saline bag by my ankle, the cold, darkness of this room Greg felt he had to hide in, away from society, and I wondered if this was my future, this life of solitude. Except the Beast had Max, and we just, maybe, killed Max, and so who would deliver our saline? Our meat?

Or people to eat, Dr. Watson said, clearly addicted like I was trying not to be.

I stood up, feeling my ankles strong, my body perfectly normal after eating Max, and looked over to the lifeboat where the Beast no longer was. In a show of no compassion, his body was huddled over his brother, his half tongue scooping blood out my ex-boyfriend's neck, flowing down his throat. The sound of lapping, the sound of the semi-tongue digging through and licking at tendons, Max's choking sobs, and Greg's grunting. I wanted to vomit, and, finally I did, a gross spew of blood and who knows what else, ejecting itself onto the ground, too little too late.

Greg turned, hearing my upchuck hitting the sandy cement and looked at me, a half face of horror. I remembered my ultimate goal in all of this. Feeling the sunlight and the warm air coming through the door, I turned and ran, hearing Greg slip on the bloody vomit behind me.

As soon as I hit the open air, though, I saw my hands in front of me as I ran. They moved up and down for balance, but they were covered in blood which was probably a no-no to go out in public in. Covered in gore as was I, instead of running out toward town, toward all the strangers who might not have a good sense about what was going on, I ran the opposite direction toward the beach, toward the ocean. The kids laughing in the distance were way too in the distance since there were no lifeguards at this dead end—there was no safe swimming. The water was two hundred yards of hard running through soft sand, and I felt my thighs burn from never having jogged like this before.

Greg howled behind me, his animal call bouncing off the sky, and I could just imagine that half tongue swilling at the air like a charmed baby snake, and I ran faster, and when the cold ocean water surrounded my ankle, I raised my legs higher in the air, and I churned, and when I was knee deep in the water, I knew how cold it was going to be, but I didn't care, and just before I got waist-deep, a wave came along, and I dove.

I didn't think about being covered in blood and the possibilities of sharks. I didn't think about riptides and currents. I didn't think about how there was nowhere to swim to other than around the southern tip, and maybe back to the bayside. I just jumped and swam.

I had killed Greg's brother and he would come after me. I knew it. I hazard a look behind me as he walks into the waves, his jaw in his left hand, his face starting a quarter of a foot higher than it should have, and what I knew was the truth—his throat, his windpipe, his lungs, an exposed hole that water would have no problem invading. I flipped to my back to watch him as I got past where the waves were breaking, and so all I had to do was inflate my lungs with air, and I could just float, and look back, and watch as he got waist deep, and then chest deep, and he put an arm into the air to break a wave before it over took him, but he kept coming.

I imagined his fear when he realized his mistake. I wasn't close enough to see his eyes, but I envisioned that they grew wide when the first wave overtook him, and the water went right down his unprotected throat into his stomach and lungs. The way the salt water would burn filling him up, the way it must feel to drown standing up. He must have been so sure that he would capture me by the time I got tired, and had to swim back, and now he suddenly became aware of the fact that there was a method to my madness, there was a plan to my escape that I had come up with as soon as I redirected my run and thought I should wash off the blood in the water, and what the water would do to Gregory.

That there was no way he could chase me without

killing himself. And there was nobody to save him on this dark part of the island.

Greg, the Beast, had no time to try and save himself. A drowning person would flail, would scream for help, try to alert someone to their conflict before succumbing to the waves, and the current, and then, beyond all hope, would breathe in their death. But, Gregory had no struggle, he had no defense, as soon as the water hit his mouth, he had swallowed it, he had filled his lungs with it, and it was only a matter of moments before his body convulsed, before some inner mechanism threw up a mouthful of water, just to get another wave to sink him again. Wave after wave, swallow after swallow, I watched as the earth reclaimed the body of the boy who had fought so hard not to die.

I had stopped swimming to watch. It wasn't lost on me that this could be my fate someday. That Greg was a life lesson for me, for how not to do things, for how far along not to get. I wasn't alone in this world, but maybe I was on this island. And if I wasn't careful, I could be the enemy instead of just a simple high school girl trying to graduate.

As Gregory floated face down in the current, letting the ocean take him wherever it wanted him to go, most probably back to shore sometime, I sank my face and body into the water. The same water they had found my brother in, just a couple blocks away.

In the end, the waters surrounding the island of Ocean City allowed my brother to be found, bringing him to shore, and they had saved me from being killed. I felt at home swimming parallel to the shore, wanting to get a couple blocks north before getting out, hopefully less bloody, and finding a phone to call my parents.

31

Didn't take too long to find a phone, not that I would need one.

As I walked up the beach toward where I parked my mom's car, I noticed the flashing lights of police cars, and I heard my father and my mother shouting my name. This time, I wasn't angry or embarrassed or sad or any of the negative emotions I've been experiencing when it came to them. My name on their voices was the sweetest sound in the world. When I climbed the wooden steps that separated the streets and the beach, I saw them, surrounded by concerned Ocean Citians, looking about, and they saw me; soaked, drenched, blood-stained clothes me, and they came running.

In a moment, I was in their arms with no concern for their own clothes, and my God did I miss their warmth, and their arms, and Mom kissed me, so Dad kissed me, and I didn't mind if they fought over who loved me the most. It seemed like they knew the horror I'd just faced, and then I realized the horror they must have faced when they found the car abandoned and Max's body and thought about Benjamin, and the last of their children that they couldn't find. Imagining this, I actually felt bad for them.

After all I went through, and it was them I felt bad for.

"Where were you?" my mother asked, finally, and I could see over her shoulder Grillings and Ispy making their way toward me.

"I was in the ocean," I responded.

"Why?" My dad asked. "Is this blood?!" He grabs my shirt and holds it out, and I look down and it's actually blood and sand and dirt, and I feel like now is not the time to get into specifics.

"Yeah, from..." I begin, but Grillings is there, her eyebrows so high on her face they look like they're escaping into her hairline. I stop talking as if I don't want the police to hear, as if I just want some private time with my parents for once.

"Ms. Jordan, may I have a word with you?" Grillings says, stopping about ten feet short.

My father puts me behind him, separating me from the police, probably wondering if he is breaking any laws by doing such a thing, but I feel his body block the sun, and I feel my mom's arm around me, holding me closer, and despite the sudden strength I got back, all I want to do is lay down on the couch, rest my feet on my Dad's knee as he sits at one end, and my head on my mother's thigh as she sits at the other, and we all just watch some stupid TV show, and be a family.

But, for right now, I'm dripping wet with salt water, covered in blood, and the police want to talk to me.

As they should, Dr. Watson says.

Right. I get that, I respond.

"We're going to wait for the lawyer to get here," my father says, staring at Grillings and Ispy.

"You got one?" Ispy asks, sucking at his teeth like something is stuck there.

"What's the question?" I ask, safely behind my father, beside my mother.

Grillings demeanor changes at the sound of my voice. She sees me as the girl that was in the hospital room, the one that she thought got attacked, but in a different way, but there was no different way in the end, was there? Attacked was attacked, and seeing me, cold, wet, and huddled for safety reminded her of herself way back when, and so she wasn't as confrontational. The anger she felt at what seemed like her town going down some proverbial tube dissipates, and she remembers why she became a cop in the first place; to punish bad guys who made people like her and me feel like victims.

"What happened?" Grillings asks, her eyebrows coming back down to shade her eyes.

"The boy who's been attacking me all weekend wasn't Max. It was his brother, Greg."

"Gregory?" My mom asks, and of course, in a town of ten thousand people, names of the children probably aren't hard to come by. I would have to ask how she knew that, before all the other questions I had to ask; such as, can they take me to the Apple store? What's my favorite television show? And if they can, tell me everything they remember about Benjamin, who may or may not have been attacked by someone like me?

"I found him in the Lifehouse on the beach, and he tried to attack me again, so I fought him off, and I ran to the ocean, where I swam away, and he tried to follow but

I think he drowned."

I excluded some very important information, I'm aware. Like one, I did not tell them about Max's involvement. I didn't bring up Max at all, because I thought if I did, I might also say how I ate his neck, and that would bring up more questions, and the police officers might not let me leave with my parents, and that is all I wanted to do at the moment. I also didn't bring up anything about my disease... yet. Why bring up something to someone whom you just met, and I didn't know what Grillings or Ispy's angles would be on it. Since I didn't know my audience, I didn't want to tell my story, and after all that I have been through, I figured that was my right, no?

"Greg drowned in the ocean?" Grillings asked, looking back at Ispy, who took out his walkie to radio, probably, the coast guard, and have them start looking for a body. I hoped they wouldn't find him for days, or they might come asking questions about his jaw. Let the fish get him like they got my brother and let us all believe poor Gregory got eaten by a shark, and not dismembered by a girl who reads a lot.

"We've been looking for Gregory for a couple weeks now. Ever since he was reported missing at his college." Grillings looked out from whence I came, deep in thought. Probably thinking how it all didn't quite make sense, yet, and who could blame her?

"How did you know he was at the Lifehouse? And why go to the Lifehouse if you knew your attacker was there?"

"I didn't. I like this pathway through the shrubs, to think. It's been a long weekend, and I just wanted some familiarity, so I hopped in my mom's car and drove down here for a short walk."

Okay, that was a straight lie. But, once you start, you can't stop, right?

"I didn't know he would come out of the Lifehouse. He probably thought I was drawn to him or something, right? He grabbed me, took me in; we fought, I fled."

"You fought him, huh?"

"Like you told me to. In the hospital room, remember? I fought him."

Grillings looked at me, a smile seeping onto her face. One where she knew I was kind of lying, but she didn't know what part. And since what I was saying was that she helped save my life, she couldn't quite completely hate what she was hearing.

"Lotta blood here," a voice said over the walkie, which broke the mood.

"How much blood?" Ispy asked back.

"I think we're looking for a body," the voice answered.

I saw everyone else's faces change to the news, but I held mine the way it was. I was in that guard house, I knew exactly how much blood was in there. I was glad Gregory had grabbed his jaw because that would probably be a question. As everyone's reactions read shock and awe, I kept mine stoic, the only question I had was, "Why?"

Looking for a body? Dr. Watson asked as well. *They should have found one.*

32

I had to go to the police station and answer a lot of questions. I fessed up to being punched and choked (I had bruises to prove it) and that I threw up, and yes, it appeared to be blood I was throwing up. They had yet to find Gregory's body, but the simple fact that my wounds were still bleeding through the gauze, and that my attacks had been well documented, and that I appeared to be an honest individual, there was no reason to arrest me or anything of the like. I do believe I made two new friends with Ispy and Grillings, and I valued that. They were just doing their jobs, protecting the people, and they didn't like the fact I was attacked any more than I or my parents did.

But, they dang sure were pretty ticked off the Lifehouse was covered in blood; a building in their city that they were trying to protect.

Later on that night, I am in the backseat of my parents' car as my father drove. The streetlights keep bouncing off the windshield, spraying the car with a sliver of light that quickly passed by and out; like a street scanner, checking on the occupants. The two people in the front seat, my father, driving, and my mother sitting in the passenger seat in her usual way of letting her head loll on the headrest. She looks out at the world, and thinks, popping her cinnamon gum.

My mom absent-mindedly puts her hand down on the center console, letting it rest there with a sigh. My father looks over, and consciously takes her hand in his. She looks at him in surprise at his touch, and he brings her hand up to his mouth and kisses it, and she smiles as she looks at him. And he smiles back to her. And I smile at witnessing the exchange and look out the back window at the city I recognize, but still don't quite know.

It's been a lot. It's been too much. And it's Sunday night, so I have school to look forward to tomorrow, which I am not looking forward to at all. The hallways filled with strangers, the need to be put together, to fit in, or I'm going to be an outcast, and knowing that I'm the only one there that might need to eat raw meat to get through third period—aren't I outcast enough? I have to go home tonight, I have to go through my stuff and try to figure out as much of my tomorrow as I can so that I'm prepared. That I can take on this life.

But I know I can't do it alone. And despite the attacks, the boy who strangled me, the feeling that I don't understand my own body, the dread of not knowing who I am or anything about me, despite how long of a weekend this has been, I lean forward in the backseat, taking off my seatbelt, and rest my elbows on the back of both of my parents' seats. They feel me there, and my father checks me out in the rearview mirror, and my mother looks back, and smiles. She takes my face in her hand, and her touch is burning, so I realize I must be growing cold again, but she kisses my cheek anyway, and I feel my eyes begin to tear up, and I toughen my lips to fight it, and I take a deep breath, and I look down at where my mother's hand fell again on the center console and my father's hand met hers there again, and I think to myself that... this is family. This is what family does....

Everything negative is temporary and the love is forever.

So, I let myself feel the fear, and the emotion, and I let the tears fall from my eyes to the center console where I focus, and I say "hey guys," as if I'm going to ask if they want to get ice cream or something, and both of them pull their focus from whatever they were previously thinking about and turn it toward me, and now it's my turn, and despite everything, I know this is the scariest moment in my life that I can remember....

But it's time.

And so, I begin to talk.

And I tell them the truth.

Epilogue

School sucks, says my stomach, and I have to remind Dr. Watson that this is only second period. That we have a whole day to go. We haven't even had lunch, yet. *It still sucks.*

My parents had walked me into school to explain to the principal, or the assistant principal, or some random lady at a desk, that I was traumatized this weekend, and they would prefer to walk me about, "just to be with me for the first couple of minutes of school," to which the lady agreed that it would be okay, and she apologized to me, and we left to walk about the building. But I didn't recognize anything or anybody.

Amelia and Gianna came up to me, not being scared of my parents behind me as everyone else seemed to be, and they put on their bravest faces, knowing what they knew because my parents called their parents last night. They smiled at me, and took my hand, and ignored how cold I must have felt, and my parents let them lead me away, telling them to try and keep an eye on me as we disappeared into the crowd of people my own age.

My backpack contained within it strips of steak that my dad thawed last night, jerky that my mom went out and bought along with a few strips of raw bacon ("For old times," my father had said, with a slight smile). They had seemed incredulous when I first told them, and then we discussed the implications of my revelation, and decided what was best was to try and keep it fed. My father would do some research into clinics that might be able to help, but we all agreed this wasn't a case for the local Ocean City hospital. We might have to go to Boston or New York or something, but that was something in the future. For now, keep me fed, keep me as normal as possible, and trust in my parents' intuition.

Gianna and Amelia were in most of my classes, so they told me throughout the day how they would handle me. They didn't ask much about the weekend, although when they found out Max wasn't the attacker Friday night, they asked if the date went well anyway. Gianna asked for her purple tank top back, and I had to tell her it was pretty much ruined. And I told them the date did go well, that he tried to show me the stars and that he was really nice the entire weekend, but that he had gone missing.

"I know, right?" Amelia said, and I found out she preferred to be called Mia, which is something I probably called her for years, but for the past two days, I only knew Amelia, so it became a habit hard to break. "A few years ago, his father goes missing. Now his mother loses both of her sons. That poor woman."

"I'm sure Max will turn up," Gianna says, rolling her eyes but keeping her smile on. "He loved his brother. He liked Alex. I'm sure he's just going through some stuff, ya know? His brother attacks his girl? That's gotta be a mind trip."

We get to a door of a chemistry lab class, and I turn around to see neither of them following me in. I cock my eyebrow up, feeling that in just three short bursts of interaction with them between classes, I'm beginning to feel somewhat normal, somewhat myself. And now here they are, letting me enter a class alone, and I don't like it at all. I wonder if I've always had this anxiety about being alone or if this is just a new thing about this weekend.

"What's going on?"

"Neither of us have this class," Amelia, I mean Mia, says.

"But don't worry, we'll be right here when the bell rings," Gianna smiles.

They see the panic on my face, and the bell rings, and they pull me in for a group hug, and the teacher of the class, who I don't recognize, and whose name I don't know because he doesn't put it up on the board after the first couple of days, clears his throat loudly, which doesn't work at first, and then asks us by name, "'Mia, Gianna, Alex, can we break it up? Two of you still have to get to class....'" And I wonder how the news of my dramatic weekend hasn't hit all the faculty, but perhaps this guy just doesn't care about the gossip in the teacher's lounge.

"Bye-eee!" Mia says, and I imitate her whole note and tone, and Gianna laughs and says the same kind of "Bye-eee!" and I turn to see that the teacher is not amused, but I don't care, because I have friends, and I'm a normal teenage girl, and nobody is going to take that away from me. Least of all some science teacher guy, right?

In all the other classrooms, I was lead to my desk by

one of my friends, but this time I was alone, and luckily the only empty seat in the room was the first place I looked, first column on the left side, midway back, so without looking around, and looking lost, I head right for it, and put my raw-meat-filled backpack down on the ground, opening it to quickly take out a notebook and pencil for note taking. I smell the meat within, which smells so good; raw meat sprinkled with a little pepper. I doubt anybody else in the class could smell it.

It wasn't like I was opening up a ziplock of fried chicken or anything, so I took another whiff, and Dr. Watson stirred inside of me, back and forth, like a seal in her tank at the zoo. I almost couldn't stand it, but I close the backpack, and sit up in my seat like a good student would.

The teacher turns to the chalkboard and begins to write the title of the next chapter, and I think about how there are midterms and finals, and I am going to have to study everything I have forgotten. Junior year was an important year, too, what with college applications coming up. Despite what I was currently going through, I was going to have to work double time to make sure my grades didn't slip, and as I sat and worried about all of this, a familiar voice sounded behind me and a row over, and I knew who it was without even looking.

"What smells so good in your bag?" he asked.

And despite Dr. Watson saying *no,* I turned around.

Acknowledgements

I began formulating my thoughts about *The Dead Life* on the playground of an elementary school in 2011 in Cleveland, OH.

Summering in Ocean City, New Jersey— I found myself a setting. Such a fantastic island that I hope takes no offense to anything I wrote. Other than the geography of the island, everything else is completely made up.

I began writing *The Dead Life* in Los Angeles, CA in 2014. It was in a subfloor studio, tucked away in the Hollywood Hills, right at the 101 exit onto Cahuenga.

I finished writing *The Dead Life* back in Cleveland, OH in 2019. In the nine years it took for Alex Jordan to take shape, plenty of people have crossed my path with opinions, questions and ideas. So much so, thanking everybody would be like reciting a phonebook. The acknowledgements that follow are people that I would almost have to put on the cover because of how much they helped this novel come to fruition.

First and foremost, to Erin Fenderbosch-Aguiar, who

stood with me on that playground and pontificated about everything zombie that was neither covered in the multitudes of movies or the plethora of books. "What happens with the baby if a zombie bites a pregnant woman?" "Are there even zombie babies?" "Why is their blood black?" "Why aren't zombie animals more explored?" "Why don't vultures eat zombies?" From question after question, Alex emerged; a girl with nothing but questions, and dead things on her mind...

Erin and I were a part of a before-and-after school program for Kindergarten to eighth graders. That and our minuscule book club of Laura Roeder (and then Sue Hart) was integral; nothing helps build a book better than dissecting others.

To my mother, Lucille Parsell, for being my first typist and editor back in fifth grade, (and buying me my first computer because she was tired of retyping up whole pages on the typewriter.) Thank you for all the red pen marks.

To my father, Allan Sprosty, who bought me my first writing software, and proudly showed off my work to all of his friends. Miss you, Dad.

To Conor Monaghan and Shannon Armstrong, who stepped up to deliver some of the most invaluable notes. Conor, who unabashedly told me what sounded like "an adult trying to sound like a kid." And to Shannon... until you, most of my readers were male telling me what a teenage girl would or would not say. Thank you for reassuring me that Alex Jordan sounded authentic, or helping me better her. If no one else was reading this, I would tell you your notes were my favorite.

To everyone who offered to beta-read: Chris Barone,

Matthew Christensen, Sarah Soll Davis, Jimmy Helms, Rebecca Hill, Sean Koltiska, Brittany Lade, Kyrstin Schilens, Brynn Severance, Judi Spitzer, Christi Vaugn, Matthew Verlei and the dozens of people on Inkitt—your excitement for *The Dead Life* is the only reason I kept going.

To Officer Hallie Beardsworth. So glad we were neighbors dozens of years ago so I could pick your criminal justice brain on all of the police work in this. Thank you for signing off on it, and keeping us all safe.

To the amazing staff at Atmosphere Press. From Nick Courtright, who took a chance (OU, Oh yeah! baby.) Bryce Wilson, who walked me through my first editor/author relationship and told me what I needed to hear. To my proofreader, Kelleen Cullison, who provided me 1,886 corrections— you're obviously a Godsend. Ronaldo Alves designed the cover, being the first person to give Alex an image, and Cameron Finch was my interior designer. They say it takes a village to raise a child, and I don't know about that. But, it obviously takes a village to make my work look good, and I appreciate all of you.

To Alex Jordan, you have been in my life for 9 years, and I have been in your head for 6 of them. Suffice to say, you're a blend of fictional reality for me. Thank you for allowing me to use your voice to make up words I think should exist, and for making me laugh through some hard times. Maybe, we'll hang out again.

Finally, to you, Dear Reader... Why... You're my favoritest person in the whole wide interweb-connected world! Especially if you have gotten all the way to here. And if you want to reach out with any questions, comments, notes or suggestions, I will be available, and would love to hear from you. Please, find me at my website- www.matthewsprosty.com. I'll get back to you as soon as I can.

So... Now, that we have come to the end... What's next in your pile to read?

Matthew Sprosty
November 2020

About Atmosphere Press

Atmosphere Press is an independent, full-service publisher for excellent books in all genres and for all audiences. Learn more about what we do at atmospherepress.com.

We encourage you to check out some of Atmosphere's latest releases, which are available at Amazon.com and via order from your local bookstore:

The Tattered Black Book, a novel by Lexy Duck
American Genes, a novel by Kirby Nielsen
The Red Castle, a novel by Noah Verhoeff
Newer Testaments, a novel by Philip Brunetti
All Things in Time, a novel by Sue Buyer
Hobson's Mischief, a novel by Caitlin Decatur
The Black-Marketer's Daughter, a novel by Suman Mallick
The Farthing Quest, a novel by Casey Bruce
This Side of Babylon, a novel by James Stoia
Within the Gray, a novel by Jenna Ashlyn
For a Better Life, a novel by Julia Reid Galosy
Where No Man Pursueth, a novel by Micheal E. Jimerson
Here's Waldo, a novel by Nick Olson
Tales of Little Egypt, a historical novel by James Gilbert
The Hidden Life, a novel by Robert Castle
Big Beasts, a novel by Patrick Scott
Alvarado, a novel by John W. Horton III
Nothing to Get Nostalgic About, a novel by Eddie Brophy
Whose Mary Kate, a novel by Jane Leclere Doyle

About the Author

Matthew Sprosty is an award-winning playwright and screenwriter living in Bay Village, Ohio. A graduate with a BFA in Playwriting from Ohio University, Sprosty has had various professional productions across the country, with his play *Malicious Bunny* being rewarded the most critical praise. Audiences and critics alike compliment Sprosty's strength in dialogue, his characters' verisimilitude and his penchant for blending genres. Altogether, the music videos for which he wrote treatments (for artists such as Timbaland, Katy Perry, Neon Trees, among others) have over half a billion views on YouTube. *The Dead Life* is his first novel.

CPSIA information can be obtained
at www.ICGtesting.com
Printed in the USA
LVHW030011280421
685732LV00007B/425